James Agee was a man far ahead of his time. When it was not fashionable to hurl lances at the middle class, he did. When it was not considered proper to write of homosexuality, he did. And when it was not good form to recall with intimate, searching detail the life of an Alabama sharecropper, he did.

In *The Collected Short Prose of James Agee*, Robert Fitzgerald, a long-time close friend of Agee's, has selected a wide range of Agee's writings, never before put into one collection. In addition to short stories, there are notes for motion pictures, scenarios, and plans for projected works which reveal the dizzying way in which fresh ideas competed for Agee's energies.

In his opening memoir to the collection, Fitzgerald sketches his portrait of the undergraduate Agee, and the later journalist, colleague, author and friend. *The New York Times* has called this essay *"in itself, a small classic in American memoirs, radiating fairness, humor, and a humane intimacy which are, quite simply beyond praise."*

More Ballantine Books
You Will Enjoy

THE COLLECTED SHORT PROSE OF JAMES AGEE

EDITED WITH A MEMOIR BY ROBERT FITZGERALD

BALLANTINE BOOKS • **NEW YORK**
An Intext Publisher

"A Memoir," by Robert Fitzgerald,
appeared in part in the November 1968 issue
of *The Kenyon Review*.

"Plans for Work: October, 1937" was first published
in *Esquire* Magazine in November 1968 under the title
"Diary of My Future." "Southeast of the Island:
Travel Notes" was first published in *Esquire* Magazine
in December 1968 under the title "Brooklyn Is."

Library of Congress Catalog Card Number: 68–29549

This edition published by arrangement with
Houghton Mifflin Company

First Printing: January, 1970

Cover Designed by Aldo Rostagno

Printed in the United States of America

Ballantine Books, Inc.
101 Fifth Avenue, New York, N.Y. 10003

FOR

JOEL, TERESA, ANDREA

AND JOHN

Note and Acknowledgments

This book was first planned in 1962 as a kind of omnibus volume in which James Agee's poems would be printed or reprinted along with selections from his prose, all introduced by a memoir that would sketch the biographical context for his several sorts of work. I did in fact complete such a book, and the publisher prepared it for the printer, early in 1964. Then there was a long delay. Among those who had helped me most and who were most closely concerned, the conviction grew that it would be better to make two volumes, one of Agee's verse and another of his uncollected prose. The merit of the original plan was to document the special case of a writer who began as an artist in verse and who then found himself most memorably in prose; but this merit, I am now persuaded, is outweighed by the greater distinctness gained for each kind of work in separate presentation, to say nothing of the fact that in bulk each justifies a volume to itself. The reader of this book should nonetheless be aware of the critical importance in Agee's life and work of the verse collected in *The Collected Poems of James Agee*, edited by me for the same publisher. For assistance in preparing the present book I am grateful to Mia Agee, the Reverend James Harold Flye, Walker Evans, Wilder Hobson, Helen Levitt, Robert Lescher, T. S. Matthews, John K. Jessup, Eunice Jessup, Ralph D. Paine, Jr., Celia Prettyman, Lillian Hellman, Leonard Bernstein, H. R. Luce, Joseph McG. Bottkol, J. L. Sweeney, W. M. Frohock, Geneviève Fabre, and David McDowell.

R. F.

Contents

PART I

A MEMOIR

by Robert Fitzgerald

A Memoir

The office building where we worked presented on the ground floor one of the first of those showrooms, enclosed in convex, non-reflecting plate glass, in which a new automobile revolved slowly on a turntable. On Sunday a vacant stillness overcame this exhibition. The building bore the same name as the automobile. It had been erected in the late 20's as a monument to the car, the engineer and the company, and for a time it held the altitude record until the Empire State Building went higher. It terminated aloft in a glittering spearpoint of metal sheathing. From the fifty-second and fiftieth floors where Agee and I respectively had offices, you looked down on the narrow cleft of Lexington Avenue and across at the Grand Central Building, or you looked north or south over the city or across the East River toward Queens. As a boom-time skyscraper it had more generous stories than later structures of the kind, higher ceilings, an airier interior. Office doors were frosted in the old-fashioned way, prevalent when natural daylight still had value with designers. In a high wind at our altitude you could feel the sway of the building, a calculated yielding of structural steel. Thus contact of a sort was maintained with weather and the physical world. In our relationship to this building there were moments of great simplicity, moments when we felt like tearing it down with our bare hands. We would have had to work our way from interior partitions to plaster shell to exterior facing, ripping it away, girder after girder, until the whole thing made rubble and jackstraws in 43rd Street. Jim was vivid in this mood, being very powerful and long-boned, with long strong hands and fingers, and having in him likewise great powers of visualization and haptic imagination, so that you could almost hear the building cracking up under his grip.

He was visited on at least one occasion by a fantasy of shooting our employer. This was no less knowingly histrionic and hyperbolic than the other. Our employer, the Founder, was a poker-faced strong man with a dented nose, well-modeled lips and distant gray-blue eyes under bushy brows; from his boyhood in China he retained something, a trace of facial mannerism, that suggested the Oriental. His family name was a New England and rather a seafaring name; you can find it on slate headstones in the burial grounds of New Bedford and Nantucket and Martha's Vineyard. These headstones in the middle years of the last century were fitted with tintypes of the dead as living reminders on the spot of what form they were to reassume on the Last Day, provided that the Day should occur before the tintypes utterly faded, as now seems not altogether unlikely. The Founder had that seacoast somewhere in him behind his mask, and he had a Yankee voice rather abrupt and twangy, undeterred by a occasional stammer. A Bones man at Yale, a driving man and civilized as well, quick and quizzical, interested and shrewd, he had a fast sure script on memoranda and as much ability as anyone in the place. He had nothing to fear from the likes of us. Jim imagined himself laying the barrel of the pistol at chest level on the Founder's desk and making a great bang. I imagine he imagined himself assuming the memorable look of the avenger whom John Ford photographed behind a blazing pistol in *The Informer*. It is conceivable that the Founder on occasion, and after his own fashion, returned the compliment.

The period I am thinking of covers '36 and '37, but now let me narrow it to late spring or early summer of '36. Roosevelt was about to run for a second term against Alf Landon and in Spain we were soon to understand that a legitimate Republic had been attacked by a military and Fascist uprising. One day Jim appeared in my office unusually tall and quiet and swallowing with excitement (did I have a moment?) to tell me something in confidence. It appeared very likely, though not yet dead sure, that they were going to let him go out on a story, a story of tenant farming in the deep South, and even that they would let him have as his photographer the only one in the world really fit for the job: Walker Evans. It was pretty well beyond anything he had hoped for from *Fortune*. He was stunned, exalted, scared clean through, and felt like impregnating every woman on the fifty-second floor. So we went over to a bar on Third Avenue. Here I heard, not really for the first time and certainly not for the last, a good deal of what might be called the theory of *Let Us Now Praise Famous Men*, a book that was conceived that day, occupied him for the next three years, and is the center piece in the life and writing of my friend. It may occur to you that if he had not been employed in our building and by our employer (though upon both at times he would gladly have attracted besides his own the wrath of God), he would never have had the opportunity of writing it. That is true; and it is also true that if he had not been so employed the challenge and the necessity of writing it might never have pressed upon him so gravely as for some years to displace other motives for writing, other ends to be achieved by writing, including those of which the present book is a reminder.

2

The native ground and landscape of his work, of his memory, was Knoxville and the Cumberland Plateau, but his professional or vocational school was one that for a couple of years I shared. You entered it from shabby Cambridge by brick portals on which were carven stone tablets showing an open book and the word VERITAS, a word—not that we paid it then the slightest attention—destined to haunt us like a Fury. The time I am thinking of now is February of 1930 in the Yard of that college where the stripped elms barely shadowed the colonial brickwork, and planks on the paths bore our feet amid clotted snow. On a Wednesday afternoon in the dust of a classroom I became sharply aware for the first time of Mr. Agee, pronounced quickly *Aygee*. We had been asked each to prepare a lyric for reading aloud. The figure in the front row on my right, looming and brooding and clutching his book, his voice very low, almost inaudible but deliberate and distinct, as though ground fine by great interior pressure, went through that poem of Donne's that has the line *A bracelet of bright hair about the bone*. It was clear that the brainy and great versing moved him as he read. So here, in the front row, were shyness and power and imagination, and here, moreover, was an edge of assertion, very soft, in the choice and reading of this poem, because the instructor for whom he was reading did not belong to the new School of Donne.

After this, Agee and I would sometimes have a Lucky together and talk for a few minutes outside Seaver Hall in the bitter or sweet New England weather. Seniority was his, then and for that matter forever, since he was a year older and a class ahead. He lived in the Yard and we had no friends in common. Older, darker, larger than I, a rangy boy, alert and gentle, but sardonic, with something of the frontiersman or hillman about him—a hard guy in more than the fashion of the time—wearing always a man's clothes, a dark suit and vest, old and uncared for, but clothes. His manner, too, was undergraduate with discrimination. He was reading Virgil that year under a professor whose middle initial had drawn down upon him the name of Pea Green William; Agee grimly referred to him strictly as Green. In the Seaver classroom with a handful of others we gave our attention to English metrics as expounded by our instructor, the Boylston Professor, who had set his face against Eliot and Pound. Faintly graying, faintly blurred, boyish and cheerful, mannerly and mild, he turned back to us each week our weekly sets of verses with marginal scrawls both respectful and pertinent. He was also good at reading aloud. Our metrical sense was educated by such things as the hovering beat of "Hark All You Ladies," and we heard the heroic couplet doomed by Romantic orchestration in "Whether on Ida's Shady Brow."

Far away from college, in the realm where great things could happen, great things had in fact happened that year: works of imagination and art in newly printed books, and these we pored and rejoiced and smarted over: *A Farewell to Arms*, most cleanly written of elegies to love in war, in the Great War whose shallow helmets, goggled masks and khaki puttees were familiar to our boyhood; *Look Homeward, Angel*, the only work by an American that could stand with *A Portrait of the Artist as a Young Man;* and *The Innocent Voyage*, from which we learned a new style of conceiving childhood. Agee and I were very fond of these books. We were also devoted to Ring Lardner and to all the Joyce that we knew. But "The Waste Land," which had made my foundations shift, had not affected him in the same way, nor did "Ash Wednesday" seem to him as uncanny and *cantabile* and beyond literature as it did to me. Here we diverged, and would remain divided in some degree, as he desired in poetry something both more and less than I did, who chiefly wanted it to be hair-raising.

In *The Harvard Advocate* that year there were poems by J. R. Agee, but to my intolerant eye they seemed turgid and technically flawed. I did not see until several years later the highly mannered and rather beautiful "Epithalamium" that he wrote in the spring. "Ann Garner" was a more complicated matter. This longish poem appeared in the quarterly, *Hound & Horn*, still known that year by the subtitle, *A Harvard Miscellany*, and edited by the princely Lincoln Kirstein, then in his last year as an undergraduate. Kirstein had known James Rufus Agee as a new boy at Exeter four or five years before, and there is a passage on Jim in his book, *Poems of a Pfc.*, finally published in 1964. "Ann Garner" had been written, in fact, while Jim was still at Exeter in 1928. Boys in prep school do not often write anything so sustained, and it is clear from one of Jim's letters what an effort it had been. In the first year of our friendship it impressed me more than any of his other verse for the ambition of the attempt at narrative with variations, not really like Jeffers but reaching like him toward myth, a vision of elemental life in the American earth.

What brought me fully awake to Agee as a writer was not this poem, callow even in its power, but a short story in the April *Advocate*. Two boys hunting with a BB gun in the outskirts of Knoxville got some infant robins out of a nest and decided they must be "put out of their misery," so while the mother bird flew shrill and helpless overhead they did the deed with stones. In puzzlement, in awe, in fascination, in boastful excitement—in shame, in revulsion. The younger boy threw up; the boys went home. That was about all, but the writer fully realized and commanded his little event. When I reread this story after thirty-three years I saw that he had put into it some of the skills and passions of his life: sympathy with innocent living nature, and love of it; understanding of congested stupidity and cruelty, and hatred of it; a stethoscopic ear for mutations of feeling; an ironic ear for idiom; a descriptive gift. No other contributor to the *Advocate* that year (in what other year?) wrote with ease, and repeatedly, prose like this:

> The birds were very young. A mildew fuzz covered their heads and backs, along their wings lay little white spikes, like hair-fine fishbones. Through the membrane globing their monstrous bellies the children could see a mass of oystery colours, throbbing faintly. The birds kicked, and gaped, and clenched their wings.

Significantly, too, the story intimated a pained interest in the relation between the actuality of birds and

9

boys—kicking and gaping—and the American institution of "Church" or weekly Christian observance. The two hunters, parting uneasily after their crime, agreed to meet at Sunday School.

3

By simply descending a flight of steps and pushing through a turnstile for a nickel you could leave the university behind and set off for the big-city mystery of Boston, where wine in coffee cups could be drunk at the Olympia or *arak* at the Ararat on Atlantic Avenue; then other adventures would follow. If the Yard was our dooryard, Boston and neighborhood were the backyard we explored, and Jim later wrote a short catalogue of attractions that he liked:

> Window table in Tremont St. Childs, brilliant Sunday midmorning; the New England Boxing Tournament, for steady unsparing (if unskillful) ferocity; Boston Common with an actor and hangover and peanuts and pigeons, midafternoon; the Common on a rainy afternoon or night; on a snowy night; on a Sailor's night; the Fenway at about dusk, fair weather; for good movie stuff: the Arlington Theatre and lampposts from just beyond the level bridge; the debouchement of the Forest Hills subway . . . Revere Beach in midwinter, for sea sounds and pure ghoulishness; East Boston for swell houses, stunted trees struck through with mordant street lamps, and general dilapidation; the Arnold Arboretum in October or May; up the Charles at midnight, down at dawn; the fishboats unloading before dawn. . . .

We lacked neither opportunity nor time for excursions like these and for a good deal of what we had to concede was Young Love. As for the university, it could be contented with a few classes a week and a few sleepless nights before exams. Considering human bondage in general and the demands of any other mode of life, it is remarkable that Agee and I both talked of breaking for freedom from this one, but we did, and he even had a plan of bumming to the Coast that spring on the chance of getting a movie job. If he had, the American Cinema might have felt his impact twenty years before it took place. I reconcile myself to things having turned out as they did. He waited until summer and went west to work as a harvest hand and day laborer in Oklahoma, Kansas and Nebraska.

Jim had been briefly in England and France in the summer of his sixteenth year, on a bicycle trip with his boyhood and lifelong friend, Father James Flye. Although he never returned to Europe, he had absorbed enough to sharpen his eye and ear for his own country. It can be said of him that he was American to the marrow, in every obvious way and in some not so obvious, not at all inconsistent with the kind of interest that some years later kept us both up until three in the morning looking through drawings by Cocteau, or some years later still enabled him to correct for me a mistranslation of Rimbaud. He took Patrick Henry's alternatives very seriously. Deep in him there was a streak of Whitman, including a fondness for the barbaric yawp, and a streak of Twain, the riverman and Romantic democrat. What being an American meant for an imaginative writer was very much on his mind. His summer wandering fell in, so to speak, with his plans.

Two short stories written out of his working summers appeared in the next year's *Advocate* and are reprinted in this book. They are the last fiction Jim published as a young man, the last he would publish until *The Morning Watch* in 1950. In both stories you may feel the satisfaction of the narrator in being disencumbered of his baggage, intellectual or cultural, urban and familar and social, and enabled to focus on the naked adventure at hand. The adventure in each case partly happened and was partly made up; the stories are pure fiction in the usual way of pure fiction, as much so as stories by Hemingway, their godfather. My point is that to conceive and feel them on his skin he had deprived himself of all the distraction that he liked—company, music, movies and books— and had lived in lean poverty like a lens. To write them, and almost everything else that he had to work on for any length of time, he took on destitution by removing himself from class-bells, Thayer Hall and his roommates and holing up in the *Advocate* office for days and nights until the job was done. Advocate House at that time was a small frame building up an alley, containing a few tables and chairs and an old leather-covered couch, all pleasantly filthy; and there were, of course, places round about where you could get coffee and hamburgers or western sandwiches at any hour of the night. A boardinghouse bedroom or an empty boxcar might have been still better.

Did he ever draw any conclusions from all this? He certainly did. He never forgot what it meant to him to be on the bum, and he managed it or something like it when he could. His talent for accumulating baggage of all the kinds I have mentioned was very great, as it was very endearing, and he spent much of his life trying to clear elbowroom for himself amid the clutter. But on the question as to whether he had any business coming back to college that year, his third and my second, the answer is Yes, and the best reason was Ivor Armstrong Richards.

In the second semester, on his way back to Magdalene, Cambridge, from a lectureship as Tsing Hua University in Peking, Richards paused at Harvard and gave two courses, one on modern English literature and the other carrying on those experiments in the actual effects of poetry that he had begun at Cambridge and had written up in his book, *Practical Criticism* (1929). Jim and I attended both courses and found ourselves at full stretch. Though he appeared shy and donnish, Richards was in fact intrepid and visionary beyond anyone then teaching literature at Harvard; when he talked about our papers he sometimes gave me the impression that he had spent the night thinking out what he would say in the morning. By pure analysis he used to create an effect like that produced by turning up an old-fashioned kerosene lamp, and he himself would be so warmed and illuminated that he would turn into a spellbinder, gently holding sway, fixing with his glinting gray eyes first one quarter and then another of the lecture room. When he spoke of the splendors of Henry James' style or of Conrad facing the storm of the universe, we felt that he was their companion and ours in the enterprise of art.

Richards' exacting lucidity and Jim's interest in the "Metaphysicals" are reflected in a poem in octosyllabics called "The Truce," printed in the *Advocate* for May, 1931, the first poem of Jim Agee's that seemed to me as fully disciplined and professional as his prose. I not only admired but envied it and tried to do as well. The image of the facing mirrors fascinated him and made its last appearance in his work twenty years later, in *The Morning Watch* and in his commentary for the film, *The Quiet One*. There is an echo in "The Truce," as there is also in one of the sonnets, of a great choral passage ("Behold All Flesh Is As the Grass") in the Brahms *Requiem*, which he sang that spring in the Harvard Glee Club; the surging and falling theme stayed in our heads for years.

Along with his stories, "The Truce" would be evidence enough—though there is explicit evidence in one of his letters—that in the spring of 1931 Jim held the English Poetic Tradition and the American Scene in a kind of equilibrium under the spell of Richards, and lived at a higher pitch, but at the same time more at ease with his own powers, than in any other college year. He was elected President of the *Advocate* and thus became the remote Harvard equivalent of a big man on campus. We still saw one another rarely aside from class meetings, but had now one or two friends in common including Kirstein and a superb girl at Radcliffe, a dark-eyed delicately scornful being who troubled him before she troubled me; I can still see his grin of commiseration and tribute.

4

In the world at large where the beautiful books had happened, something else had begun to happen that in the next few years fixed the channel of Jim Agee's life. I was in England in '31–'32 and saw nothing of him that year, when he got his degree, nor in the next year when I was back at Harvard to get mine. What gradually swam over everyone in the meantime was an ominous and astringent shadow already named by one cold intellect as the economic consequences of the peace. Worse evils and terrors were coming, but at the time this one seemed bad enough, simple as it was. People had less and less money and less and less choice of how to earn it, if they could earn any at all. Under a reasonable dispensation a man who had proved himself a born writer before he left the university could go ahead in that profession, but this did not seem to be the case in the United States in 1932. Neither in Boston nor New York nor elsewhere did there appear any livelihood appropriate for a brilliant President of *The Harvard Advocate*, nor any mode of life resembling that freedom of research that I have sketched as ours at Harvard. In the shrunken market the services of an original artist were not in demand. Hart Crane and Vachel Lindsay took their lives that spring. Great gifts always set their possessors apart, but not necessarily apart from any chance to exercise them; this gift at that time pretty well did. If a freshman in '29 could feel confined by the university, in '32 it seemed a confinement all too desirable by contrast with what lay ahead—either work of the limited kinds that worried people would pay for, or bumming in earnest, winter-bumming, so to say. Agee thankfully took the first job he could get and joined the staff of *Fortune* a month after graduation.

During the next winter, back in Cambridge, where my Senior English tutor was studying *Das Kapital* and referred to capitalist society as a sick cat, we heard of Jim working at night in a skyscraper with a phonograph going full blast. Thus a writer of fiction and verse became a shop-member on a magazine dedicated by the Founder to American business, considered as the heart of the American Scene. It is odd, and, I think, suspicious that even at that point in the great Depression Jim did not live for a while on his family and take the summer to look around. Dwight Mac-Donald, then on the staff of *Fortune*, had been in correspondence with Jim for a year or two and had bespoken a job for him on the strength of his writing—which incidentally included a parody of *Time*, done as one entire issue of the *Advocate*. The man who was then managing editor of *Fortune* was clever enough to recognize in Agee abilities that *Fortune* would be lucky to employ, and he would have had it in him to make Jim think he might lose the job if he did not take it at once. I do not know, however, that this occurred. What else Jim could have done I don't know either; but again at this time there was the alternative of Hollywood, and there might have been other jobs, like that of forest ranger, which would have given him a healthy life and a living and left his writing alone. Now and again during the next few years he would wonder about things like that.

At all events, he hadn't been on *Fortune* three months before he applied for a Guggenheim Fellowship, in October, 1932. Nothing came of this application, as nothing came of another one five years later. In the '32 application (of which he kept a carbon copy among his papers) he proposed as his chief labor the continuation of a long satirical poem, *John Carter*, which he had begun at Harvard, and said he would also perhaps finish a long short story containing a "verse passacaglia." The title of the story was to be "Let Us Now Praise Famous Men;" I never saw and have not recovered his draft of it. For opinions of his previous writing he referred the judging committee to Myron Williams, an English teacher at Exeter, Conrad Aiken and I. A. Richards. For opinions of *John Carter* he referred them to Archibald MacLeish, Stephen Vincent Benét, Robert Hillyer, Theodore Spencer, and Bernard DeVoto. Phelps Putnam, he said, would also be willing to give an opinion. If awarded a fellowship he would work mainly on the poem, "which shall attempt a diversified and comprehensive reflection and appraisal of contemporary American civilization and which ultimately, it is hoped, will hold water as an 'Anatomy of Evil.'" He would work on it "as long as the money held out" and he thought he could make it last at least two years.

"I don't think I would spend much time about any university," he said; "I expect I would live in France, in some town both cheap and within reach of Paris." It is a fair inference from this that in October, '32, he did not yet know that he would marry Olivia Saunders in the following January. Both in October and January he must have considered that he had a good chance of a Guggenheim. On his record he was justified in thinking so. Yet in the last sentence of his "project" for *John Carter* his offhand honesty about the prospect of never finishing it may have handed the Guggenheim committee a reason for turning him down.

The two long sections that he got written, with some unplaced fragments, have been printed in *The Collected Poems of James Agee.* His hero, never developed beyond conception in the poem as it stands, would have owed something not only to Byron's Don Juan but, I think, to the Nihilist superman Stavrogin in *The Possessed* of Dostoevsky, a novel we were studying with Richards in the spring of '31—greatly to the increase of hyperconsciousness in us both. Jim's fairly savage examination of certain Episcopalian attitudes and décor—and even more, the sheer amount of this—indicates quite adequately how "Church" and "organized religion" in relation to awe and vision, bothered his mind. Another value, almost another faith, emerges in the profound respect (as well as disrespect) accorded to the happy completion of love. When Jim spoke of "joy" he most often meant this, or meant this as his criterion.

5

Moderate ambitions may be the thing for some people at some ages, but they were not for James Agee, and certainly not at twenty-three. To make "a complete appraisal of contemporary civilization," no less, was what he hoped to do with his long poem. Now the Founder, Henry Luce, with his magazines, actually held a quite similar ambition, and this accounts for the mixture of attraction and repulsion in Agee's feeling for his job. Attraction because *Fortune* took the world for its province, and because the standard of workmanship on the magazine was high. Also because economic reality, the magazine's primary field, appeared grim and large in everyone's life at that time, and because by courtesy of *Fortune* the world lay open to its editors and they were made free of anything that in fact or art or thought had bearing on their work. Repulsion because that freedom in truth was so qualified, because the ponderous and technically classy magazine identified itself from the start, and so compromised itself (not dishonestly, but by the nature of things), with one face of the civilization it meant to appraise; whatever it might incidentally value, it was concerned with power and practical intelligence, not with the adventurous, the beautiful and the profound—words we avoided in those days but for which referents none the less existed. At heart Agee knew his vocation to be in mortal competition, if I may put it so, with the Founder's enterprise. For *Fortune* to enlist Agee was like Germany enlisting France.

Nevertheless he had now three uninterrupted years of it. One blessing was the presence on *Fortune* of Archibald MacLeish, a Yaleman like the Founder and one of the original editors, but also a fine artist who knew Jim for another, respected him and helped him. MacLeish in 1932 was forty and had published his big poem, *Conquistador*. Being experienced and distinguished, he could pick the subjects that appealed to him, and being a clearheaded lawyer-turned-poet, he wrote both well and efficiently. His efficiency was a byword on *Fortune*. Requiring all research material on cards in orderly sequence, he merely flipped through his cards and wrote in longhand until five o'clock, when he left the office. Often enough other people, including Jim, would be there most of the night.

I had a brief glimpse of the scene when I got to New York in the summer of '33. The city lay weary and frowsy in a stench of Depression through which I walked for many days, many miles up and down town, answering ads, seeing doubtful men in dusty offices, looking for a job. MacLeish got me an interview with a rather knifelike *Fortune* editor who read what writing I had to show and clearly sized me up as a second but possibly even more difficult Agee, where one was already enough. Staring out of the window reflectively at Long Island he told me in fact that the Founder had taken a good deal from Agee, allowing for Agee's talent, but that there were limits. Back in MacLeish's office I waited while he, the old backfield man, warm and charming as ever, called up Jim. So Jim came in and we poets talked. One subject was the current plight of Kenneth Patchen, a poet dogged by misfortune. Archie also mentioned Hart Crane, whom he had once persuaded *Fortune* to take on for a trial. Hart had been completely unable to do it. It did not cross my mind that this had any relevance to me. I felt elated over my visit, and Jim took me home to dinner.

The basement apartment on Perry Street had a backyard where grew an ailanthus tree, and there under the slim leaves we sat until dark, he and Via and I, drinking I don't remember what but I imagine Manhattans, a fashion of the period. After dinner we went to the piano and sang some of the Brahms *Requiem*. Then he got out his manuscripts, read from *John Carter*, and read a new poem, a beauty, "Theme with Variations" (later he called it "Night Piece"). *Fortune*, I suppose at MacLeish's suggestion, had assigned him an article on the Tennessee Valley Authority, and in the course of preparing it he had gone back that summer to the countryside of his boyhood: hence, I think, this poem. In that evening's dusk and lamplight neither of us had any doubt that we shared a vocation and would pursue it, come what might. We were to have a good many evenings like it during the next three years while that particular *modus vivendi* lasted for Jim Agee as office worker and husband.

Jim must have thought *Fortune* would have me (*Time*, instead, had me, but not until February of '36), because at the end of August when I was temporarily out of town I had a letter from him that concluded: "I'm wondering what you'll think of a job on *Fortune*, if you take it. It varies with me from a sort of hard, masochistic liking without enthusiasm or trust, to direct nausea at the sight of this symbol $ and this % and this *biggest* and this some blank billion. At times I'd as soon work on *Babies Just Babies*. But in the long run I suspect the fault, dear *Fortune*, is in me: that I hate any job on earth, as a job and hindrance and semisuicide."

His TVA article appeared in *Fortune* for October. It opened:

> The Tennessee River system begins on the worn magnificent crests of the southern Appalachians, among the earth's older mountains, and the Tennessee River shapes its valley into the form of a boomerang, bowing to its sweep through seven states. Near Knoxville the streams still fresh from the mountains are linked

and thence the master stream spreads the valley most
richly southward, swims past Chattanooga and bends
down into Alabama to roar like blown smoke through
the flood-gates of Wilson Dam, to slide becalmed along
the crop-cleansed fields of Shiloh, to march due north
across the high diminished plains of Tennessee and
through Kentucky spreading marshes toward the valley's end where, finally, at the toes of Paducah, in one
wide glassy golden swarm the water stoops forward and
continuously dies into the Ohio . . .

Soon after this Luce called him in and told him that
he had written one of the best things ever printed in
Fortune. It was characteristic of the Founder to ac-
knowledge this; it was also characteristic of him to indicate, as Agee's reward, the opportunity to write a
number of straight "business stories" whereby to
strengthen his supposed weak side. The first of these
concerned The Steel Rail, and according to Dwight
MacDonald, the Founder himself buckled down to
coach Agee in how to write good hard sense about the
steel business.* Eventually he gave up and the job
went to someone else, but the article as it appeared in
December retrained traces of Jim's hand:

Caught across the green breadth of America like
snail paths on a monstrous plantain leaf are 400,000
. . . steel miles. If, under the maleficent influence of
that disorderly phosphorus which all steel contains,
every inch of this bright mileage were suddenly to
thaw into thin air . .

---

* A story later got around that the Founder for a time considered
sending Agee to the Harvard Business School. "That story," Luce wrote
to me in 1964, "is quite plausible—though I do not actually recall it.
A problem in journalism that interested me then—and still does—is to
combine good writing and 'human understanding' with familiarity with
business."

6

During that fall and winter and the following year we pretty often had lunch or dinner together. I would call for him in his lofty office, or I would look up over my typewriter in the newspaper city room where by that time I worked and see him coming down the aisle from the elevator. He would come at his fast loose long-legged walk, springy on the balls of his feet, with his open overcoat flapping. We would go to a saloon for beer and roast beef sandwiches. I wish very badly that I could recall the conversations of those times, because in them we found our particular kind of brotherhood. Both of us had been deeply enchanted and instructed, and were both skilled, in an art remote from news writing, an art that we were not getting time or breath to practice much. You would underestimate us if you supposed that we met to exchange grievances, for of these in the ordinary sense we had none. We met to exchange perceptions, and I had then and later the sense that neither of us felt himself more fully engaged than in talk with the other. My own childhood enabled me to understand his, in particular his schooling at the monastery school of St. Andrew's in Tennessee. We were both in the habit of looking into the shadow of Death. Although we came of different stock and from different regions, we were both Catholic (he, to be precise, Anglo-Catholic) by bringing-up and metaphysical formation; both dubious not to say distressed about "Church"; both inclined to the "religion of art," meaning that no other purpose, as we would have put it, seemed worth a damn in comparison with making good poems. Movies, of course, we talked about a good deal. My experience was not as wide as

22

his, my passion less, but we admired certain things in common: Zasu Pitts in *Greed* and the beautiful sordidness of that film; the classic flight down the flights of steps in *Potemkin;* Keaton; Chaplin. We saw, sometimes together, and "hashed over," as Jim would say, the offerings of that period: the René Clairs, the Ernst Lubitsches; *The Informer; Man of Aran; Grand Illusion; Mayerling; The Blue Angel; Maedchen in Uniform; Zwei Herzen* . . .

The various attitudes covered by "taking care of yourself" interested Jim Agee, but rarely to the point of making him experiment with any. Rubbers, for example, he probably thought shameful and never wore in his adult life; on the contrary, in that period, his shoes both winter and summer were often worn through, with cracked uppers. But he had some conventional habits and impulses. He wore a hat, a small one that rode high on his shock of dark hair. For several entire weeks in '34 he gave up cigarettes for a pipe. The episode of the pipe was the last effort of that kind that he would make until many years later when he cut down smoking after his first heart attack.

Another thing he did with Via was to keep a catboat at City Island and go out there to sail and swim on Sundays in summer. I think he had been on the swimming team at Exeter; at any rate he had an enviable backstroke. On one of these Sunday excursions when I went along I remember that we amused ourselves during the long black blowy subway ride by playing the metaphor game: by turns each describing an inanimate object in such a way as to portray without naming a public figure. Jim developed a secondhand silver flute into Leslie Howard, and a Grand Rapids easy chair into Carl Sandburg. Later that evening we had a memorable and I suppose comic conversation about whether or not the Artist should

Keep in Shape. In the course of this I quoted Rémy de Gourmont to the effect that a writer writes with his whole body, bringing immediate and delighted assent from Jim, but not to the inference I myself would draw. His own body seemed so rugged and his stamina so great that I thought he could overlook his health and get away with it. The truth is that he was not as rugged as he looked. He had an inclination to hemophilia that had nearly cost him his life when he had his tonsils out in 1928, and at Exeter, too, he had first hurt his heart trying to run the mile. He never mentioned any of this.

Many-tiered and mysterious, the life of the great city submerged us now, me rather more, since I had no eyrie like his but all day long spanieled back and forth in it and at night battered at my deadlines; and I think Jim envied me the unpretentious but hard craft I had got into. Whatever other interests we had, one became fairly constant and in time inveterate: the precise relation between any given real situation or event and the versions of it presented in print, that is, after a number of accidents, processes and conventions had come into play. The quite complicated question of "how it really was" came before us all the time, along with our resources and abilities for making any part of that actuality known in the frames our employers gave us. Of those frames we were acutely aware, being acutely aware of others more adequate. Against believing most of what I read I am armored to this day with defences worked out in those years and the years to follow. Styles, of course, endlessly interested us, and one of Jim's notions was that of writing an entire false issue of the *World Telegram* dead-pan, with every news item and ad heightened in its own style to the point of parody. He could easily have done it. Neither of us felt snide about eye-witness writing in itself or as practiced by Lardner or Hemingway; how could we? We simply mistrusted the journalistic apparatus as a mirror of the world, and we didn't like being consumed by it. Neither of us ever acquired a professional and equable willingness to work in that harness. For him to do so would have been more difficult than for me, since he had a great talent for prose fiction and I had not. After being turned down for the Guggenheim, in fact, he thought of trying to publish a book of his stories, and went so far as to write a preface for it.

"I shall do my best to stick to people in this book," he wrote. "That may seem to you the least I could do; but the fact is, I'm so tied up with symbols and half-abstractions and many issues about poetry which we'd better steer clear of now, that it is very hard for me to see people clearly as people . . . someday, if my life is worth anything, I shall hope to give people clearly in clear poetry, and to make them not real in the usual senses of real, but more than that: full of vitality and of the ardor of their own truth . . ."

But he dropped the idea of publishing any stories at that point. Instead, with MacLeish's encouragement, he gathered the best of his old poems together with some new ones to make a book, and in October, 1934, in the Yale Younger Poets series, in which MacLeish and Stephen Vincent Benét were then interested, the Yale Press published *Permit Me Voyage*.

7

Of how I felt about Jim's book then, it is perhaps enough to say that at bad times in the next year or two I found some comfort in being named in it. So far as I can discover, none of the contemporary comments on it, including the Foreword by MacLeish, took much notice of what principally distinguished it at the time: the religious terms and passion of several pieces, rising at times to the grand manner. In two of his three pages MacLeish did not refer to the book at all, being engaged in arguing that neither of the current literary "programs," America Rediscovered and Capitalism Be Damned, mattered in comparison with *work* done. As to Agee, "Obviously he has a deep love of the land. Equally obviously he has a considerable contempt for the dying civilization in which he has spent twenty-four years." But he said nothing of the fact that Agee's book appeared to be the work of a desperate Christian; in fact, he rather insisted on saying nothing, for he concluded that by virtue of the poet's gift, especially his ear, and his labor at his art, "the work achieves an integral and inward importance altogether independent of the opinions and purposes of its author."

This was true enough, but some of the poems were so unusual in what they suggested as to call, you might think, for a word of recognition. One gusty day years later, as we were crossing 49th Street, Jim and I halted in the Radio City wind and sunlight to agree with solemnity on a point of mutual and long-standing wonderment, not to say consternation: how rarely people seem to believe that a serious writer means it; he means what he says or what he discloses. Love for the land certainly entered into *Permit Me Voyage;* contempt for a dying civilization much less, and contempt here was not quite the word. It could even be said, on the contrary, that a sequence of twenty-five regular and in some cases truly metaphysical sonnets rather honored that civilization, insofar as a traditional verse form could represent it. The most impressive things in the book were the "Dedication" and the "Chorale," and what were these but strenuous prayers? They could have no importance, because no existence, independent of the opinions and purposes of the author.

A sense of the breathing community immersed in mystery, exposed to a range of experience from what can only be called the divine to what can only be called the diabolical, most intelligent in awe and most needful of mercy—a religious sense of life, in short—moved James Agee in his best work. If in introducing that work the sensitive and well-disposed MacLeish could treat this motive as unmentionable, that may give some idea of where Agee stood amid the interests and pressures of the time. It must be added that those interests were also Agee's, and that those pressures he not only profoundly felt but himself could bring to bear.

Four years at Harvard had complicated out of recognition his youthful Episcopalianism (he preferred to say Catholicism), but he hated polite academic agnosticism to the bone. In one *Advocate* editorial as a senior he had even proposed Catholicism as desirable for undergraduates. The poem, *John Carter*, that he had begun there, and would have carried on if he could, was to be an "anatomy of evil" wrought, he said, by an agent of evil in the "orthodox Roman Catholic" sense. At twenty-five, after two years in New York, he published an openly religious book of poems. MacLeish was not alone in ignoring what it said; the reviewers also ignored it. It was as if the interests and pressures of the time made it inaudible.

Inaudible? Since I still find it difficult to read the "Dedication" and the "Chorale" without feeling a lump in my throat, I do not understand this even now. If he had been heard, surely a twinge of compunction would have crossed the hearts of thousands.

But the book itself, Jim's poems in general, remained very little known or remarked during his lifetime, and for that matter are little known even now. One reason for this, I am well aware, is that in the present century the rhymed lyric and the sonnet for a time seemed disqualified as "modern poetry." Jim was aware of it, too; so aware that his sequence ended with a farewell to his masters, the English poets:

My sovereign souls, God grant my sometime brothers,
I must desert your ways now if I can . . .

The concluding poem in the book, the title poem, was indeed a conclusion, but it enfolded a purpose.

My heart and mind discharted lie—

with reference, that is, to the compass points, religious, literary, and other, within which at St. Andrew's, at Exeter, at Harvard and in New York he had by and large lived and worked. This was more than the usual boredom of the artist with work that is over and done with. He turned away now from Christian thought and observance, and began to turn away from the art of verse. Yet his purpose was to rechart, to re-orient himself, by reference to the compass needle itself, his own independent power of perception. his own soul . . .

8

Therein such strong increase to find
In truth as is my fate to know.

Everyone who knew Jim Agee will remember that in these years there grew upon him what became habitual almost to idiosyncrasy: a way of tilting any subject every which way in talk, with prolonged and exquisite elaboration and scruple. He was after the truth, the truth about specific events or things, and the truth about his own impressions and feelings. By truth I mean what he would chiefly mean: correspondence between what is said and what is the case— but what is the case at the utmost reach of consciousness. Now this intent has been delicately and justly distinguished from the intent of art, which is to make, not to state, things; and a self-dedication to truth on the part of Shakespeare or Mozart (Ageean examples) would indeed strike us as peculiar. On the other hand, with philosophy dethroned and the rise of great Realists, truth-telling has often seemed to devolve almost by default upon the responsible writer, enabling everyone else to have it both ways: his truth as truth if they want it, or as something else if they prefer, since after all he is merely an artist. Jim Agee, by nature an artist and responsive to all the arts, took up this challenge to perceive in full and to present immaculately what was the case.

Think of all that conspired to make him do so. The place of Truth in that awareness of the living God that he had known as a child and young man and could not forget. The place of truth at the university, *Veritas*, perennial object of the scholar's pains. New techniques for finding out what was the case: among them, in particular, sociological study, works like *Middletown* in the United States and *Mass Observation* in England, answering to the perplexity of that age, and the "documentary" by which the craft of the cameraman could show forth unsuspected lineaments of the actual. (An early and what would appear a commonplace example of this craft, *The River*, by Pare Lorentz, excited Agee and myself.) Then, to sicken and enrage him, there was the immense new mud-fall of falsehood over the world, not ordinary human lying and dissimulation but a calculated barrage, laid down by professional advertisers and propagandists, to corrupt people by the continent-load. Finally, day by day, he had the given occupation of journalism, ostensibly and usually in good faith concerned with what was the case. In the editing of *Fortune* all the other factors played a part: the somewhat missionary zeal of the Founder, a certain respect for standards of scholarship, a sociological interest in looking into the economic conditions and mode of life of classes and crafts in America, an acquiescence in advertising and in self advertisement, and, of course, photography.

The difficulties of the period were, however, deepened by an intellectual dismay, not entirely well-founded but insidious under many forms: *What was the case* in some degree proceeded from the observer. Theoretical in abstract thought for centuries, this cat seemed now to have come out of the bag to bewitch all knowledge in practice: knowledge of microcosmic entities, of personal experience, of human society. Literary art had had to reckon with it. To take an elementary example, Richards would put three x's on a blackboard disposed thus ∴ to represent poem, referent and reader, suggesting that a complete account of the poem could no more exclude one x than another, nor the relationship between them. Nor were the x's stable, but variable. *Veritas* had become tragically complicated. The naïve practices of journalism might continue, as they had to, but their motives and achievements, like all others, appeared now suspect to Freudian and Marxian and semanticist alike; and of what these men believed they understood James Agee was (or proposed to make himself) also aware. Hence his self-examinations, his ambivalences ("split" feelings) on so many things. As he realized well enough, they could become tedious, but they were crucial to him and had the effect that what he knew, in the end, he knew with practiced definition. It must be added that the more irritated and all-embracing and scrupulous his aspiration to full truth, "objective" and "subjective" at once, the more sharply he would know his own sinful vainglory or Pride in that ambition, in those scruples; and he did. Few men were more sensitive to public and private events than he was, and he would now explore and discriminate among them with his great appetite, his energy, his sometimes paralyzing conscience, and the intellect that Richards had alerted. I am of course reducing a long and tentative and often interrupted effort into a few words.

I named three books arbitrarily as stars principal in our first years at Harvard; I will name three more, arbitrarily again, to recall the planetary influences after graduation. In the spring of '34, after Judge Wolsey's decision, Random House published *Ulysses* for the first time legally in America, and even if we had read it before, as Jim and I had, in the big Shakespeare & Co. edition, we could and did now read it again, in a handier form suitable for carrying on the subway. Or for the Agee bathroom, where I remember it. Joyce engrossed him and got into his blood so thoroughly that in 1935 he felt obliged, as he told a friend of mine, to master and get over that influence if he were ever to do anything of his own.

Céline's *Voyage au Bout de la Nuit* was our first taste of the end-of-the-rope writing that became familiar later in Miller and later still in Beckett. Malraux's *Man's Fate* had another special position. This story, with Auden's early poems, counted as much as the

Russian movies of Eisenstein and Dovzhenko in sway-
ing Jim toward Communism. The attraction in any
case was strong. The peaceful Roosevelt revolution
had only begun; there was a real clash of classes in
America. I had myself, in a single day of reporting,
seen the pomp of high capitalism to be faded and
phoney at an NAM convention in the Waldorf, and
the energies of laboring men to be robust and open at
a union meeting. On one side of his nature Jim was
a frontiersman and a Populist to whom blind wealth
and pretentious gentility were offensive. Besides this
he had the Romantic artist's contempt, "considerable
contempt," for the Philistine and for what were then
known to us as bourgeois attitudes—though he distinguished between the human souls that inherited
them. For poverty and misery in general he had a
sharp-eyed pity. The idea of a dedicated brotherhood
working underground in the ghastly world held his
imagination for several years—spies amid the enemy,
as Auden had imagined them; at the same time he
had no great difficulty in seeing through most of the
actual candidates for such a brotherhood, including
himself. The Party fished in vain for Agee, who by
liking only what was noble in the Revolution liked
too little of it.

9

Embedded in *Fortune* for those years are several of
Jim's best efforts at telling how things really were. As
in the description of the Tennessee River, these are
most often concerned with American landscapes and
American living. In September, 1934, for example,
there was this opening to an article on the Great
American Roadside:

. . . This continent, an open palm frank before the sky against the bulk of the world. This curious people. The automobile you know as well as you know the slouch of the accustomed body at the wheel and the small stench of gas and hot metal. You know the sweat and the steady throes of the motor and the copious and thoughtless silence and the almost lack of hunger and the spreaded swell and swim of the hard highway toward and beneath and behind and gone and the parted roadside swarming past. This great road, too; you know that well. How it is scraggled and twisted along the coast of Maine, high-crowned and weak-shouldered in honor of long winter. How in Florida the detours are bright with the sea-lime of rolled shells. How the stiff wide stream of hard unbroken roadstead spends the mileage between Mexicali and Vancouver. How the road degrades into a rigorous lattice of country dirt athwart Kansas through the smell of hot wheat and this summer a blindness and a strangulation of lifted dust). How like a blacksnake in the sun it takes the ridges, the green and dim ravines which are the Cumberlands, and lolls loose into the hot Alabama valleys. How in the spectral heat of the Southwest, and the wide sweeps of saga toward the Northwest, it means spare fuel strapped to the running board. . . . Oh yes, you know this road; and you know this roadside. You know this roadside as well as you know the formulas of talk at the gas station, the welcome taste of a Bar-B-Q sandwich in midafternoon, the oddly excellent feel of a weak-springed bed in a clapboard transient shack, and the early start in the cold bright lonesome air, the dustless and dewy road . . .

In October of the same year, on *The Drought*:

That this has been by all odds the most ruinous drought in U. S. history is old stuff to you by now. So are the details, as the press reported them, week by broiling week, through the summer. But all the same, the chances are strong that you have no idea what the whole thing meant: what, simply and gruesomely, it was. Really to know, you should have stood with a Dakota farmer and watched a promissory rack of cloud take the height of the sky, weltering in its lightnings . . . and the piteous meager sweat on the air, and the earth baked stiff and steaming. You should have been a lot more people in a lot more places, really to know. Barring that impossibility, however, there is the clear dispassionate eye of the camera, which under honest guidance has beheld these bitter and these transient matters, and has recorded this brutal season for the memory of easier time to come . . .

These quotations must suffice, and they are not carelessly chosen. In 1935 he did a thorough re-examination of the TVA, published in May, and a study of Saratoga, New York, published in August. These and other examples of sheer ability won him a taste of the freedom he craved. Beginning in November, *Fortune* gave him a six months' leave of absence, most of which he and Via spent in Florida on a small coastal island, Anna Maria, south of St. Petersburg and Tampa.

In a notebook of his, half-filled with jottings of that winter I find the first entry amusing at this distance: it was a name and an address—*The New Masses*—later canceled out by a scribble. He was now steadily devouring Freud and recording his dreams. "Read Freud until midnight" is an entry several times repeated. There are pages like Stephen's or Bloom's waking thoughts in Ulysses. There are notes and self-injunctions about writing. For instance:

My need for tone, tension & effect in writing limits me very badly. Yet cd. be good. But in many ways needless effort. And in many ways false. Its attempt in long run: to give, at once, frame and fluescence to pic. of universe. Seem to feel I have no right to give

the looseness till is established the tightness wherein
it moves . . . Must throw brain into detail. And into
fearlessness, shamelessness & naturalness abt writing . . .
Poem or prose in line between The Barge She Sat In
and a social report of a wedding. What was worn.
Who was there. etc. / Bks not of one thing—stories,
poetry, essays, etc. / but of all, down to most casual . . .

In December he wrote some ottava rima, a few stanzas
mocking something Sir Samuel Hoare, then British
Foreign Minister, had said in the course of diplomacy
that winter over the Italian war against Ethiopia. It
was the last spasm of *John Carter*. He read *Crime and
Punishment*, Caroline Spurgeon on *Shakespeare's
Imagery* and *The Counterfeiters*. Gide, he wrote,

. . . makes me realize more clearly than I have for a
long time what a damned soft and uncertain customer
I am. Had again, still have, though now my head and
purposes are woolly, feeling of necessity to go plain to
the bone and stay there. The 40-day fasts and that
kind of thing. Misnamed virtues: they clear you:
which is a state of grace or virtue. / Virtual / feel in
many words, suddenly like little puffs of light, nowadays, the shine and silver quality wh. is equivalent
(EQUIVALENT is such a word) to a whole certain tone in
Bach. Does Bach and don't many composers reduce to
2 or 3 dominant tones? & I don't mean idioms either.
Same with writers. Mozart's very skillful chromatic developments & returns that an ear holds a lot less surely
than much trickier 20th Century stuff. Analyze (can
you) quality of excitement in minuet of Jupiter. Sense
of a full orchestra in a Beethovenish way of being full,
even in 1st measure when woodwinds have it. Mozart's
queer "darker" music, something like Hopkins' love of
the dappled, the counter, original, spare, strange. In
some rather homely themes of scherzi—and, likelier to
turn up in them than in slo mvts & finales? 1st mvt of
G-minor has some of it, too. Also vide great values of

the prosy & verbose line in poetry, & of bromide almost. Note some of Mozart's more strenuous & some of his more tossed off slow mvts; lyrics in Songs of Innocence; many passages in Schubert; quite a few in Beethoven . . .

Among many entries on music, there is one noting "the great beauty of West End Blues" and another, written firmly with a fresh pencil as if he wanted badly to get it down:

Swing music is different from any contemporary Art Mouthpiece. Barring straight folk stuff and vaude & burlesk adlibbing, runs roughly this way. Writing last had this freedom in Elizabeth's time, with something half like it but crippled in Byron. Sculpture of Africans has it. Music lost it (roughly) with Mozart. Beethoven had but did not use and finally buried it. The 19th and 20th centuries are solidly self-conscious and inhibited. Only swing today is perfectly free and has in its kind a complete scope. Some directors have it. Eisenstein does or did. Disney does or did. Chaplin did. There may be bits of it in some surrealist art. With words, does Perelman have some? and Groucho some? and Durante some? But all pretty much of a kind: not at all capable of wonderful lyric scope of swing. Can words spoken or written possibly break through it again, break through and get free . . .

He worked on some of the poems that were published over the next three years or so, on some that were never published or worth publishing, on others that have not survived. He drafted autobiographical material that would serve him years later in the novel published after his death, as the following entry indicated:

Have been working (c. 12–15,000 words) on the footloose in Knoxville idea. Don't know.

One entry of great importance, because it stated an obsession that had its relevance to everything and especially to "Church" and Christianity, was this:

> Truth goes much less far than falsehood: at every transition, more misunderstanding comes aboard: gradually becomes handleable by those too corrupted by falsehood to handle bare truth. Radium into lead.

I have been quoting these notes generously in the hope that you will hear at least remotely a voice in them and get at least an inkling of what his talk was like. But one final entry I will quote as a thing in itself, comparable to one of Hopkins' beautifully delineated studies of nature in the *Notebooks*. This was during a walk on a misty night under an almost full moon down the beach on Anna Maria.

> Surf as rounded point, coming in at acute angle, running along its edges on shallow sand with tearing glistening sound, like drawn zipper opening. Then around pt., meet surf broadside. In darkness you see it, well out on the dark, explode like opening parachute, and come in. Another kind: where in 2-3 parts on single line it whitens and the white widens—again the glistening zipper action—till all white meets and in it comes. Also: smallish tendons of it, private to themselves, bearing up (no white) and smacking themselves straight down on hard sand beneath a few inches of water with great passion and impact, PFFUHHH. Also, lovely and violent, competent folding-under of seam, pursing as of lips, when wave crest falls so prematurely as to undermine its own back: so you get a competent, systematic turning under in long lines. Also sink and drying of water in sand as shallow wave draws down.

In May, 1936, some time before the great day of the assignment in Alabama, Jim and I journeyed together to Bennington to read our verses to the college. In that budding grove he was almost inaudible, as usual when reading his own or other poems, but then as a kind of encore he did a parody of a southern preacher in a hellfire sermon, and this was more than audible: it brought down the house. I have not found it in manuscript, but I have included in this book a prose parody of the same period, to show the sort of thing he occasionally did. You do not hear much of his parodies. You do not hear much, either, of his mimetic powers, great as they were, though years yater he had a bit part as a "vagrant" in one of his movies. At the time I am thinking of, one of his best acts was a recital of "When the lamp is shattered" in the accent and pitch of rural Tennessee.

We saw a good deal of one another all that spring—by this time I was married and working for *Time*—but by midsummer he was gone into the deep South with Walker Evans on the tenant farmer job. Walker has written very well about that in his short foreword to the 1960 reissue of *Let Us Now Praise Famous Men.*

Jim's passionate eye for the lighted world made him from boyhood a connoisseur of photography, and among all photographers I think the one who had moved him most was Mathew Brady. The portraits and Civil War photographs of Brady were a kind of absolute for him, calling him and sounding in him very deeply. Another near-absolute was the photography in von Stroheim's *Greed*; he especially loved the burning-white powdery kind of sunlight produced by the "orthochromatic" film of that period. These kinds of studied finality and fiery delicacy in images of contemporary existence he found above all in the photographs of Walker Evans. Their work together that summer made them collaborators and close friends for life. It is strange that Jim never wrote much about Evans' photographs. Perhaps this was because only a couple of years later the Museum of Modern Art held a big Evans exhibition for which Lincoln Kirsten wrote a full and handsome introduction. Jim did write, in 1942, an introduction for a proposed book of photographs by another artist he admired, Helen Levitt. For a full and pondered statement of what photography meant to him. you will do well to consult this book, *A Way of Seeing*, finally published in 1965 by the Viking Press. The heart of what he wrote is this:

"The artist's task [in photography] is not to alter the world as the eye sees it into a world of esthetic reality, but to perceive the esthetic reality within the actual world, and to make an undisturbed and faithful record of the instant in which this movement of creativeness achieves its most expressive crystallization. Through his eye and through his instrument the artist has, thus, a leverage upon the materials of existence which is unique . . ."

After the summer in Alabama I should guess that he got his *Fortune* piece done in September or October, and I remember it hanging fire in the autumn, but I can't be sure of these dates. Why did the magazine in the end reject the article that the editor, knowing Agee and therefore presumably knowing more or less what to expect, had assigned him to write? Well, one reason was very simple: the editor was no longer the same man. He was no longer the same man because *Fortune*'s repute in the Duquesne Club and the

Sky Club and the Bohemian Club—in those places, in short, where subscribers met—had been damaged by what appeared to the subscribers as a leftward drift in the contents of the magazine. In 1935 Jim's piece might have been printed, but in 1936, by the excellent disposition of Providence, the new editor, not much liking his duty, did his duty and turned it down.

Now all hands at last had more than a glimmer of a fact I have alluded to earlier—that Agee's vocation, at least at that point and as up to that point meditated by himself and inflamed by his recent experience, was in competition with *Fortune*. It appeared that the magazine, committed of course to knowing what was the case, had had the offhand humanity and imagination and impertinence to send an ex-President of the Harvard *Advocate* into the helpless and hopeless lives of cotton tenant farmers, but that it did not have the courage to face in full the case he presented, since the case involved discomfort not only for the tenants but for *Fortune*. Anything but that. Well and good, this gave him his chance to show *Fortune* and everyone else how to treat the case: he would make the assignment his own and make a book of his own on the tenant farmers. His friend Edward Aswell at Harper & Bros. induced that firm to offer Agee and Evans a contract and an advance, but for the time being Jim did not accept it, fearing that it might affect the writing. He remained loosely attached to *Fortune*. I believe no high words passed.

In 1937 he was in and out of the office on three jobs. The most interesting took him to Havana on an excruciating Caribbean "vacation cruise," of which his narrative, appearing in September as "Six Days at Sea," was a masterpiece of ferocity, or would have been if it had been printed uncut. He had become grimmer about American middle-class ways and desti-

nies, and would become grimmer still. His inclination
to simple cleanliness, for example, turned to anger for
a while as he discerned meanness and status and
sterility even in that.

In the good poems of this period, the one to his
father in *Transition,* the one called *Sunday: Outskirts
of Knoxville,* and some of the lyrics in *The Partisan
Review,* he did things unachieved in *Permit Me Voyage.* But most of the topical poems in quatrains,
published or unpublished, are not so good. He never
did as well in this vein as in the epigrammatic "Songs
on the Economy of Abundance" that he had sent to
Louis Untermeyer for the 1936 edition of *Modern
American Poetry.* His skill with traditional meters
declined; it remained, now, mistrusted and for long
periods unused, or used only casually and briefly. The
Auden-MacNeice *Letters from Iceland* came out that
year with a section of brilliant Byronics, and if Jim
had had any intention of going on with *John Carter*—
as I believe that by now he did not—those pages might
have dissuaded him. Auden's unapproachable virtu-
osity may, in fact, have had something—not much,
but inevitably something—to do with Jim's writing
verse more seldom. "Seen this?" he came in saying one
day, with a new book in his hand, and read aloud the
Auden poem that opens with such beauty:

> Out on the lawn I lie in bed,
> Vega conspicuous overhead,
> In the windless nights of June . . .

In the Bickford's Cafeteria at Lexington and 43rd,
over coffee at some small hour of the morning, we
read together and recognized perfection in a set of
new lyrics by Robert Frost in *The Atlantic;* one was
the short one beginning:

I stole forth dimly in the dripping pause
Between two downpours to see what there was . . .

Perfection of this order Jim now scarcely any longer tried for in verse.

Under one strain and another his marriage was now breaking up; I remember the summer day in '37 when at his suggestion we met in Central Park for lunch and the new young woman in her summer dress appeared. It seems to me that there were months of indecisions and revisions and colloquies over the parting with Via, which was yet not to be a parting, etc., which at length would be accomplished as cruelly required by the laws of New York. Laceration could not have been more prolonged. In the torments of liberty all Jim's friends took part. At Old Field Point on the north shore of Long Island, where the Wilder Hobsons had somehow rented a bishop's boathouse that summer, a number of us attained liberation from the *pudor* of mixed bathing without bathing suits: a mixed pleasure, to tell the truth.

One occasion in this period that I remember well was a public meeting held in June, 1937, in Carnegie Hall, by a "Congress of American Writers," a Popular Front organization, for the Spanish Loyalist cause. Jim and I went to this together, and as we took our seats he turned to me and said, "Know one writer you can be sure isn't here? Cummings." MacLeish spoke, very grave. His speech was a prophetic one in which he might very well have quoted "Ask not for whom the bell tools: it tolls for thee." Then he introduced Hemingway. It must have been the only time in his life that Hemingway consented to couple with a lectern, and as a matter of fact he only stood beside it and leaned on it with one elbow. Bearish in a dark blue suit, one foot cocked over the other, he gave a running commentary to a movie documentary by Joris Ivens on a Spanish town under the Republic. Jim Agee hoped for the Republic, but I don't think he ever saluted anyone with a raised fist or took up Spanish (my own gesture—belated at that). He had joined battle on another ground.

In October he put in his second vain application for a Guggenheim Fellowship. His "Plans for Work" (of which he kept a carbon) are printed in this book and will give you an idea of his mood at the time, maverick and omnivorous as a prairie fire, ranging in every direction for What Was the Case and techniques for telling it. As in '32 he did not fail to indulge in those gratuitous honesties (now about Communism, for instance) that would make it tough for the Guggenheim committee. I do not know how he lived that winter, or lived through it.

Not, however, till the spring of '38 did he take the Harper's contract and settle down with Alma Mailman, in a small frame house at 27 2nd Street, Frenchtown, New Jersey, to write or rewrite and construct his book. Jim wrote for the ear, wanted criticism from auditors, and read to me, either in Frenchtown or in New York, most of the drafts as he got them written. There isn't a word in *Let Us Now Praise Famous Men* that he—and I and others—did not ponder many times. Frenchtown was then quiet and deep in the dense countryside, traversable whenever and as far as necessary in an ancient open flivver; they had a goat, God knows how acquired, in the backyard; there was a tennis court in the town. Jim played an obstinate and mighty game, but wild, against my obstinate and smoother one.

He labored all summer and fall, through the Sudeten crsis and the international conferences and the Nazi mass meetings at Nuremberg and elsewhere that sent the strangled shouting of *Der Führer* and *Sieg Heil, Sieg Heil* in an ominous rhythmic roar over the radios of the country. He labored into the winter. I have found among his things a journal in which he noted on December 1st that when the rent was paid he would have $12.52 in the world and in the same breath went on with plans for his wedding to Alma later that month. In January or February *Fortune* came to the rescue with an assignment: the section on Brooklyn in an issue to be devoted to New York City. For the rest of the winter and spring they moved to a flat in St. James Place, taking the goat with them. When Wilder Hobson went to see them once he found that the neighborhood kids had chalked on the front steps: "The Man Who Lives Here is a Loony."

11

In the living room or backyard of that place I heard several drafts of his prose on Brooklyn, and by some accident kept two drafts in a file. Twenty-four years later these turned out to be the only vestiges of this work in existence. In this case, too, *Fortune* found Jim's article too strong to print and it did not appear in the New York issue (June, 1939). *Fortune's* editor, however, appreciated this labor. As epigraph to the tamer article (by someone else) that finally got into print, the editor lifted one lyric sentence from Jim's piece and quoted it, with attribution. The version printed in this book is Jim's preliminary draft: *Southeast of the Island: Travel Notes*. The later version prepared for *Fortune* editing on May 15, 1939 (by the "ditto" process, which produced a number of legible copies) was shorter by nearly half and lacked the particularity of the earlier piece. Compression and generality served him well in one passage only, funny and biting if you remember that *Fortune* was rather given to Ripley-like statistical play:

> Courtship and marriage are difficult matters to speak of, and it will be the better part of valor not to speak of them, beyond remarking that no park has ever been more eloquently designed beneath the moon for its civic purpose than Prospect; that more homes are owned in Brooklyn than elsewhere in New York City; that there are more children per capita; that the divorce rate is only . . . per cent per head that of Manhattan; that there are 48,000 electric refrigerators in Flatbush alone; and that if all the perambulators in Brooklyn were pushed end to end, at the pace of a walking mother, they would soon reach three times around the origin of species, the history of religion, the cause of imperialistic war, sexual ethics and social fear, and the basis of private property and universal prenatal spiritual suffocation . . .

After the Brooklyn interlude, the Agees returned to Frenchtown for the summer. Some weeks before we heard Mr. Chamberlain's weary voice declaring that a state of war existed between His Majesty's Government and Nazi Germany, Jim Agee's manuscript of a book entitled *Three Tenant Families* was in the hands of the publishers. The war began, and the German armored divisions shot up Poland. In the Harper offices Jim's manuscript must have appeared a doubtful prospect as a rousing topical publishing event. The publishers wanted him to make a few domesticating changes. He would not make the changes. Harper's then deferred publication; they could live without it. He was broke and in debt, and in the early fall he learned that fatherhood impended for him in the spring. I had just fallen heir to the job of "Books" editor at *Time*, so we arranged that he should join me and the other reviewer, Calvin Fixx, at writing the weekly book section, and he and Alma found a flat far over on the west side somewhere below 14th Street.

Now for eight or nine months we worked in the same office several days and/or nights a week. Early that year or maybe late the year before, I can't remember precisely when, the Luce magazines had moved to a new building called the Time & Life Building in Rockefeller Center between 48th and 49th Streets (now superseded by a later and of course bigger and better T & L Building farther west). We had a three-desk office on the twenty-eighth floor with a secretary's cubbyhole. Our secretary, or "checked," with a girl I had known in 1934 when she was Lewis Gannett's secretary on the *Herald Tribune*—a crap-shooting hoydenish girl who used to get weekly twenty-page letters from a lonely and whimsical young man in a San Francisco YMCA, by the name, then unknown, of William Saroyan. In the years between '34 and '39 Mary had been in South Africa and had come back statelier but still *au fond* not giving a damn; her father was an Episcopal canon. She kept track of the review books and publication dates and spotted errors in what we wrote. The other reviewer, Fixx, was a Mormon, a decent, luminously inarticulate man engaged in living down some obscure involvement in the Far Left. He knew a great deal about that particular politics and history, now a great subject for "re-evaluation" after the Ribbentrop-Molotov embrace. Each of us read half-a-dozen books a week and wrote reviews or notes—or nothing—according to our estimates of each.

Jim Agee of course added immeasurably to the pleasure of this way of life. If for any reason a book interested him (intentionally or unintentionally on the author's part) he might write for many hours about it, turning in many thousands of words. Some of these long and fascinating reviews would rebound from the managing editor in the form of a paragraph. We managed nevertheless to hack through that barrier a fairly wide vista on literature in general, including even verse, the despised quarterlies, and scholarship. With light hearts and advice of counsel we reviewed a new edition of the classic *Wigmore on Evidence*. One week we jammed through a joint riview of Henry Miller, for which Jim did *Tropic of Cancer* and I *Tropic of Capricorn*, both unpublishable in the United States until twenty years later. Our argument that time was that if *Time* ought to be written for the Man-in-the-Street (a favorite thought of the Founder), here were books that would hit him where he lived, if he could get them. In all our efforts we were helped by T. S. Matthews, then a senior editor and later for six years managing editor and a friend to Jim Agee.

Not because I idolize Jim or admire every word he ever wrote but again to show his mind at work, this time in that place under those conditions, I will quote the first paragraph of his review of Herbert Gorman's *James Joyce* and the final paragraphs from his review of *The Hamlet* by William Faulkner.

> The utmost type of heroism, which alone is worthy of the name, must be described, merely, as complete self-faithfulness: as integrity. On this level the life of James Joyce has its place, along with Blake's and Beethoven's, among the supreme examples. It is almost a Bible of what a great artist, an ultimately honest man, is up against...

> Whatever their disparities, William Faulkner and William Shakespeare share these characteristics: 1) Their abundance of invention and their courage for rhetoric are bottomless. 2) Enough goes on in their heads to furnish a whole shoal of more temperate

writers. 3) By fair means or foul, both manage to play not for a specialized but for a broad audience.

In passages incandescent with undeniable genius, there is [in *The Hamlet*] nevertheless not one sentence without its share of amateurishness, its stain of inexcusable cheapness.

12

Of the physical make and being of James Agee and his aspect at that time, you must imagine: a tall frame, long-boned but not massive; lean flesh, muscular with some awkwardness; pelt on his chest; a long stride with loose knee-joints, head up, with toes angled a bit outward. A complexion rather dark or sallow in pigment, easily tanned. The head rough-hewn, with a rugged brow and cheek-bones, a strong nose irregular in profile, a large mouth firmly closing in folds, working a little around the gaps of lost teeth. The shape of the face tapered to a sensitive chin, cleft. Hair thick and very dark, a shock uncared for, and best uncared for. Eyes deep-set and rather closely set, a dull gray-blue or feral blue-gray or radiantly lit with amusement. Strong stained teeth. On the right middle finger a callous as big as a boil: one of his stigmata as a writer. The hands and fingers long and light and blunt and expressive, shaping his thought in the air, conveying stresses direct or splay, drawing razor-edged lines with thumb and forefinger: termini, perspective, tones.

His capacity for whiskey, as for everything else, was very great. I saw him once or twice violent with drink, but I never saw him disabled by it and don't know anyone else who ever did. As a rule, with every drink he only became more interested in any subject or line of action—any except going home and going to bed. A little conviviality was enough to get his comic genius off the ground and into such flights as his one-man rendition of the Bach Toccata and Fugue as arranged by Stokowski—a magistral act in which varieties of fruity instrumentation were somehow conveyed by voice and gesture, e.g. the string section by a flapping left hand and "fiddle-faddle, fiddle-faddle, fiddle-faddle." At the invention of American place names, or personal names, Jim had no peer; one of his best compositions, brought off while wandering late at night with Wilder Hobson, was the man's name, "George F. Macgentsroom." Very rarely, he might follow through with an inspiration from one of those evenings. In his war against middle-class folkways he struck a happily premeditated blow at the Christmas card custom by sending out, one Christmas, a card bearing as its olde winter scene a photograph of a pair of polar bears in innocent copulation, with season's greetings.

At the piano he sat well back and more than erect, head withdrawn and watchful, eyes downcast over the length of arms and fingers in hard exertion at the keyboard. It was the old upright that his grandmother had given him; I think he had it for twenty years. When he played he would have the whole form of the sonata or whatever it was before him in his mind. Battered conclamant notes, quite a few near misses, very little sweet shading or pianissimo. At his writing he looked the same: his left hand pinning down at arm's length a stack of yellow second sheets, leaning far back from it frowning (by this time he was getting far-sighted; he tried, but discarded, some steel-rimmed glasses), power flowing through the sharp pencil into the tiny closely-organized script. Wholly focused on it, as I remember him in warm weather once, oblivious of the closed office window behind him, stifling in a fog of cigarette smoke, with a small pure space cleared before him amid mountains of litter.

He wore blue or khaki work shirts and under the armpits there would be stains, salt-edged, from sweat; likewise under the arms of his suit jacket, double-breasted dark blue, wrinkled and shiny. He was too poor to afford a lot of laundering, and he didn't believe in it, anyway. After the baby arrived in March, '40, I remember one big scene in which Jim was engaged in spooning Pablum into Joel. The father sat, all elbows and knees, in an arm chair upholstered in some ragged and ancient fabric that had grown black absorbing through the years the grime of New York. The infant in his lap mouthed with a will at the Pablum but inevitably gobs of it splattered down even on the richly unsanitary arms of the chair, whence Jim would scoop it in long dives lest it drip—irretrievably, you could hope—on the floor.

The time was about over for all fragile arrangements and lightness of heart. In those days the German airborne troops were taking Norway. There was nothing we could do about it. One fine day in late spring, playing tennis with Jim on some courts south of Washington Square, I broke a bone in my instep. *Life* with a wealth of illustration assured us that General Gamelin was the flower of military science and the French army the finest in Europe. Within a week or so it looked as though *Life* had exaggerated. While I was still getting around on a plaster clubfoot the British were evacuating Dunkirk and the panzers were going through the Ardennes. The dress parade of the German army down the Champs-Elysées was reported by the *World-Telegram* with a photograph of the Arc de Triomphe and the headline ICI REPOSE UN SOLDAT

FRANÇAIS MORT POUR LA PATRIE. I looked at this and
realized that so far as I was concerned a decade had
come to an end, and so had a mode of life, to flatter
it by that term, that included working for *Time*. To
see what could be done about my *modus vivendi* in
general, I turned over "Books" to Agee, Fixx and
Whittaker Chambers and departed, taking my first
wife away to the west and eventually to Santa Fe for
the winter. There I settled down on my savings to do
unnecessary and unpaid work for the first time in five
years. I had resigned. Taking no offense, and with
great accuracy of foresight, the people at *Time* made
it a leave of absence until a year from that October.
I intrude these details because I am about to quote a
few passages from Jim's letters to me during the year.
At some point in the spring or summer Houghton
Mifflin, to their eternal credit, accepted the manuscript that Harper's had released to him. Well, from
a letter in December:

> . . . Excepting Wilder, whose getting-a-job has done
> him a favor as leaving-it has you, everyone I see, my-
> self included, is at a low grinding ebb of quiet despera-
> tion: nothing, in most cases, out of the ordinary, just
> the general average Thoreau was telling about, plus
> the dead-ends of one of the most evil years in history,
> plus each individual's little specialty act. I don't think
> I'll go into much if any detail—for though I could
> detail it blandly and painlessly and some of it is of
> 'clinical' interest, it could possibly have an intrusive
> and entangling effect. So I can most easily and
> honestly say that it isn't as bad as I've perhaps sug-
> gested, except by contrast with health and free action—
> is, in fact, just the average experience of people liv-
> ing as people shouldn't, where people shouldn't, doing
> what people shouldn't and little or nothing of what
> people should. Journalists, hacks, husbands, wives,

sisters, neurotics, self-harmed artists, and such. Average New York Fall.

The book is supposed to be published January or February—no proofs yet, though. I now thoroughly regret using the subtitle (Let Us Now Praise Famous Men) as I should never have forgotten I would. I am rather anxious to look at it, finished and in print—possibly, also, to read it in that form—but I have an idea I'll be unable to stand to. If so, it might be a healthy self-scorching to force myself to: but that's probably my New England chapel-crank blood. Mainly, though, I want to be through with it, as I used to feel about absolution, and to get to work again as soon as I can. I am thirty-one now, and I can conceivably forgive myself my last ten years only by a devotion to work in the next ten which I suspect I'll be incapable of. I am much too vulnerable to human relationships, particularly sexual or in any case heterosexual, and much too deeply wrought-upon by them, and in turn much too dependent in my work on 'feeling' as against 'intellect.' In short I'm easily upset and, when upset, incapable of decent work; incapable of it also when I'm not upset enough. I must learn my ways in an exceedingly quiet marriage (which can be wonderful I've found but is basically not at all my style or apparent 'nature') or break from marriage and all close liaisons altogether and learn how to live alone & keep love at a bearable distance. Those are oddly juvenile things to be beginning to learn at my age: what really baffles me is that, knowing them quite well since I was 15, I've done such thorough jobs in the opposite direction. Well, nothing would be solved or even begun tonight by any thing I wrote or thought, or at any time soon: my business now and evidently for quite a while to come is merely to sit as tight and careful as I can, taking care above all to do no further harm to others or myself or my now virtually destroyed needs or hopes, and doing a timorous or drastic piece of mending when or wherever there seems any moment's chance to. I haven't been very intelligent—to say nothing of 'good'—and now it's scarcely a chance for intelligence or goodness—only for the most dumb and scrupulous tenacity. On the whole, though, it's time I had a good hard dose of bad going, and if I find I'm capable of it the winter will be less wasted than it otherwise might be. Meanwhile, though, I find I'm so dull I bore myself sick. A broken spirit and a contrite heart have their drawbacks: worst of all if at the same time the spirit is unbroken and ferocious and the heart contrite only in the sense of deep grief over pain and loss, not at all in true contrition . . .

I thought *The Long Voyage Home* quite awful . . .

I feel very glad you like the reviews. I wish I did. As a matter of fact I have hardly judgment or feeling, for or against, and on the whole, not a bad time with the job, except a general, rather shamed feeling, week by week, that with real intelligence & effort I could do much better, whatever the limitations of space and place. Then a book as important as Kafka's *America* can't even get reviewed, and I shrug it off again . . .

The magazine you write of [an imaginary one.— R. F.] makes my mouth water. I spend a lot of time thinking of such things and of equivalent publishers. They really existed in France and Germany and even in England. The fact that they don't here and I suppose won't ever, by any chance, makes me know just a little better what a fat-assed, frumpish hell-on-earth this country is. Last stronghold of just what . . . But I do love to think about magazines like that. And the writing *can* be done—the only really important thing—whenever and wherever qualified people can cheat their inferiors out of the time it takes. Thank God you're getting it . . .

That is the longest excerpt. A shorter one, from a letter of February or March (he never dated his letters) :

... I'm in a bad period: incertitude and disintegration on almost every count. Somehow fed up and paralytic with the job; horribly bad sleeping rhythm; desperate need to live regularly & still more to do new work of my own; desperate knowledge that with all the time on earth I could as I spiritually feel now be capable of neither ... Alma is in Mexico—so is Joel—nominally, presumably, perhaps very probably, that is broken forever. And so far, I am not doing the one thing left me to do if it is ever possibly to reintegrate: entirely leave knowing Mia. It is constantly in the bottom of my gut—petrifying everything else—that I must, and will; and I still do nothing. A kind of bottomless sadness, impotence and misery in which one can neither move a hand nor keep it still without some further infliction on one or another ... For some doubtless discreditable reason it is of some good to speak of it, but I hope I don't do so at your expense, in sympathy or concern (I've known such things to derail me) —There is truly no need; as I say, I'm only too detached and anesthetized.

I delayed 2 months in all this trouble, in correcting proofs, but all is done now so I presume the machinery is turning. Don't yet know the publication date though.

Another one from about June, 1941:

Your last letters have sounded so thoroughly well in the head and health and so exciting in potentiality, that the thought of its shutting-off in a few more months, with your return to work, has made me probably almost as sick as it makes you.

I think this could be rather easily solved as follows: What with one expense and another I shall nowhere near have paid off my debts by October and so will nowhere near be free to quit work and get to my own. So why don't I continue at this work and you continue at yours, for 6 months or 8 or a year (we can arrange that) during which I could send you and Eleanor $100 a month.

That would be very scrawny to live on in most parts of this country; but apparently in Mexico would be: in Mexico City an adequate poverty; elsewhere an amplitude. This would, then, involve living where perhaps you might rather not; but a living, and free time, would be assured. And when I am able to quit work, if you are ready or need to come back, you could do likewise for me on some general equalization—

I think that by this or some such arrangement we & others might really get clear time when we are ripe for it, and it seems a better chance than any other—What do you think? . . .

Another a bit later:

. . . Nothing on earth could make me feel worse than that you should for any reason whatever have to come back now that you are ripe for so much.

As for the money, I feel as you do, that it belongs to him who most needs it at a given time—your need for it for the next year or so is far out of proportion to any I could have short of a year or so of freedom first, and greater too than you would be likely to have again, without a long stretch of preparatory freedom. I think neither of us should think twice about your later paying me back—that is a wrong conception of the whole thing. I'll be able to take care of myself, one way or another, when my time comes for it—meanwhile I'll be best taking care for things I care for most, if I can make freedom and work possible for you when you can make the best use of it.

I'm talking badly out of turn in all this walking-in and urging—I hope you can forgive it. It seems terribly crucial to me that you stay free at this particular time, and criminal if you don't . . .

Chambers is still moving Books at *Time*—Stockley does Letters, and an occasional review. If you should come back—which God forbid—I imagine I could get switched to movies & you could replace me here . . .

13

I hope an occasional reader will understand that the foregoing private things are quoted after long hesitation and at the expense of my heart's blood. I think I am aware of every way in which they—and he, and I—can be taken advantage of. Jim Agee's agonies and his nobleness are equally the affair of no one who cannot keep still, or as good as still, about them, and there is no chance that all of you can. But some of you can, and some of you are thirty or thirty-one and hard beset and bound to someone in brotherhood, perhaps in art, and you may see that the brotherhood you know is of a kind really wider than you may have thought, binding others among the living and the dead. It is best, at any rate, that you should have the living movement of his own mind about his New York life and the dissolution of his second marriage, and it is essential that you should see proof of selflessness in a man who often appeared self-centered, and often was.

Before the publication of *Let Us Now Praise Famous Men,* just before I returned to New York, I received the book in September, '41, for review in *Time.* When Jim got word of this he wrote at once, airmail special, to make sure whether I had been consulted, whether I had time to spare for it, and whether if, consulted or not, I did have time and would write the review, we shouldn't agree that he would not read it. I wrote a review but the editor who had invited it thought it was too stiff and reverent (he was right) and sent it back. He reviewed the book himself, recognized great writing in it, but classified it as "a distinguished failure." By this he, as an old Fortune editor, did not really mean that if *Fortune* had done it it would have been a success, but

that was true: it would have been objective and
clearly organized and readable and virtuously restrained, and would have sounded well and been of
small importance beyond the month it appeared. A
failure on the contrary it consciously was, a "young
man's book," and a sinful book to boot (as Jim called
it in a letter to Father Flye) and was thereby true to
the magnitude and difficulty of the case including the
observer. It is a classic, and perhaps the only classic,
of the whole period, of the whole attempted *genre*.
Photographs and text alike are bitten out by the very
juices of the men who made them, and at the same
time they have the piteous monumentality of the
things and souls represented. Between them Agee and
Evans made sure that George and Annie Mae Gudger
are as immortal as Priam and Hecuba, and a lot closer
to home.

I refused to take about a quarter of Jim's already
mortgaged income, as he proposed, and returned to
work for *Time* from October, '41, to May, '43, when
to my relief I joined the Navy. That October of my
return he got "switched to movies," all right, and the
last and perhaps the best phase of his life began. He
and Mia Fritsch, who was to be his third wife, moved
into the top-floor flat on Bleecker Street where they
lived for the next ten years. Before I went to Fort
Schuyler I managed to revise my manuscript of poems
and put them together in a book, but not until Jim
had commented on each in the most minute and
delicate written criticism I ever had.

How more than appropriate, how momentous, it
was that after 1941 James Agee had "Cinema" for all
occupation could scarcely have been realized to the
full by anyone, but a few of us at least felt uncom-
monly at peace about Jim's employment. He loved
movies more than anyone I ever knew; he also lived

them and thought them. To see and hear him describe a movie that he liked—shot by shot, almost frame by frame—was unquestionably better in many cases than to see the movie itself. Once when I was driving him across the Brooklyn Bridge in an open Model-A, he put on beside me such a rendering of Jimmy Cagney in a gangster film that I had to take my eyes off the road and give him my close attention. There must have been moments on that ride when we were both absolutely uninsurable.

He had wanted for years to do a scenario for Chaplin; whether he ever did more than imagine it, I have been unable to find out. By the late 30's he had, however, not only written but published two scenarios, both stunning exercises in what must be called screen-writing as literature. Both are published in this book.

The first, entitled "Notes for a Moving Picture: The House," was printed by Horace Gregory in a collection called *New Letters in America*, in 1937. Detailing ever shot and every sound, second by counted second, with his huge sensuous precision and scope, he constructed a screen fantasy for the camera, his angelic brain, before whose magnifying gaze or swimming movement a tall old house disclosed its ghastly, opulent moribundity until blown and flooded apart in an apocalyptic storm. Compare this with the efforts of more recently "rebellious" young men if you want to see how close to artistic non-existence most of these are.

His second scenario was published in the first number of a review, *Films*, edited by Jay Leyda in 1939. In this one he merely (if you could use that word of anything Jim did) transposed into screen terms the famous scene in *Man's Fate* in which the hero, Kyo, waits with other Chinese Communists to be thrown by the Nationalists into the boiler of a locomotive. I am told that Malraux, who thought he had got everything out of this scene, thought again when he read the Agee script.

Concerning his movie reviewing for *Time*, T. S. Matthews has told me of one incident. Matthews as managing editor late one Sunday evening received and read a cover story Jim had written, on Laurence Olivier's *Hamlet*, and in Jim's presence indicated that he found it good enough, a little disappointing but good enough and in any case too late to revise; he initialed it for transmission to the printer (*Time* went to press on Monday) and in due course left for home presuming that Jim had also done so. At nine the next morning Jim presented him with a complete new handwritten version. Fully to appreciate this you would perhaps have to have felt the peculiar exhaustion of Sunday night at *Time*.

Jim Agee, however, had now found a kind of journalism answering to his passion. Beginning in December, '42, he began the signed movie column for the *Nation*, every other week, that Margaret Marshall, the literary editor, invited and backed, and that in the next several years made him famous. He began to be called on at *Time* for general news stories to which no one else could do justice. Whatever he wrote for the magazine was so conspicuous that it might as well have been signed. In the Western Pacific I recognized at once his hand in *Time*'s page-one piece on the meaning of Hiroshima and Nagasaki:

> . . . In what they said and did, men were still, as in the aftershock of a great wound, bemused and only semi-articulate, whether they were soldiers or scientists, or great statesmen, or the simplest of men. But in the dark depths of their minds and hearts, huge forms moved and silently arrayed themselves: Titans, arrang-

ing out of the chaos an age in which victory was already only the shout of a child in the street.

. . . All thoughts and things were split. The sudden achievement of victory was a mercy, to the Japanese no less than to the United Nations; but mercy born of a ruthlessness beyond anything in human chronicle. The race had been won, the weapon had been used by those on whom civilization could best hope to depend; but the demonstration of power against living creatures instead of dead matter created a bottomless wound in the living conscience of the race. The rational mind had won the most Promethean of its conquests over nature, and had put into the hands of common man the fire and force of the sun itself . . .

. . . The promise of good and of evil bordered alike on the infinite—with this further, terrible split in the fact: that upon a people already so nearly drowned in materialism even in peacetime, the good uses of this power might easily bring disaster as prodigious as the evil. The bomb rendered all decisions so far, at Yalta and at Potsdam, mere trivial dams across tributary rivulets. When the bomb split open the universe and revealed the prospect of the infinitely extraordinary, it also revealed the oldest, simplest, commonest, most neglected and most important of facts: that each man is eternally and above all else responsible for his own soul, and, in the terrible words of the Psalmist, that no man may deliver his brother, nor make agreement unto God for him.

Man's fate has forever been shaped between the hands of reason and spirit, now in collaboration, again in conflict. Now reason and spirit meet on final ground. If either or anything is to survive, they must find a way to create an indissoluble partnership.

Enough, and perhaps more than enough, has been said by various people about the waste of Jim's talents in journalism. It is a consolation and a credit to his employers that on this occasion, as on some others, he was invited and was able to dignify the reporting of events.

14

When I got back to New York in 1946 I found Jim in a corduroy jacket, a subtle novelty, and in a mood far more independent than before of Left or "Liberal" attitudes. He had become a trace more worldly and better off (I'm sure Matthews saw to it that he was decently paid) and more sure of himself; and high time, too. His years of hard living and testing and questioning had given him in his *Nation* articles a great charge of perceptions to express. His lifetime pleasure in cinema had made him a master of film craft and repertory. He had had some of the public recognition that he deserved. Most important of all, I think, this critical job had turned his mind a few compass points from the bearing Truth to the bearing Art. He was ready to take a hand, as he was soon to do, in the actual and practical making of films.

We were never estranged, but we were never so close again, either, as we had been before the war. The course of things for me (here I must intrude a little again) had not only broken up my own previous marriage and way of life but had brought me back in astonishment, with a terrific bump, into Catholic faith and practice; and though Jim intensely sympathized with me in the break-up, he regarded my conversion with careful reserve. He saw an old friend ravaged and transported by the hair into precisely the same system of coordinates that he had wrestled out of in the 30's. Or rather, not precisely the same. For in my turn I had reservations, now, about the quality of his old vision. It struck me that for him it must have been a matter of imagination and empathy, a profound and sacramental sense of the natural world, but only a notion of the incommensurable overhead, the change of light and being that leaves a man no fulcrum by which to dislodge himself from his new place. With my all-too-negative capability and other flaws, I could easily have been self-deceived, as he must have imagined. I was not, however. At any rate, I now wanted to lead a kind of life that Jim had rejected and, in his own and general opinion, outgrown; and there was (at most) one art that I might practice, the art of verse that he had likewise left behind.

All the same, the memory of what he had aspired literally to be, in college and for the first years thereafter, could return now and again to trouble him. One day in 1947 when he and Mia brought their first baby, Teresa, to spend an afternoon with my wife and myself, he handed me the two very sad and strange sonnets on the buried steed, published three years later in *Botteghe Oscure* and now included in the collection of Agee's poems recently edited by myself. His hand at verse had barely retained but not refined its skill, and there is a coarseness along with the complexity of these and other late sonnets. Two or three of the final poems are very beautiful, though. "Sleep, Child" certainly is, and so is the peerless Christmas ballad in Tennessee dialect (but I am not sure how late that one is, and have no clue as to when it was written).

The last verses that he wrote were some rather casually attempted drafts, by invitation, for a musical that in the late winter and spring of 1955 Lillian Hellman and Leonard Bernstein were trying to make of *Candidate*. Both playwright and composer felt that these drafts wouldn't do, but Miss Hellman is not sure that Jim, who was more desperately ill than he knew, understood this before his fatal heart attack on

May 16th. "He was not a lyric writer," Miss Hellman says. "Good poets often aren't." At my distance I find the episode fairly astringent. In their most nearly completed state, the drafts appear in Agee's *Collected Poems* at the end of Part IV. They may be compared with the lighter lyrics by various hands, mainly Richard Wilbur's, for the show as produced in December, 1956.

Helen Levitt has told me that only a year or so before his death in 1955 Jim seriously said to her that poetry had been his true vocation, the thing he was born to do, but that it was too difficult; on the other hand, work in films was pure pleasure for him. I think he had in mind the difficulty for everyone—not only for himself—of making true poetry in that time; I think, too, that what he was born to do, he did.

Jim's leaning to self-accusation does not seem to me very deplorable, however. It was, rather, part of what gave him his largeness among his contemporaries, most of whom were engaged in pretending that they were wonderful and their mishaps or shortcomings all ascribable to Society or History or Mother or other powers in the mythology of the period. I gather that he got cooler and tougher about everything in his last years, in particular about love. Before he went to the Coast, in the late 40's, he wrote a draft scenario, never worked up for production or publication, in which with disabused and cruel objectivity he turned a camera eye on himself in his relations with women.

After my wife and I moved away from New York in the summer of 1949, we saw him only once again, for an evening, in the following spring. His last letter to me was from Malibu Beach in 1952: I had written to say how much I liked *The African Queen*. Of his final years I can have little to say. (I had been in Italy for two years when the shocking cable came to tell me of his death). I am told that young men in New York began heroizing him and hanging on his words, but late one night at a *Partisan Review* sort of party a younger writer in impatience saw him as "a whisky-listless and excessive saint." I myself felt my heart sink when I began to read *The Morning Watch*; the writing seemed to me a little showy, though certainly with much to show; and I wondered if he were losing his irony and edge. It is pretty clear to me now that he had to go to those lengths of artifice and musical elaboration simply to make the break with journalism decisive. He never lost his edge, as *A Death in the Family* was to demonstrate—that narrative held so steadily and clearly in the middle distance and at the same time so full of Jim's power of realization, a contained power, fully comparable to that in the early work of Joyce. Let the easy remark die on your lips. Jim arrived at his austere style fifty years and a torn world away from Edwardian Dublin and Trieste; if it took him twenty years longer than it took Joyce, who else arrived at all?

The comparison with Joyce is worth pausing over a moment more. Each with his versatile and musical gift, each proud and a world-plunderer, each choosing the savage beauty of things as they are over the impossible pieties of adolescence, each concerned with the "conscience of his race." Agee had less icecold intellect; he could not have derived what Joyce did from Aquinas. He had, of course, nothing like Joyce's linguistic range. His affections were more widely distributed and perhaps dissipated. He inherited the violence that Americans inherit: a violence, too (it will not have escaped you), no more directed against office buildings, employers and bourgeois horrors than against himself. The cinema that interested Joyce in its infancy had by Agee's time become a splendid art form, a successor perhaps to the art of fiction, and who else understood it better than he? The record is there in two volumes. Joyce had more irony, but Joyce, too, sentimentalized or angelicized the role of the artist. In all Agee's work the worst example of this is in the scenario of *Noa Noa,* and anyone can see that script becoming at times a maudlin caricature of the artist-as-saint.

Jim's weakness and strength were not so easy to tell apart. Consider, if you will, his early story, "They That Sow in Sorrow Shall Reap." Through weakness, through not being able to do otherwise, the boy narrator brings the laborer to the boardinghouse and so precipitates the catastrophe that leaves the scene and people in ruins. Or it is entirely through weakness? Is it not also through a dispassionate willingness to see his microcosm convulsed for the pure revelation of it, for an epiphany that he may record? Was it weakness later that kept James Agee at *Fortune,* or was it strategy and will, for the sake of the great use he would make of it? Ruins were left behind then, too, but in New York journalism of the 30's no one created anything like the Alabama book. Likewise, no weekly reviewer of the 40's created anything like the body of new insights contained in his *Nation* film pieces. Again, no writer of film pieces prepared himself to write for cinema with such clean and lovely inventiveness (barring the instance I have noted). Finally, no scriptwriter except possibly Faulkner exercised, or learned, in film writing the control over fiction that went into *A Death in the Family.* When you reflect on his life in this way, weakness and strategy, instinct and destiny seem all one thing.

In one of the best novels of the 60's, a charmer by a Southerner, I find a sentence running like this, of cemeteries that at first look like cities from a train passing at a slight elevation: ". . . tiny streets and corners and curbs and even plots of lawn, all of such a proportion that in the very instant of being mistaken and from the eye's own necessity, they set themselves off into the distance like a city seen from far away."* It is an Agee sentence, so I conclude that his writing has entered into the mainstream of English. But I share with him a disinclination for Literary History and its idiom. Jim may be a Figure for somebody else, he cannot be one for me.

> This breathing joy, heavy on us all

—it is his no longer; nevertheless, I have written this in his presence and therefore as truly as I could. Quite contrary to what has been said about him, he amply fulfilled his promise. In one of his first sonnets he said, of his kin, his people:

> 'Tis mine to touch with deathlessness their clay,
> And I shall fail, and join those I betray.

In respect to that commission, who thinks that there was any failure or betrayal?

---

* From *The Moviegoer*, by Walker Percy.

PART II

EARLY STORIES

Death in the Desert

Between Springerville and Magdalena lie one hundred and forty miles of desert so deathly that no sane man will undertake them on foot. Accordingly the outskirts of Springerville are scattered with bums, strung out singly along the road and quite frankly waiting for luck.

The night before I had covered nearly two hundred miles, had arrived at about dawn in St. John's and had been five hours getting here. I bought a can of sauerkraut and a loaf of bread at an A. & P., found a quiet spot behind a church, and took my time with my day's meal. I couldn't do much else, as a matter of fact: my jaw was so swollen I could hardly chew. After a cup of coffee in a lunch bar, I fished out a cigarette. I had only four left and a long jump ahead, so I went back to the A. & P. and bought two packs. I was all set, now. I strolled out of town by the eastern highway. The first two cigarettes got some support from breakfast, the third was flat, and the fourth half made me sick: it was getting hotter minute by minute, and my ear was beginning to pound in grand style.

Bums lined the road at intervals of a hundred yards or so. I took up my position at the far end of the line, about half a mile from town. For a while I talked with a peg-legged man of perhaps sixty; he spent his winters with his niece and her husband in St. Louis. In the summers he got out of their way. His luck was always good, he said—too damned good. This summer he'd been through St. Louis twice already. Unless he did somehting about it, he'd be there again inside of a week. Did I have a cigarette? Thanks. He'd run out that morning. No, he didn't see his niece, either time he was in St. Louis. He'd tried that, three summers ago—just dropped in for supper one night. They'd given him supper and told him to get the hell out, did he think this was cold weather? I was a young fellow, and he wanted to pass on some advice, which was to let well enough alone. All the while, as he talked, he watched the cars come up the road, and flicked his thumb eastward as each one approached. He stood always with his peg leg toward town. Before long a Chandler, after running a half-mile gauntlet of men, slowed down for him. He took another cigarette and was gone.

For the rest of us, rides came more slowly. My ear was too sore, by now, to make talking a pastime. I sat down on my coat and decided that it was rather less than necessary on days like this. After a couple of hours, I considered the manifold advantages of being conspicuously a cripple. After another hour I had the idea of holding up a sign:

SORE EAR

PLEASE

This request seemed a little ambiguous, and a lousy idea at best. As always, I kept watch on the license plates, and as always, had unreasonable hopes of luck from cars of my own state. In the four hours I waited one Maine car passed; it didn't even slow up. So, once more, I enjoyed being pretty sore at Maine. Since I had no right to be, I got a good deal of fun out of it. It was also gratifying to get seven reinforcements to my theory that of all motorists those of Pennsylvania are least hospitable to bums.

Man by man, the line was dwindling. There was no foretelling your luck: half a dozen trucks and ratty Fords might pass; then a new Buick or even, sometimes, a Pierce-Arrow, would stop for one of us. I began to wish I had shaved; sometimes it makes all the difference between a truck and a Pierce-Arrow—and sometimes it doesn't. With my ear in the shape it was, I'd have been willing to travel in a tux or a green gauze chiton for the sake of a good ride. A Transcontinental Bus came piling eastward, just one jump ahead of its blind trail of dust. Two out of three bums stepped into the road and waved frantically. The driver and some of the passengers laughed and waved back. This show of democracy on their part cheered me up, but not for long; my ear was too sore for sustained good humor. A little later a Chrysler with Purdue stickers tore through. Riding in the rumble seat beside a white sweater and an open clean collar and three weeks' fine golden down was a young Polack I had run into in Omaha. He looked back, and waved and grinned from a hundred yards ahead. I persuaded myself that his ride was good for at least a thousand miles, and managed to get thoroughly griped at the world in general. He could damned well have gotten his boy-friends to pick me up. If there wasn't room, well, I'd ridden the running-boards before, and I could do it again. I had a fairly good time elaborating the various phases of this: and about then a car slowed down.

It was a Buick touring car from Oklahoma, five or six years old and in need of paint, but apparently capable of speed. It was funny that even in my present condition, I could be snooty about my cars, but I was; and so is every bum. Few bums, however, are snooty enough ever to refuse a ride.

I climbed into the back seat. There was a boy of ten, asleep in the far corner.

"Thanks," I said, and began to dig a hole in the mass of suitcases, pop bottles and soiled blankets. The man got under way, and drawled into the windshield, "Just move that baggage around any way you like."

"Thanks."

"How far you going?" his wife asked.

"Maine."

"Maine? Gee, you got a long ways to go, ain't you?"

I laughed at that as if it was news to me, and said, "Yeah. But I've come a long ways, too."

He said, "Yeah, I reckon that's right," went into a huddle with himself, and said, "Why? Where'd you come from?"

"The Coast . . . Tia Juana, last."

"Oh, yeah, there. That's a pretty hard place, they tell me. Lots of gambling, lots of liquor, there, huh?"

I was a little too shot to give him his idea of Tia Juana, and said, "Oh, not so bad as it's painted."

"Not, huh?"

His wife heaved around, and said, "Oh. It's not so bad as it's painted, huh?"

"No ma'am," I shot back.

We all thought things over for a few minutes. Then he said: "Been working?"

"Some in the wheat fields, first of the summer." I began to think fast. Was I going to college or working, or in High School?

"What do you do at home? In school?"

"No, not right now. I been out of High School a couple years. Just doing jobs as they turn up."

"You aim to go on to college?" the man said.

"Well, I don't rightly know. I been thinking some of going to State of Maine, this fall; but I don't know."

His wife leaned round again, got firmly settled, and said: "I want to give you a piece of advice: you go ahead to college. You won't never regret it."

"Well, I know," I said, "education—."

"Education is a great thing," her husband stated. "I sure wisht I'd had the sense to complete mine."

"Well, I know it is if you go at it right. But trouble is with a lot of these college fellows, when they get out in the world they got to unlearn everything they ever learned."

"I do' know. Maybe you're right," he mourned. "But I aim to give my boy the best he can get."

"You must know the Stein Song, don't you?" The woman brightened.

"Oh—no, not very well."

"Can you sing it? Come on, sing for us." She began to hum it.

"I'd wake up your boy."

"Oh, you can't wake him up. Come on, sing it."

I felt a little foolish. "I'd rather not."

"Aw, let him be. He don't want to sing that song."

"That's a pretty song." She encouraged me by smiling and singing more loudly.

"I'm kind of sick," I despaired; and that was no lie. "It would hurt me to sing."

"What's wrong?"

"I've got a boil in my right ear."

"A what?"

"A boil. It's terrible sore. I can't hardly chew my food."

"A boil in his ear. I never heard of nothing like that, did you, Joe?"

"Sure I have, and so have you. What'd you think was wrong with Dob Foster, last spring?"

"Oh did he have a boil in his ear?"

He turned his head, and said, "You better see a doctor."

"It'll be all right in a day or two."

"Oh, I'd see a doctor if I was you. Dob Foster didn't get no relief till he seen the doctor."

"I've had them before. They don't last long with me."

"Well . . ."—and he disposed of ears and began on doctors. He proposed that they are a blessing to humanity. I admitted the probability of this. He embellished this theme, and by way of "but by jinny a doctor ain't always the thing," modulated to a passage on the efficacy of herbs. His wife said her mother could vouch for the power of certain charms, and her cousins in Arkansas wouldn't have a thing to do with doctors. I tried to get her going on charms and queer cures, but she had nothing new on this. Her husband insisted that doctors are a blessing to humanity and that he never yet seen a charm work. I said well, I didn't know about that, and told of Maine a lie or two I had picked up in Tennessee. His wife cheered up right away, and went over her ground *in re* charm cures. He said she was just ignernt, that was all; and after twenty minutes on this matter they got round to the value of education in general, and from that to the fact that I'd better see a doctor. If I didn't want to see a doctor, why then there were other cures, she didn't care what Joe said. Joe said she could think up cures darn quick for a woman that had never even heard of boils in the ear, five minutes ago. She said she reckoned what was good for ear-*ache* was good for boils in the ear. He said that was an entirely different matter, that any fool could tell her that. She said, could tell her what? He said my God didn't she know what they'd been talking about all this time? She said well! it was too hot to think straight anyhow. He said if her brains were so weak they couldn't stand a little heat she'd a damn sight better stayed home. She said well! she liked that and besides, Centerville, Oklahoma wasn't no icebox. He wanted to know what the hell that had to do with it. She said if he had to cuss at her like that he'd much better quit talking. I felt like telling them both to go to hell, but I found I was half asleep anyway. After a little backing and filling to keep their self-respect, they shut up. Joe allowed her the last tag, and she said nothing when he increased speed ten miles an hour. So they were both fairly happy, but not nearly so pleased as I.

Joe visibly chewed tobacco, but I wanted to smoke; so I offered him a cigarette. That gave him the satisfaction of calling my attention to his preference. When that was over, I set fire to a Lucky and slouched down until I sat on my kidneys. My face was crawling with fatigue, and now my nose began to itch unbearably, as it does when I am very hot and tired and unwashed. I mauled it meditatively, and smoked several Luckies, and was quite contented. I gave my ear all possible comfort in my cupped hand, and once more felt the film-thin globe of lead build around my brain. This was the state that passed for sleep, most of the time, now that I was bumming. In a lazy, ticklish way, I was acutely conscious, but nothing could worry or interest me. I was, rather, passively amused at anything. The dark cage of the Buick and the two backs before me were like shadows against the great screen of the desert. I could hear the two backs talking from time to time, but it meant nothing to me. The man said God, wasn't it hot, and the woman agreed with him. I thought Oh, Yeah? and felt quite witty. After a while he said they still had ninety-seven miles to go. She wondered if the water really would last them through. Well, the man at the filling station said so, didn't he? I thought, ask the man at the filling station; he knows and knows and knows. The man at the filling station is trained to help you. He is not only your servant but your dear friend. He loves you and you love him. God how you love him. Kindly report any discourtesy. That was a howl, too. I performed one of my favorite tricks, and saw two skeletons in the front seat. One wore a dirty sleeveless dress and remarked that it sure would be good to get back to Oklahoma. The other manipulated the steering wheel, and its skull chewed tobacco mournfully. I allowed this skull to sprout horns, and they were very funny until I realized that the lady skeleton couldn't possibly fulfill her requirements. So I dehorned the man.

The car slowed down and the skeletons sprang into flesh. Nothing I could do prevented it.

"Need any help, brother?"

I looked out. Two men and a good-looking girl were working on a tire.

"No thanks. Just a flat."

"Got a spare?"

"It's OK. We mend our own tubes," the girl said. She was tall, and darkly blond.

Oh, you mend your own, huh? I thought. Talented girl. Great girl to have around the house. "Please, sir: I majored in domestic science and eugenics. May I be your bride?"

As we started again I leaned out and smiled at her. She grinned and waved and I waved back.

The car was from Massachusetts, and I wished they

had picked me up. I also wondered if they were from Boston or Cambridge, and speculated on my chances of seeing the girl again. In spite of all I could do, they seemed pretty thin; so I dropped back into my skeleton routine. But the girl kept breaking in on this train of thought, and I found that a confusion of lovely flesh and Oklahoma bones wasn't as amusing as you might think. So I thought of other swell girls I had seen once and never seen again, and of the very few girls I had not, strictly speaking, lost, and I became rather unhappy; and after a while, with the feeling that all this was pretty sour, I set myself to remembering good walks I had taken.

I could remember a path through Tennessee woods; every turn of it, and every fork; and the place I used to leave it for a trickling ravine that ran down into Shake-Rag Hollow. There was a flat of sand half way down, printed with exciting tracks that I could never identify. Once, a little farther down, I had come suddenly upon a king snake and a rattler, fighting. There had been a silver flash and flex of sinew scattering last year's leaves, and in the end the rattler lay shuddering with a broken back, and slowly, head first, the king had eaten him and crawled into the dark laurels with rattles still purring between his jaws. I had walked home a little sick at my stomach. The fight was very fine, and I ran it through, now, two or three times. There were abandoned coal mines in the hollow; shale and slate and coal were naked and flaky about the tumbled shafts. If you kicked a black stone it fell away in sheets like a broken book. The sheets were one great clear weave of black ferns, every vein and feather of them distinct. They were giants, but they could never have been larger than the ferns in the drop below, that sprang and drooped in the half-light, a sinister ferocious green. It was somehow too terrifying to know that they too would sink into the earth, that this blaring green would be flattened into blackness. Above the ferns the forest leaves lay on the air in wide silver planes; but there was nothing awful in the thought of their death; for I had never seen and could not conceive such foliage stamped on stone. I tried now, knew I would fail, and failed, to feel about it as I had when I was eleven. But the feeling now was so flat, so anaemic, that once had smoked with reality. Waning moons and the wind against trees, obsidian arrow-heads and my Babylonian tablet, the swell of a New Hampshire hill, and water from God knows where forever striking granite forever bound in Maine, the fixed swerve and distance of stars . . . all these things and all things else were categorized and filed away with their proper emotions and their proper metaphors: and in all the world and in all experience there was little enough that was remarkable. I could no longer get excited over these things; I could no longer even think of them without a slight sickened feeling of shame, without ending by laughing at them and at myself.

Something or other is something else again on all fours. Professor Lowes is Professor Babbitt on all fours. Professor Babbitt is Aristotle on all fours. Aristotle on all fours is a sight for sore eyes. How about ears? Your ear, or my ear, or anybody's ear? If you wore your ear around your neck you'd change it oftener. If you ate eggs with your knees you'd look to your garters, if you wore any garters. Personally I think this discussion is getting a little, well. Ah, then, you are a prig. For my part, I think it's just great to see our boys and girls discussing their little problems, heart to heart. Don't you think Sex is interesting, Elvira? I do. It's my hobby. Sex and Stamps. But Sex is lots more fun. Where would we be without it?

Probably off shooting pool somewhere, if at all. Or following the ponies. Every healthy American boy follows the ponies. Pick yourself a good, healthy pony with a sense of humor and a knowledge of cooking, and you have the ideal mother of your children. None of these frills, son. Or a brisk set of backgammon and a cold shower will turn the trick.

The car went over a bump, my elbows slipped, and I struck my ear with the heel of my hand. It felt as if I'd torn half my brain out, and I yelled.

"Hurt?" Joe said.

"Little bit."

His wife said: "It must have hurt you something awful. You drive slower, Joe."

That made Joe pretty sore. He said nothing, and he did not slow down: I knew he was sore at me because his wife had seen fit to register an objection in my behalf. He had as low an opinion of me as if I myself had asked him to slow up. I felt like socking them both; but I had just enough sense to keep quiet.

I couldn't doze now, and I couldn't think; I simply sat there, enclosing the agony of my ear and half-numb fatigue and a simmering gripe at everything on earth. It was terribly hot. The smells of hot oil and hot stale clothing were like a blow in the face, and the wrinkling air on the desert was one great shiver of heat. I decided I might as well get back in Joe's good graces.

I said: "Wouldn't be so good, walking through this, would it?"

"I reckon it wouldn't."

I knew I'd never have been fool enough to try such a walk, but it wasn't my place to bring that up.

Joe said: "I don't reckon many fellers would be fool enough to try walking it, though."

"They'd be crazy if they did. This is one place you've got to wait for a ride, if it's a week coming."

"Well, you were pretty lucky," Joe said complacently.

"Yes. You sure were lucky." So his wife was getting back on his good side, too. For no reason at all, I was fairly disgusted with both of them.

"I sure am glad of the ride," I said; and we all let it go at that. I sat looking at the two backs, recognizing the cheap condescension and the thin antagonism, and not particularly giving a damn.

Far ahead there was a black speck, and as we came nearer it was moving, and was a man, and the man was limping toward us and waving wildly.

"Good God Almighty," Joe said. "How did he ever land out here!"

I was wondering myself. None of us spoke, for there was something about it that shut our mouths. But Joe got all the speed he could out of the Buick, and very soon we were all sure that the man was black.

"Why, it's a nigger," the woman said.

Joe nodded. It was a nigger all right, and every second we saw him more clearly. A nigger, an exhausted nigger, very tall, and with terrible effort limping toward us. He was grinning and crying and laughing, and the noises he made were strange and unintelligble. For some shameful reason, the effect was grotesquely funny, if indeed there was any effect.

There was little on Joe: enough to make him slow down the car; enough to make him hesitate and do a little thinking; enough, in the end, to make him drive past the man, slowly shaking his head and gathering into his original speed. As it became obvious that he did not intend to stop, his wife turned toward him as if jerked by a cord. Her mouth hung open in a silly way. As we passed, it was thus: Joe looking straight

ahead, jaw set over his quid, and head wagging definitively. It was thus: His wife staring at him in naked
amazement, her mouth open as if she were dead. It
was thus: I watching the two of them and the boy
asleep in his corner and the nigger in the road; and
feeling excited and horrified and ill and quite unable
to think. It was thus as we passed: The nigger's
laughter and weeping still alive on his face, as a
machine still runs when the power is cut off; the
laughter and the weeping frozen in a mask and gone;
then only an astounded blackness and marbled eyes
and a bestial burnt stalk of tongue; and then, as
suddenly, he was moving again and letting out
wheezing yells, pleading still and still demanding that
God bless us; he was running after us, desperately
running after us with both arms hooked and waving
in the crisping air. His face was gone and his body
shrank with the desert, and he progressed eastward
and after us with mad and jerky running, like a small
black mangled frog. He was still running, he was a
speck that seemed not to run, he was gone and I knew
he still ran and still waved and still demanded that
God bless us.

The woman did not speak, and I could not. After
a time Joe said: "I don't aim to pick up no damned
nigger."

"Why, Joe you ought not to talk that way. That
poor nigger was one of the Lord's creatures, same as
you and me." It was wonderful how quickly she had
calmed down.

"I don't know about that, but if you think I'm
going to allow any damned nigger in the same car
with my wife, you got another thing coming."

"But Joe. It ain't as if he was all right, near a town
or anything. Way out here in middle of nowheres . . ."

"I don't want to hear another peep about him, see?"

As he drove on, he talked in jerks: "What was he doing out here in the middle of nowheres, I'd like to know. Yes sirree, that's what I'd like to know . . . Wasn't out there for no good reason. No doubt about that . . . I reckon someone had took pity on him, picked him up. Then, by glory, he got fresh . . . they had to boot him out. That's the trouble with these damn niggers . . . never will learn to let well enough alone . . . Why it wouldn't even be patriotic to pick up a feller like that . . . How do you know he ain't a dangerous criminal?"

His wife cut in: "You'd a picked him up, if he was a white man."

He started to say a number of things, and finally got out: "Well, what if I had? I didn't, did I? Think I'm going to let some damn sweaty nigger stink up my car? Well I'm not, and the sooner you get that through your head the better.

"I don't know as I'd have picked him up, if he *had* been a white man. This car's crowded, right now.

"I'm no damn nigger-lover.

"Let some of these nigger-loving Yankees pick him up, if they want to. Some of them will do anything, just to favor a nigger."

"You ain't even Christian."

"By God, I'm as good a Christian as the next man, but I ain't no nigger-lover."

"That ain't . . ."

He stopped the car and turned and glared and shouted at her: "Now that's just about enough. I'm pretty damn sick of all this bugling about some filthy nigger that didn't know enough to stay home and let well enough alone. I ain't a Christian, huh? By Jesus Christ, I'll learn you to talk like that to me. Now it's my advice to you to keep your trap shut. My Holy God, I never heard the like of it in my life! I don't want to hear another word about that black bastard. If you care so much about him, maybe you'd like to trot back and look after him. I don't know as I'd put it a-past you."

And he drove on. After a minute she said: "You ought to be ashamed to talk to me like that, Joe Tate."

"Shut up."

There was no more talking.

I have said that during the incident of passing the man, I was "quite unable to think." This is not quite true. The truth is, that my mind was one chaotic wash of nervous emotion, in which thought could at best merely drift aimlessly and shortly sink. But I thought: and my thoughts were chiefly of my own responsibility in this matter, and, more vaguely, of the fact that I was spontaneously jolted by the incident as I was by few things, of late years. These thoughts, disconnected at first, in time took on substance and form; they drew from the conversation I have recorded above; they begot themselves and built upon themselves. The fact that, according to Joe, the car was crowded already, became, for a time, very important to me. I was the extra man in the car. I was the reason why an exhausted Negro remained in the desert near death. I could offer my place; I could refuse to ride any farther, unless something were done to help him. I realized, all the while, that my presence here had nothing to do with Joe's refusal to take him in, and at length this truth reduced that sport of conscience to its logical absurdity. I knew, quite soon, that there was nothing for me to do; yet I felt compulsion to say what his wife had tried to say, and a great deal more. In purely abstract argument I had talked myself red-eyed and ready for murder, on this matter of the Negro and and his place; and now, when I was involved in actuality, I could say nothing and do nothing; and my silence made me confederate in a monstrous wrong. His contemptible wife, in her half-minded fashion, had dared to speak what she felt on the matter; and I . . . I did not dare. The thin fact that I was dependent upon this man's charity: that closed my mouth. What business had I to say anything, pro or con? And another thought built upon this: there would be something cheap and mock-heroic in anything I might do, and I despised mock-heroics. And on this built another thought: we had all exaggerated the Negro's plight. With reasonable certainty, someone would pick him up. The little melodrama that had seemed so shatteringly important, was really in no sense melodrama. I had been fool enough to get excited about it in the first place, and by now I was thankful that I had not paraded my idiocy in talk. There was no tragedy here; only after a manner of speaking was there drama. From now on, I would be proof against any such cheap emotional pitfalls. No sort or condition or twist of humanity deserved such weakness. For there was, indeed, no real tragedy in life. Tragedy was the perennial flower of the ego, and the ego is inconsequent manure.

I was rather proud of this quasi-epigram; it occupied my mind, now, for quite a while; it bred other cool and soothing generalizations; and the mass of them did me a great deal of good.

In due time, I admitted these definite facts: I was heartily sorry for my cheap weakness. It was much more to the point to take care of myself; and this I had managed quite creditably to do. I was tired, I needed sleep, my present occupation was bumming. The desert was broad and hot and deadly, and I was extraordinarily weak with the pain of my ear. If I had spoken out of turn, I might conceivably have been dropped in the road without more ado. As it was, I was in reasonable comfort, and I was letting well enough alone.

That was enough for the present as I think it over now, I can see no flaw in my course of reasoning. I feel, at times, that I thought too much. Certainly for a little while, I thought clearly and well; so clearly and so well that thought assumed substance and shape. It was as if my brain had been dipped in lead, that cooled and thickened and moment by moment bound more securely, so that before long I was sleeping soundly for the first time in several days.

"That was the state that passed for sleep, now that I was bumming." But this fool-proof shell outlasted sleep and several mild calamities, and is as serviceable today as it was the day I bought it.

[From *The Harvard Advocate*, October, 1930]

They That Sow in Sorrow Shall Reap

The house, which was on a main street, near the tracks, and convenient to work, was painted a remote white; barrenly fonted the street, but possessed along one side a comfortable ledge of porch sparsely trellised with morning-glories; appeared to be small, but was rangy and subdivided into many small rooms. The floor of each room was covered by linoleum of one restless pattern; and each lodger's room contained a bed, a bureau, a shallow closet, a straight chair, and, upon request, a table. Throughout the house there was a flat smell of linoleum made warm, this first evening, by the sun. In every bedroom there were clean curtains; a rhomboid of light was projected upon each opposite wall, and across this the sun had stencilled a shifting lace of shadow. As I waited in my bedroom, the sun, descending, cramped the rhomboid of light, and urged the plaque of shadow and light toward the ceiling. The house was extremely clean. I lay across the clean counterpane, very tired, but lying tensely, in the hope that I might not print the counterpane with uncleanliness. I was slippery with rust and clay. I lay on my back and watched the sunlight tilt upward through the pane, and with vague impatience heard a tired man making himself clean in the one bathroom; and knew that other tired people were impatient and were waiting; and breathed the clean odor germinated on the warm linoleum; and saw a sharp gable shoulder cut the sunlight.

This place was so clean; in one corner which the sun never struck I could see traces of a mop; and the linoleum was not ridged through by boards beneath; its checker pattern was everywhere sharp; and shifty, because my eyes were tired; but clean, and pleasant; and altogether the house was far better than the Eagle Hotel. I got up and looked resentfully at the bed, which I had creased with red dirt. It was my turn to wash. I took a bath, shaved with unusual care, and tried to free my hair of rust and clay; and went downstairs feeling very clean and complacently tired, like a patient ready for the operating table.

In the parlor, the boarders sat in a circle, patient but unrelaxed, and silent. The room was ornamented with pampas-plumes, and with nodular vessels of iridescent glass. There was a piano, carefully dusted, and with open music, and with an air of long desuetude. The room was quiet, except for a clock and the irregular ticking of wicker chairs. Between the next room and the next was a hurry of footsteps, and the clash and arrangement of tableware; but here, silence, and people, most of them still unrelaxed, still in poise like birds about to take wing. There were two men; the laborer looked down at his linked hands, which resembled scrubbed roots; the other, younger, a man of forty, furtively ran his nails one beneath another, while he sat self-consciously beneath his thinning hair. The two older women leaned back, now, with knees unflexed; the younger woman maintained an air of anxiety; she sat straight, with knees snapped crosswise like a closed purse. The people were tired, and without emotion they received once more the deliberate edge of evening.

Mrs. Stevens came to the door to say, "Supper is ready," and with abrupt commotion the six of us filed in to the table, where already an old man was standing guard.

The food was abundant and pridefully cooked. Large bowls of it, consumed, were removed, and came again replenished. The woman who carried them said to each boarder, "Good evening," (then calling him by name) ; "This has been a beautiful day." And she would say no more. The old man her husband, who sat with the meat pie at the head of the table would add, "Yes, a beautiful day. Can't I help you to something, Miss Silk?" She, who had sat primly as a closed purse, would with difficulty reply, "No. Thank you." And in her silence a blush would thicken across her forehead. The old gentleman said next, "Nor you, Mrs. Bixby?" at the same time nodding inquiry toward the third woman. After this, whatever the result, he would smile with embarrassment, and restore his attention to his own food.

He was a handsome old gentleman. His features were aquiline and finely regular; his cleft lower lip and chin were opulent and weak, and the whole face was drawn into a sort of perfection by a recently combed and waxed moustache. There was in his face a flicker of forgotten arrogance; and in his appearance was a suggestion of continued vanity; for his hair, shining white and fine as a child's, was most carefully set back from his shield-like forehead; and he wore the sort of "sport" shirt that boys wear; a shirt whose collar flared buttonless away from his strong youthful throat. His hands were abnormally small and veinless; as much as possible he kept them folded in his lap. As I have remarked, he spoke very little, but he smiled continually, as if at his own happiness, and he seemed unduly eager to resolve all uncertainties with his own calm.

I found this beauty, this unexpected youthfulness, somehow sinister. As I watched him, however, this repellence vanished, for he showed only gentleness and kindliness, and embarrassing humility, and shortly, I was aware of his remarkable serenity. For, each time his wife was in the room he smiled and watched her as she moved about, and his eyes blazed with peace.

He was especially anxious for Miss Silk's ease, and this, though futile, was praiseworthy. For Mr. Harbison, oblivious of his thinning hair, was brimming over with good fun and pleasant quips. The fun, much of it at Miss Silk's expense, was delivered to the table at large, as were the pleasant quips. A few of the

better-turned quips were repeated so that Mother
Stevens, in the kitchen, might hear them. They were
carelessly deflected by six at the table, but each one
struck Miss Silk solidly and with fine effect. A miserably shy woman of twenty-five, she looked straight
into her plate and, for fear of her own voice, said
nothing. When she was forced to reply to Mr. Stevens,
or to a kind question from Mrs. Bixby, she grew red
with mortification as she contemplated the rude
brusqueness in her voice.

As the boarders, soothed by good food and by a
coolness expanding on the air, became more talkative,
it was easier to remark their various interrelations.
Mr. Harbison, I understood quickly enough, had ap-
propriated the role of star boarder; this he was
granted without jealousy and without recognition. He
sat opposite Mr. Stevens at the foot of the table, and
fought a routine battle of wits best comparable to
shadow-boxing. The two older women worked in the
office of the canning factory, and were friends of long
standing. From time to time Mrs. Bixby, the more
gregarious of the two, made casual efforts to engage
Miss Silk in conversation; she weathered each failure
far more happily than did the young woman. The
laborer said very little and paid much attention to his
manners, furtively watching Mr. Harbison's use of
knife, fork and toothpick. There were, too, certain
unchanging group attitudes: mild hostility toward
Harbison, tolerance toward the laborer, and a rather
disturbing disregard of Mr. Stevens. I felt a faint
curiosity concentrated on me, and a gathering apa-
thetic distrust as Mr. Harbison subtly drew me out.
Mr. Habison gathered, from my replies, that I was
the scion of a wealthy house, a student in Harvard,
working for my health, trying to live down my education, rather a snob, and possibly about town for no

good purpose. It was a good thing, he informed me, for a young man to get out and see the world a bit, to mix with all sorts; it would convince me that life wasn't all silver spoons and things. The only way to rise in the world was to start at the bottom and get to know your fellow man. I would find that there were very fine traits even in those poor souls bruised by fortune and left by the side of the road.

(The laborer took his spoon from his cup and looked ashamed.) I made no effort to reinform him or anyone else. Harbison sailed on, inexorably misinterpreting and advising and, I could see, preparing a lecture on his philosophy of life. But even when most drunk with vast ideas, he did not allow himself to forget his duty to his disciples. After every particularly memorable statement he glanced away from me, and asked Miss Silk if that was not so.

Meanwhile, Mr. Stevens, sensing as much guile as sincerity in Harbison's conversation, pitied me in my bewilderment; a number of times he smiled encouragement toward me. As we left the table and moved toward the porch, Mr. Harbison fell into step beside me, asking for my criticism of Mother Stevens' cooking; and Mr. Stevens followed.

There was no safe answer to such a question, and I grew cold in the shadow of Harbison's tall surmise, so I hung back a little and allowed him to overtake Miss Silk. This act, I could see, crystallized various suspicions he had unwillingly entertained. I was glad enough of that; with only a sharp feeling of pity for Miss Silk, I leaned against a porch post and lighted a cigarette.

"This has been a handsome day."

"Yes. Fine."

It was Mr. Stevens who spoke.

"We don't get many days like it."

"No, you're right."

"Most of this summer has been very rainy, very unpleasant."

"It has been pretty lousy."

He smiled brightly. "Yes, it has been very unpleasant, exceedingly unpleasant. But today has been splendid."

"Yes, it's been a lovely day. We don't get many like it."

"I have a feeling we are in for a good spell, now, though. Not a cloud in the sky, all day."

"It has been very clear, today."

He was anxious, for some reason, to talk; but some sixth sense told us that the weather was a delicate subject, and had best be spoken of no more.

"Do you care for a cigarette?"

"No, thank you; I have never touched tobacco in any form." He smiled apologetically and added, "But thank you very much, just the same."

"Surely."

"I don't in the least frown upon smoking, you understand. And I don't take faith in this stuff and nonsense about its doing any physical harm. Only, I don't like to form habits, as one is likely to do with smoking, don't you think?"

"Yes, I think you're right. I know it's a habit with me."

He was very liberal, for several minutes, on the whole matter of smoking and other habitual vices. I liked the old man but, just because I preferred to be alone, I said as little as I politely could in reply. Just when the subject ran encouragingly dry, and I was getting ready to take my leave, he said, "You are satisfied with everything here?"

I assured him that I was. He was very glad: he and his wife tried to make everything as clean and attractive as could be. They were particularly anxious that the young folks should be happy. It was hard, he knew, being young and a long way from home. He had been young himself once, and it had been a great comfort to him when older people were nice, and tried to make everything, although there was no place like home, like home.

"Young people should appreciate it," I said, without mentioning any names. Mr. Stevens' eye showed more understanding than I had bargained for and, genuinely ashamed, I added that I most certainly did.

Immediately reassured, he said with eagerness that I was to feel just like one of the family. We exchanged appreciations and wore through a discourse on loneliness, during which his concentration upon speech gave way before a crescent eagerness. Across his left cheek, I saw the flutter of some irrelevant sinew, and the nicely curled moustache was wry and twitching. At the same time a ticklish, cold weakness filled through the roots of my spine.

"It's been a fine day," he said, "but very hot."

"Not so bad."

"It must have been very hot working."

"Not so bad."

"Is your work pretty heavy?"

"Digging a ditch and handling iron, today."

"That must have been hot, on a day like this. Are you used to such work?"

"Not very. But it wasn't bad."

"Not bad, eh? Ah, my boy, when you're young you can stand up to any sort of work."

I said nothing.

"A fine, strapping young fellow like you. You can stand up to anything, can't you?"

His shaky small hand closed upon my arm. "Let me feel your biceps. Ah, what a fine, strapping young fellow. See, I can't reach half around it." He slipped one arm across my shoulders, and his own shoulder, hard and hot, clenched against my chest. For a moment pretense was lost to him, and his eyes, narrowed, brilliant with lust, asked me: "Is everything understood?"

Everything was quite well understood. I smiled back like one of the family a bit embarrassed at such demonstrativeness, freed myself without too much obviousness, lighted a cigarette, and said: "I guess it's about time I went in town, I promised to meet some friends."

I went in through the dining-room and upstairs for matches. I could hear Mr. Stevens washing the dishes. I hurried out the front door. As I passed the porch, the old gentleman smiled and waved; I pretended not to see him. When, in spite of myself, I looked back, he had gone in.

2

The mind is rarely audience to experience in perfection; rarely is it granted the joy of emotions and realities which, first reduced to their essential qualities, are then so juxtaposed in harmony and discord, in sharp accentuation and fluent change, in thematic statement, development, restatement and recapitulation, as to achieve in progress a continuous, and in consummation, an ultimate beauty. As a rule, experience is broken upon innumerable sharp irrelevancies; emotion and reality, obscurely fused and inexplicably tarnished, are irreducible; their rhythms are so subtly involved, so misgoverned by chance, as to be beyond analysis; and the living mind, that must endure and take part, is soon fugitive before, or else, however brave, falls to pieces beneath this broad unbeautiful pour of chaos.

The experience referred to is objective; the same difficulties hold in the case of subjective experience. The true sum of experience is, as a rule, an inconceivably complex interpenetration of subjective and objective experience. And the true sum and whole of experience is doubly chaotic.

It is therefore fortunate that most minds are constructed to float. However rigorous the weave of currents, however huge the plunge of waves, they are forever near the surface. And it is fortunate, God knows, that minds which anatomize experience are given the mercy of a million moods: these complement and relieve one another, and those which are not wholly proof against pain at least shift the weight of experience to a fresh area of the mind. That mood of sustained callousness and irony which I thought one desert afternoon had perpetuated in me, still serves me well. Although it has achieved a few complexities of perception which may perhaps enrich it, it remains my habitual state of mind, it dilutes experience to a fairly palatable beverage of dubious concoction. But, when I attempt to make real use of these instruments of perception, I realize two things: my own weakness and diffuseness of mind, and the fearful unarrangement of life realized with such completeness and sincerity as my mind may be capable of.

But certain moods, if kept as clear as possible of deflecting intellect, reflect a selection and arrangement of experience which approaches beauty: beauty of form, of emotion, of shadowy idea. The experiences during my first meal here, and just after, seemed casual enough as they occurred; Mr. Stevens' revelation struck away that mood, and, after long modulation of moods in my mind, the whole thing, as it occurred, emerged with symmetry and beauty.

But my relation to this progress of experience is broken, is never sure. In the first place, I work nine hours a day, and that violently different life seems severed from this. Then, even when I am here, so much that happens is utterly without direct significance. For instance, I talk with old Stevens every night. All our conversation, because of my avoidance, is oblique to the essential in his mind. In fragments, and by implication, I have been able to recreate his life; and I find the man as a whole pathetic, and appealing, and somehow very important. The mere unfortunate fact of his perversion is, or should be, beside the point. The important things are the complete frustration of a mind that wished to be fine and could have been good, the dwindling, for many years, of his life as an entity, his still persistent eagerness for knowledge, for the company of educated people, and this incredible tranquillity that has come with his old age. As a preacher in Maine, as a fugitive from misunderstanding, as a miserably unsuccessful grocer in this town, he can scarcely have known tranquillity. But now, as he says, he finds time once more for reading, and for music. He reads vastly and without discrimination, and he plays the piano with two fingers. Now permitted, at last, complete nonentity, he is happy. He sits at table quiet and meek, and says little, like a good child. Apparently, he worships his wife, though they have little to say to each other. He seems to have discovered some private formula for complete contentment: yet (discounting his wooer's flattery) he is genuinely grateful for my company, for the chance to talk about books, any books, for the chance to hear music played, however badly, with ten fingers instead of two. I scarcely know whether to be glad for this, or sorry to have wrought as I have upon his ancient illness.

His wife has had a strange life. In the parlor, their wedding picture is hung. In many ways, the old man still resembles the young one there, with curled mouth, and brave moustache, and arrogant Websterian posture. But the girl who stands beside him in full pride of her beauty, intelligence and aggressiveness are frozen in her eyes, and all beauty has departed the body and the grey pebble of a face; and the woman who has time, now, only for swift patience and for thorough housecleaning, for a proper but minimum politeness; and time never for a friend, or for any glint of affection—what bitterness and what unswerving loyalty have wrought this unaccountable change? Can any memory lie behind that unequivocal mask?

What resurgencies may engulf them both, when, each Sunday, they drive away into Maine? Or, is their mutual calm delicately adjusted beyond unbalancing?

I am far from my beginning. I wonder how, or if, I can return to it.

There is no return, and no use returning. I have tried to work out to my own satisfaction, some aspects of the mind's reaction to experience. I have tried to match this reaction with the patterns of music; the idea is incongruous; I should be kicked for trying it. My mind is hopelessly weak and tangential; time and again, as above, I fail to carry one idea through; before I realize it, I am whirled along the rim of another—and so on—ad nauseam.

Yet, from time to time, I am aware of a definite form and rhythm and melody of existence: however fluctuate and intermittent its progress may be, it *is* a progress; out of long, contrapuntal passages of tantalizing and irreconcilable elements there emerges sometimes an enormous clear chord. And at that moment—or, rather, through its reverberations in our brain, the whole commonplaceness of existence is transfigured—becomes monstrously powerful, and beautiful, and significant—assuming these qualities validly but unanswerably—and descends through tangled discords, once more into commonplaceness, with nothing answered, nothing gained, and heaven undisturbed.

I suppose the essentials of which this music is compounded are the facts as they are, tempered by sternness and pity and calm. We are eight people in this house; we are endowed with as many different minds, or souls, and with as many different machines for attacking existence, and defending ourselves against it. The full vision of existence is forever denied us. We live dimly in the center of being, and thence we perform the most ordinary duties, and avoid others; to some extent we guide our lives, to some extent are guided by them; and the whole object of life, whatever it may or should be, is hidden beyond a profound and inescapable confusion of egoism and of altruism and of evil and of good. And so, when these myopic people, concentrated upon their daily tasks, upon their food, or upon their rest, or upon their little loves, their little cruelties, their little aspirations; when, caught in these flimsy inescapable cogs, they are contemplated in their unrealized relation to the timeless severance of the vast radiance of life, and the enormous shadow of death, they become magnificent, and tragic, and beautiful.

I read carefully what I had written; carefully, and slowly, tried to clarify the ideas, to give them some proper connection, to discover any single coherent thought. When I finished I was sick with exhaustion and self-conempt; I wanted to beat my face to bits. I crumpled the sheets into a fistful and looked for a match; and stopped. It was the only attempt I'd ever made to get at the bottom of anything. It was a horrible failure—but in another mood something might come of it, something might be clear in it.

I lay down and read the second act of *The Cherry Orchard,* and realized once more that here, that melody was caught, and that great drama had been made of it. How, I could not tell.

Although it was very late, and I had to get up at six, I felt it necessary to walk. It was a fine night. After two miles of walking, my brain still felt like a shooting gallery. I returned to my room and went to sleep.

3

The morning was very hot and blue, the blue fading as the heat and light increased. Heat rilled above each fragment and long spine of metal, and shimmered like clear smoke over the grass and dusty streets. The gravel showed cool and dark as our shovels turned it; but almost immediately it was white. The white light grew so wide that it was painful to look into the sky.

To my right, as I turned for each new shovel-load, I saw the half-bushel scoop slicing deep into the gravel, moving in no slower rhythm than my own square-nosed shovel. Before the second truck was loaded, the new man had struck bottom. I turned toward him and together we cleared out solid footing. The truck moved out, and we all rested in the band of shade to one side of the car, drank the already tepid water, and smoked.

Of the many jobs laborers were assigned, this was by all odds the best. Digging a ditch, or screening sand, you took your time, but worked continuously, with one eye on the foreman or his suspected direction of appearance; here, you worked furiously for a few minutes, in the surety of ten minutes of solid loafing. There was much talking during these ten minutes, and ordinarily, I joined in it and enjoyed it. Today, however, I lay flat on my back and said little. It had been nearly two when I returned from my walk; the need for sleep and the extreme heat were like tightening bolts in my temples; they persuaded me to a black and painful concentration upon the problems which had arisen the evening before. I could no longer fix upon any one idea or fragment of idea. A few words burred so constantly in my brain that they spun themselves free of all meaning; and problems, words, phrases, the uncertain nature of my own mind, the lives and the ruling moods of the people in the house, frozen clear of verbal thought, assumed various geometric forms; and these in their turn underwent change, and emerged as long silver arches, thin as rods; none touched, but a current quickened each, and flickered on the intermediary darkness, and they sent forth a low and hideous multitone.

Not one arch was complete.

Despite this resonant pattern I could see and hear a little. I heard voices as one does beneath fathoms of ether; and I saw the man new on the job, prostrate on the cinders, one knee angled to the sky, head resting in a flexile sling of joined hands and bent arms. He was long and heavy and hugely powerful, and his head seemed fashioned of great plates and ridges of iron, strongly joined. When we heard the truck coming he opened his clear unintelligent eyes, smiled by drawing his mouth into a line, and towered into a magnificent repatterning of strength.

He showed some concern over my lack of skill and

economy in handling my shovel. During the next rest he offered me a cigarette, and I learned that he came from Lebanon. During the next he asked me, without that leering which is apology, whether I knew any women in town. A little Canuck made the question funny for himself; the new man saw no humor in it; he said: "Do you know any?" "My women are in Manchester," said the Canuck, among other things. "Then you'd better pipe down," said the new man. The Canuck piped down.

"I've got a Chevrolet," the new man said. I told him that women were hard to find in this lousy town. He replied, "I'll find them."

He said very little; he even swore little. He never suspected the existence of humor; he suspected the existence of nothing, I think, except women, work, food and rest.

He was staying, he said, at the Eagle Hotel. He agreed with me that it was a bad place. During the next rest, he asked me whether I knew of a cheaper place that was any good. I replied that I was staying at a cheaper place, that was very good, and that I believed there was room there. It was quite near the tracks; if he liked, we could go over and see.

And as I spoke, I felt my bowels turn to ice; but I continued to speak.

At noon, therefore, after eating lunch, we went over. We stood at the side door, on the porch.

"What's your name?"

"Grafton."

I stepped inside. From the hall I could see the long table. Miss Silk, the keeper of records, and the old gentleman were here at noon. They were broadly separated, at their regular places. As Mrs. Stevens came in from the kitchen I caught her eye and nodded. She smiled faintly, set down the food, and came to the hall.

"Fellow out here wants to board," I said, "if there's room."

As she crossed to the door I could see beyond the fine white hair, swept by sunlight.

"Mr. Grafton," I said.

She looked at him through the opening screen. For an instant her face lost its quietude, and I was staring at merciless pain and fear. Then, with composure, she slowly said: "How do you do, Mr. Grafton. Yes, I am sure there will be room. I hope you will be comfortable."

"That's good," said Mr. Grafton.

"Shall I show you your room?"

"Don't bother," I said. "We'll get his stuff after work."

"The end of the hall, on the second floor," she said to both of us. And to me, "Thank you."

I watched her as she turned and closed the door and went into the dining-room.

"Sure," I said.

I said to Grafton: "Supper isn't till six. We'll have time to move your stuff then."

"Sure," he said.

By mid-afternoon we had the car cleared, and were back on the big job. I wheeled gravel to the mixer; he was at work digging a ditch in tough clay. Even late in the afternoon it was hot, but the coldness inside me persisted in spasms, and throughout spaces of rest, I was shivering; and watching the town clock, the hands cutting slowly their wheels on the sunlight.

At five I met Grafton, and we drove to the Eagle Hotel in his Chevrolet. As we came downstairs the younger clerk spoke to me:

"How do you like it, up on Water Street?"

"It's OK."

He grinned doggishly. "How do you like the old gent?"

As we drove through the town, among the stores, among the houses, I wondered how spotted those square miles were with knowledge of the old man and his secret.

We lugged Grafton's meager baggage to the room at the far end of the hall. The room was smaller than mine, but like mine, very clean.

"I guess the can is empty," I said. "We'd better hurry up and wash." As I walked to my room, Miss Silk was going downstairs; she looked up and quickly down; and her reddening face disappeared.

My mail was on the bureau; a letter from my mother, and a card from August. My mother wrote that the sea had been lovely all day, and that my sister found life very dull this summer. She was going dancing tonight though. It would be so good to have me home. August wrote that during one week there were five Chaplins and three Garbos in Berlin, and much rain.

I got my razor and soap and towel, and went into the bathroom. Grafton, standing in his work shoes and Sunday pants, was noisily washing. His head and his naked back and shoulders were a great keystone of corded muscle.

It was late, so after washing I shaved also from the bathtub spigot.

"How old are you?" said Grafton, mowing his cheek.

"Twenty."

He snorted. "I'm twenty myself. I'd have to shave twice a day, to keep down my beard.

"Who's the woman went downstairs?"

"Oh, she's no good. Silk's the name."

"Silk, huh?" He was puzzled. After a minute he said, "That's a funny name."

"Yeah."

We got dressed, and walked downstairs and into the parlor. Everyone was clean in the clean parlor, and waiting for supper, sitting patiently but unrelaxed; with labor past, with hands unbusied, with mind unmolested, they sat very tired waiting for their food and for their few hours of quiet and for their few hours of sleep; and for the next morning, and for the next evening, and for a Sunday, and for another week and Sunday; for autumn and for winter, for spring and for summer; for another year, for another ten; for the slow chemistry of change and age; for the loss of fluids and pigments and tissues, of senses and wits, of faculties and of perceptions; for the silencing of all clamor and for the sealing of all sight; for the final levelling of all desire, of all despair, of all joy, of all tribulations; for the final quelling of all fear and pride and love and disaffection; for the final dissolution of the flesh and of all that flesh must suffer, sickness of soul and body, fast-withering delight and clouded love, unkindness and grief and wrong beyond reckoning; for the final resolution of all the good they had wrought, and all the ill; they sat resting after battle, with quiet hands and unperceiving eyes, without emotion to receive once more the deliberate edge of evening.

Mr. Stevens sat with the roast beef at the head of the table; Mrs. Stevens served food, and was busy between two rooms. She greeted each boarder briefly, and the old gentleman added, "A handsome day, but very hot," and asked Miss Silk if he could help her to anything. Miss Silk was sick with mortification, and stared at the center of her plate. Mr. Harbison was pleasant to Miss Silk, and quite the life of the party.

Mrs. Bixby and Mrs. Thompson, her friend of long standing, talked quietly and frequently dabbed their mouths with their napkins. Mrs. Stevens came in with more food, and glanced at me and at Grafton, and went out with an empty dish. Mr. Stevens watched her as she moved about the room, and his eyes were bright with serenity. The laborer, Frank Woods, scraped butter from his clean shirt, and was more deliberate in his eating. Mr. Harbison asked Miss Silk for an appointment in some sequestered grove. Miss Silk grew fiery red and said nothing. Grafton ate quickly and with thoroughness, glancing up as he bit, like a dog. I could scarcely eat; a cold weight was in my belly, the fork was cold to my touch, my temples were numb.

I was watching Mr. Stevens. He sat at the head of the table like a good child, meek, happy and silent. As much as possible, he kept his hands in his lap. His silky white hair and white face, and the white sport collar, were bright across the dimming air. From time to time he glanced toward me, and smiled; and he smiled at Grafton.

Supper was over; we all strolled toward the porch.

"Play something," Mr. Stevens said. "Play the piano."

I was blind with suspicion and fear, and anxious to counter such schemes as he might have. I replied that Grafton and I were going straight into town.

We stood, therefore, at the back of the porch. Nearer the street, the others sat to talk.

"Let's go," I said.

"Let's have a cigarette," said Grafton, and offered one to Mr. Stevens.

The old gentleman refused politely, and added that he had never touched tobacco in any form. To

Grafton's silence he replied that it had been a hot day, but a handsome one.

That was true, I said. I was watching the sky; the sunset was unusual; night was rising from east and south and north, like an immense black hood; its edge was apparent against the day. Across the world from us there was an edge of dawn and freshness; there Greece shivered into light; but over a broadness of sea and plain, sharp mountains and the thistled light of cities, enormous shadow prevailed, and over us the shadow hung.

This in an instant I saw, and pitied the nine gathered in the house.

The old gentleman's arm slipped round my shoulder, and as he openly fondled me, he said that we were all one big family, and that Grafton must feel perfectly at home, perfectly at home.

I did nothing and said nothing. There was nothing to do or say. Grafton stood a little away from us, and I saw amazement piercing his stupidity; and scorn, and incredulity. The old man babbled on, and I watched them both, and waited.

His cheek was twitching like a snake killed before sundown; his eyes were glassy and bright with lust; I felt his body trembling, and saw the trembling as, chattering inanely, he swung me toward Grafton, slid an arm about him, and called us his fine boys, his fine boys. And I saw the fine boy stand quietly, his eyes narrowing, the jaw muscles shifting and freezing; while a vein grew full and hard, and sprawled crooked on the old gentleman's forehead. Grafton stood in quiet; then drew away, and with flat palm struck across the mouth the old man, who, mouth flashing blood, for an instant assumed in all amazement the Jeffries sparring stance, with amazement gone raised supplicating tiny hands like a Moslem mole, while,

face all blood and streaming tears, he shrank among
the sorrowing flowers of morning bitterly crying, and
with dependent hands fluttering before head;

while boarders rose from their chairs and looked in
amaze and impended to interfere, then drew back and
quickly, but staring back, removed from the porch
and roomward made kind haste;

and two across the street stopped to stare;

and a second time the boy raised lowered arm
through an arc and with flat palm struck through
hands the old man's mouth; who, bawling abomi-
nable brat, splayed evening with weeping;

while with crashed plate and rushing footsteps

—murderous anger moving me with all strength I
struck the boy, behind the ear; he turned and dealt
upon my cheekbone his fist and power, that with split
skin and shrouded purpose I sank against wall and
floor, Defender of What?

—the old woman his wife ran toward him, nothing
saying, seeing none but him, and in her face revealed
unfathomable sorrow, fear and love, and two lives,
broken late in this their day, that otherwise had closed
in tranquillity—

—while in tallness and dignity around the corner
stalked Grafton—

and five stared from across the street,

and the old woman haled the old gentleman into
the kitchen,

and six stared from across the street,

and I recollecting complete consciousness, was
frozen in a pratfall, with face bleeding, watched
curiously in my sudden aloneness by six people.

I got to my feet and, through the nearest door and
the parlor of books, music and strange wedding picture, upstairs to my room, but straightway to the bathroom with towel and handkerchief, to wash the cut

across my cheek. It was not deep, and after a short time I stanched the blood. In the mirror I saw one with swollen temple and battered cheek, with dark stupid eyes which shone with no zeal for living. I started for my room. As I opened the bathroom door, another door opened, at the far end of the hall. Grafton, with his baggage, walked slowly toward me, and I toward him. We looked fully at each other, and, as we met in the middle of the hall, paused, as if in delicate balance, still looking at each other, without animosity, without regret, without emotion of any sort; then, after the instant's pause, walked on, I into my room, he down the stairs and out of my future existence.

I changed my shirt and sat down, weak, on a chair in the center of the room. I was within a hollow cube. It seemed to me that from five sides of this cube came excited whispering; and from the sixth, beneath me, came two sounds: the sound of dishes being washed in haste; and the sound of quiet but profound weeping.

It was beyond my endurance, at the time. I left the house and the town, and walked out to a high hill, from which I watched other hills, and fields heavy with crops, and wooded land, and the distant town, as they lay beneath the night. I was unable to think, and after a little while I did not try to. I stayed on the hilltop for a long while, and returned with mind quiet because unoccupied by thought; and, after packing, went to sleep.

I was early at the table, conspicuous because I was not in my work clothes. Mrs. Stevens said nothing. She did not speak to any of the boarders as, one by one, they came in. Nor did the boarders speak, either to her, or to each other. They carefully avoided looking directly at anyone, and methodically ate what was set before them. Covertly, Mr. Harbison watched me; he said nothing. Mr. Stevens was not at the table; nor was a place set for him. From the kitchen, from time to time, came the sound of a hoarse whisper.

While everyone was still at table, Harbison rose and beckoned to Mrs. Stevens, and they withdraw to the parlor. Their conversation was not audible, but the tone and intention of Harbison's voice, and the tinkle of money withdrawn from a pocket, were quite well understood by all of us.

For the spark of pleasure her liberation would give me, I was watching Miss Silk. I think we all were. Her eyes were quiet and comprehending; her face without expression, as we heard him ascend and descend the stairs. When the front door closed, however, and his footsteps were no longer audible, there was change: in her face, which lost calm and became in some ways a leaf in late autumn; and in her eyes, which grew large and alarming to look upon, and dark with tears. As she lost all control of her emotions, she rose, gnawing at her hand, and hurried from the room. The two women looked at each other, and in silence followed her. The laborer and I continued to eat, he because of a good appetite, I because of his presence. Finally he rose, looked at me with curiosity and kindness, and set out for work.

I stood up and waited for Mrs. Stevens. She came to the door, stopped, and waited for me to speak.

I had nothing to say, and I began to speak words which had no process from my mind:

"I've heard there's very good work near Manchester. They pay fifty an hour there."

Mrs. Stevens looked at me.

"It's road work."

Mrs. Stevens looked at me.

After a few moments I paid her nine dollars, the

price for a week's board and lodging. She pulled open a cupboard drawer, opened a cigar-box, and fumbled for change.

"That is right for a week, isn't it," I said.

She counted all the change in the box. "You haven't been here a week," she said. "Your week is up tonight." She gave me a bill. "Have you a quarter?"

I had only a dime in change.

"Don't mind it," I said. "Never mind it, please."

"You shall have the breakfast, then," she said. "Free." In the kitchen I heard an old man, trying to cry quietly. She let her hands fall. I put the dollar and the dime into my pocket. The weeping was suddenly very loud. There was a scuffle across the linoleum, and Mr. Stevens burst through the door. Half the fine moustache had been shaved off, and there were strips of plaster on his lips. He took my right hand in both his, and, with no further attempt to control his sobbing, he spoke rapidly through his tears.

It was a burst of mangled oratory, a sort of ex-sermon, ornamented with quotations from the Bible and with misquotations from Victorian poetry; a much prepared and half-forgotten sermon, upon kindliness, and brotherly love, upon the Christian virtues. This it ceased to be, and became lamentation for his own great sins, and loud praise of me, the whole was tinged with involuntary salaciousness, and with the sort of flattery supposedly employed by those whose love is hopeless.

Meanwhile, he looked earnestly into my eyes; and his wife watched us both.

I do not think my expression changed, during the several minutes he talked on. He found no encouragement, and no hope of encouragement, and at last he stopped, and, still clutching my hand, merely looked at me, his tears in balance.

Both of them looked at me. They were waiting for me to speak. Anything I might have said would have been better than silence; I knew that then; but there was nothing to say. There was nothing. I merely stood and looked back at them, and as I looked, I saw understanding come to fullness in their minds.

I saw that the old man understood this: although you could not do as I wished, you were kind to me. I was happy in your company, and in talking to you. But you were not truly kind, and you did not truly understand. You deceived me with your kindness. You really despised me in secret, as openly you despise me now. Nobody, nobody on earth has even understood it, has even been kind, and nobody ever will.

I saw that the old woman understood this: you despise my husband. The only feeling you have for the whole thing is hatred and disgust. I can't blame you, you are like the whole world in that: but since you hate my husband, I hate you.

The old man, with this understanding to cherish, burst into new wild weeping, and retired to the kitchen. His wife waited, until after a moment, I turned, and walked into the parlor. I heard her go into the kitchen.

I stopped for a minute, and looked at their brave wedding photograph; then took my baggage and walked northward from the town.

On the farms, people had been at work for hours. At about nine I climbed to the hill I had visited the night before, left the road, and came to the crest. The sun was high enough, now, to be free of hills and of the tall clouds along the east. The blue was slowly paling into intense light. On a farm to my right, they were cutting a little patch of wheat. Slowly the machine breasted the standing grain, and left a new band of flatness behind it.

Between sky and countryside the sunlight glanced, like a broad sheet of glass; all that I saw lay stunned beneath its clarity, save only the nearer woodlands and the grain, which swarmed and shifted with devious breezes. The sunlight, elsewhere pure and calm, was shrill upon small twisting streams, and upon far-scattered weathervanes, and upon the town clock and steeples in the town, and upon the track tangential to the town. I saw the town hall, where Miss Silk would be busy with county records; I saw the canning factory, where the two older women were at work. Beyond the town, a road was torn up, for a little space; there, the laborer was at work. In some side street, Harbison was mending shoes. Beyond that grove, the new grade-school was rising by degrees; there, Grafton was finishing his ditch. On Water Street, near the tracks, the old woman would be about her housework, by now.

The header had made a full round, now; it was turning the corner to go around again. A few more rounds, and the entire patch would be cut.

[From *The Harvard Advocate*, May, 1931]

PART III

SATIRIC PIECES

Formletter 7G3

[*Letterhead: a small oval head of Lincoln framed by the word Stability.*]

IN THE GLOAMING

Dear Bereft Ones:

Untimely frost has taken, a sinking sun has closed, that fairest floweret of the field? At such an hour, the young mother kneels at her Golgotha; her young husband can only stand by helpless. Such is no time for practical thought: yet such thought must be taken. One would cherish forever that poor blossom, withered though it be: surely, surely, it must not go so quickly. Aye, but the withered rose corrupts the water: nor society, nor our baser instincts, can stand aloof. That little one must indeed be put away: and that quickly, before the grieving dew be dried. Yet surely not just tossed aside: nay, laid away with fitting honors.

Let Montmorency bear your grief. Since 1879 our firm, our little band, has schooled itself in just such sorrowful tasks. Perhaps a beloved parent, a dear helpmeet, has known ere now The Montmorency Touch. If so, you will know us as gentlest priests of mourning, ready, oh, eager to bear your unbearable burthen, expert in carrying out your dearest wishes. Those who have known us will not forget: but will like birds return to the old beechwood. Those who have known us not have joy before them: tender, and tearful, yet a joy.

Mother, weep on: such tears are healing. Father, give it no single thought. You have only to reach for the telephone: leave all the rest to us. Our rosewood burial at 5 m.p.m., cosmetics and floral horseshoe included, comes at $1500; $75 extra for glass panel. For those in more straitened circumstances our walnut service at 15 m.p.m., minister and chairs not furnished, comes at $700; a sad bargain even the poorest of us will be happy to afford our departed. As for those distorted souls whom tender urging cannot soften, there is a jackpine burial at 50 m.p.h., on any sufficiently rainy afternoon, at $198 spot cash. (Needless perhaps to say, Montmorency seldom suffers this bitter embarrassment.)

Ah, but for those whose hearts beat highest in the certitude of incorruptibility, a glorious resurrection, and an ultimate reunion On That Beautiful Shore, we can but recommend our furnaces, "the hottest north of H——l," our lovely Grecian Urns with facsimile autograph by the poet John Keats, which are in themselves an honor to any mantelpiece. Ah, ah, in the words of The Poet, what joy more tender than "To have one's dear one ever near one!" The cost is only $2000.

Now, now, while the sun's rays grow level and fade; while the dear witsy one dwoops his eyes in the last tweet tleep ere Morning breaks eternal, muzzie, daddy, div it no second thought: weep on, weep on, secure in the knowledge that the Montmorency Ovens have guaranteed that itt bittykins of dod's heavum the tweetest and most total of all sanitary napkins.

[Unpublished. C. 1934]

Dedication Day

(Rough Sketch for a Moving Picture)

On an afternoon in the early spring of 1946, in the noble space between the Washington Obelisk and the Lincoln Memorial, crowds, roped off from a great square, watched the statesmen, diplomats, military officials, scientists, clergymen, college presidents, newsreel cameramen and *Life* photographers who had assembled upon special platforms, under the unsteady sunlight, and under the uneasy motions of the flags of nearly all nations, to dedicate the heroic new Arch which was for all time to come to memorialize the greatest of human achievements.

The Arch, which had been designed by Frank Lloyd Wright, was the master-builder's sole concession to the Romanesque; at that, he had made it proof against frost, earthquakes, and the inscription and carving of initials. Glistering more subtly than most jewels—for it was made not of stone but of fused uranium—it stood behind the billowing, rainbow-shaded veil which as yet concealed its dedicatory legend, like some giant captive royal slave of antiquity, face masked, the body nude.

From loudspeakers fairly successfully concealed within the Arch, or sprouting tall above the wide, renewing lawns like rigid quartets of zinc morning glories, poured a special performance of the choral movement of Beethoven's Ninth Symphony, in a new translation by Louis Aragon and Harry Brown, done under the supervision of Robert E. Sherwood, conducted by Arturo Toscanini in Studio 8-H in Rockefeller Center, where an invited audience watched the dedication ceremony on the screen of television's first major hookup.

Even by still not wholly perfected television, it was a stirring sight. The many preliminary speeches, to be sure, had been rather more protracted and less satisfying than speeches on great occasions generally are; for it was not clear either to the speakers or to the listeners precisely why or to what purpose or idea the Arch had been raised, and was to be dedicated: they labored, rather, purely under an irresistible obligation both to indicate their recognition of a great event by erecting a permanent altar to it, and to sign their names to the moment in a few authorized words—as is still found necessary by many people, for instance, when a dead man is buried. The speeches, accordingly, were more notable for resonance, eloquence, and on every speaker's part a most scrupulous courtesy and optimism, than for understanding, far less communication of understanding. But once the speeches were over, the ceremony was a peculiarly simple one and achieved, as several Europeans and many of the more sophisticated natives were afterward to agree in semi-privacy, a level of good taste hardly to be expected of ordinary Americans.

All it amounted to, in the long run, was a moment of silence, during which only the restive flags and the sighing of the great veil especially distracted the eye. It involved, on the part of Maestro Toscanini (who was playing as even he had never played before), a Grand Pause, just before that majestic instant in Beethoven's Symphony in which the basses, endorsed by trombones and emulated by soprani, intone the lines:

> *I embrace ye, O ye Millions!*
> *Here's a kiss for all the World!*

—lines upon which, after earnest discussion whether to substitute for the somewhat fulsome and perhaps over-Teutonic word *kiss* the sturdily alliterative, more Whitmanesque and manly, more comradely, altogether healthier word *wink,* the retranslators had agreed that it was impossible to improve. During this pause, also, it was possible to hear the subdued rattle of Latin as four ravenous Cardinals raced towards the Consecration in all but perfect unison, their voices blended with that of the Pontifical Benediction, relayed from Rome; a group of eminent Protestant clergymen, each, between his closed eyes, pinching the bridge of his nose between thumb and forefinger as if adjusting an invisible pair of pince-nez, knelt each on one knee at the spread center of a new lawn handkerchief; the most prominent and progressive of American Reformist Rabbis all but inaudibly intoned *Eli, Eli,* intimately, into a neat small microphone; the twenty best Allied marksmen of the Second World War presented their rifles; and many members of many national bands lipped their reeds and mouthpieces or, heads bowed to deft fingertips, tested their drum-heads and ravanastrons.

The climax was simple indeed. Dressed in white organdie, an exquisite little girl, recently judged the healthiest three-year-old in the United States (for it had been quickly and courteously agreed, shortly after the termination of lend-lease and Mr. Herbert Lehman's three hundred and seventy-first appeal to Congress in regard to U.N.R.R.A.'s more urgent needs, that no other nation should enter competitors), upon receiving a soft shove from her mother, a former screen star, and a whispered "Now, Lidice," toddled alone into the open, along the sulphur-pale grass, towards the great Arch, bearing in her right hand a taper which had been lighted from a light which had been taken from the light which burns eternally in Paris, above the Tomb of the Unknown Soldier. At the same moment, from a small hole at dead center of the pavement beneath the Arch (an orifice bound by a platinum facsimile of Martha Washington's wedding ring), and from the center, as well, of an embossed lucite medallion which, within a zodiacal wreath, indicated the direction of, and the air mileage to, the capital city of every civilized nation, shyly, rather the way the early worm might try the air in an especially lyrical Disney cartoon, stood up a few inches of gleaming white cord. As the child approached, her bladder a trifle unstabilized by privilege, the Cardinals, and the Monsignori and Papal Knights who served as their acolytes, could not perfectly restrain the sideward sliding of their eyes; among the Protestant clergymen there were several who saw what happened through the rainbow swarming of their eyelashes; the Rabbi's vocal chords thickened, necessitating a slight clearing of the throat, during which he forgot to turn from his microphone; a few even of the superbly disciplined riflemen (and women) uncrossed their eyes from the muzzles of their weapons; one of the musicians permitted his instrument, a tuba, to emit a strangled expletive; a boy on the outskirts of the great crowd could be heard hawking Good Humors, which were not moving very satisfactorily, for the day was chilly; a woman, moaning, fainted, falling double over the rope; and an Eagle Scout, masterfully brocaded with Merit Badges fiercely repeating to himself his terrifying last-minute change of instructions (for it had been decided only in afterthought, in bitter and desperate haste), *No! No! Not Taps! Not Taps!,* raised his bugle to his beardless, though freshly, and electrically, shaven lips.

And now the child stooped, in one of the more rudimentary postures of ballet, and, extending her sanctified taper, touched the bright cord with the flame; and in the exquisite silence there began, audible even to the distant boy who stopped saying Good Humor in the middle of the first syllable, a faint, searching, rustling noise, not unlike that which a snake elicits as he retires among dead leaves. And now, while the musicians poised their instruments and the marksmen slanted their rifles upward; and while the Cardinals slowed or accelerated a little as need be, in order to reach their genuflections, and the threshing of the bells, at the precisely proper moment; and while, in New York, the Maestro held one hundred and seventeen instruments and nine hundred and forty-three pairs of eyes suspended as by one spider-thread from the tip of his baton; and while the woman who had fainted was softly and quickly shunted toward the rear of the crowd; and while the voice of America's Number One Commentator continued its description, in such expert unobtrusiveness that although he was thrillingly audible to every one among the millions in his unseen audience, not a single person among the onlookers could hear a word he said, though nearly all were straining with all their strength, in order that they might know what was happening before they read it in the late editions, which were even now being purchased along the periphery of the crowd; while all these things were transpiring, or held themselves balanced intense in readiness, trembling, the chosen Scout, who in innumerable rehearsals had perfected a rendition of Taps so heartrending that, in recorded form, with hummed accompaniment by Bing Crosby, the Andrew Sisters, the Ink Spots, and the Westminster Choir, it had already sold better than a million disks, did as best he could, disconsolately, lacking rehearsals, with Reveille, which he had had no occasion to play since camp broke up the previous summer, and which many people agreed he managed really very prettily, considering the circumstances. As his last note melted, the twenty marksmen fired the first of their twenty-one salutes, flicking the silver-gift padlocks from a long rank of cages which exhaled a brilliant flock of homing doves, somewhat frustrated in their breathing by wired-on imitation olive-branches, and banded with appropriate messages with which, after wheeling briefly, luminous against the clouds, they set off in haste for the several and all-inclusive quarters of the globe; the Cardinals genuflected; their bells threshed; the Rabbi collapsed his microphone stand and smoothed his hair; the woman who had fainted opened her eyes, gazed up the sharp chins of sympathizers and, with a heartsick groan, miscarried; the clergymen rose from their knees and carefully folded and pocketed their handkerchiefs; the Good Humor salesboy resumed business; and in perfect synchronization the military bands of forty-six nations and the

National Broadcasting Symphony Orchestra and the Westminster Choir attacked respectively their respective national anthems and their continuation of the Choral Symphony, all somewhat modified, in the interests of euphony, by Morton Gould, but virtually all still recognizable to the untrained ear; and the iridescent veil, its release cords pulled, on a signal from James Bryant Conant, by the President of the United States, Charles de Gaulle, a reluctant veteran of the Chinese Purchasing Commission, and undersecretaries from the Embassies of the other two of the Big Five, sank laboring on the March air from the crest of the Arch, revealing, in Basic English, the words:

THIS IS IT

A soft cheer of awe moved upon the crowd; then a flowering of applause like the rumination of leaves before rain: for this secret had been successfully kept, and very few of those on the outskirts had managed to buy extras until the veil fell.

Below the legend, the Eternal Fuse continued to exude and to consume itself, one inch above the pavement at the rate of one inch per second. The fuse was chemically calculated continuously somewhat to intensify the noise of its consumption, enough to be distinguishable to anyone who kept attentive vigil for so much as twenty-four hours; at the end of precisely one hundred years, it was further calculated, this penetrating whisper, grown continuously more acute never dynamically more loud, would become audible at the point most distant from its origin, on the planet. Some stayed, now, and held vigil; others, many, listened a half hour, even an hour, then lost patience; slowly, towards the early neons, the crowd dissolved. Few were left, at dusk, to witness the lowering and folding of the flags.

During the earlier stages of planning the Memorial there had been considerable discussion whether the fuse should burn down at the rate of an inch per hour, or even per day; but an inch per second had ultimately been agreed on not only as peppier and somehow more in keeping, but also because this rate of consumption measurably helped solve, or at least proved awareness of, certain delicate social and economic problems. Some 7,200 feet of the fuse would be consumed each day; approximately 4,897.6 miles, which amounted to roughly 322.17 bales of cotton each year. The cotton would be the finest Egyptian long-staple, grown by members of a Sharecropper's Rehabilitation Project in one of the richest of the condemned areas of the Delta. Bales would be furnished alternately by a white and a Negro family, and would be purchased at cost, the cash to be applied against the interest on Rehabilitation Loans. The purchase of the chemicals used in impregnating the fuse, a mere few tons of those substances so recently and abruptly rendered obsolete for military use, was, to be sure, a mere token, but as such it assured various embarrassed manufacturers of archaic munitions of the Government's enduring sympathy and concern for their welfare. Moreover, the manufacture of the fuse itself made gainful and honorable employment available to a number of persons otherwise unemployable, and added no little not only to the symbolic dignity but also to the human warmth of the entire Project. For beneath the Arch, in a small, air-conditioned, irradiated workshop so ingeniously contrived by Norman Bel Geddes that it was possible for those who found it more efficient to do their share from hospital beds or even, a few of them, from streamlined baskets, the fuse was manufactured on the spot. Its creators, who were by unanimous agreement among those in charge of the Memorial called Keepers of the Flame, worked perpetually, wheeled in and out, as shifts changed, through silent tunnels of tile and plastic, by women physicians who had been rendered redundant by the termination of hostilities. They were at all times visible even while they slept, to tourists who used other tunnels, through thick walls of polarized glass. The tourist admission fees, even though ex-servicemen and children in arms were to be passed at half price for the next two years, would clearly better than pay both the initial cost and the maintenance of the Project; the surplus monies were to be applied toward the relief of those who should have neglected to redeem their War and Victory Bonds by 1950.

One of these twelve-hour shifts (for the work was light) was composed of such disabled winners of the Distinguished Service Cross, the Congressional Medal of Honor, and the Navy Cross as did not wish to be a burden on their communities or to languish in Veterans' Hospitals, and as were alert to the immense therapeutic value of honest work. It was required of them only that they wear their uniforms and decorations, during working hours, and, as a reminder and incentive to youth, show their wounds, scars, or stumps. They were paid whatever their rank and injury entitled them, in pension. The other shift was composed of depreciated but surviving collaborators in the experiments at Hiroshima and Nagasaki, who had been forgiven, and were, indeed, aside from a few unfortunate incidents which marred the course of their journey across the less progressive reaches of the nation, treated with marked civility, even being permitted to shake hands with Secretaries of State and of War, who laughingly apologized, through an interpreter, for wearing radiation-proof gloves and masks throughout the little ceremony. There had at first been some talk of accepting, for this work, only such Japanese as embraced Christianity, but it was generously decided, in the interests of religious toleration, that this should not be required; indeed, a number of the Nagasaki colleagues, formerly Christian, were known to have renounced Christianity; it was an open secret, even, that two of them were privately practicing the out-lawed Shintoism. This too (though care was taken that the fact should not become known among the general public) was smilingly disregarded, on the grounds that in their present occupation, and distance from the homeland, and fewness in number—not to mention the efficiency of the magnificently trained Project Guardians—no great harm was likely to come of these atavist diehards. It was required of the Japanese only that they keep on display, during working hours, those strange burns which have excited, in Americans, so much friendly curiosity—an exposure necessarily limited, of course, in a number of cases, in the interests of decency. These Japanese were paid the wages customary for prisoners of war (the funds were deposited in their names in a Subtreasury vault, their board and keep being deductible) and, in accordance with the rulings of the Geneva Convention, were required, in their eating, to fare neither better nor worse, nor other, than men in our own armed services, being forced, in fact, to ingest one can of K Rations, two four-pound porterhouse steaks, one carton of Camels, eight squares of Ex-Lax, two boxes of Puffed Rice, the juice of twelve oranges, a tin of Spam, a cup of Ovaltine, a prophylactic, a tube of nationally advertised toothpaste, and macerated or liquified overseas editions of *Time*, *Reader's Digest* and the New Testament, each, per day, plus roast beef, apple pie and store cheese on Sundays and proper supplements, including third helpings, spoon-lickings and ejaculations of "Gosh, Mom," of the special dishes traditionally appropriate to the major Holidays; all to be administered orally, rectally or by intravenous injection, as best befitted the comfort of the individual patient—a task which many of the little fellows found so embarrassing, and which the tourists found so richly amusing to watch, that even after the first few days, feeding time created something of a traffic problem.

It was agreed that in due course these invalids would be supplanted at their jobs by their children if they should prove capable of breeding and bearing them, and that such children, if their behavior should prove unexceptionable up to the age of twenty-one years, would be granted the privileges of American citizenship and of absentee voting. The male children of those veterans capable of siring them would be offered their choice between the same lifetime guarantee of gainful employment, and a scholarship at Peddie. In the event—as to some people seemed quite conceivable—that this turnover plan too rapidly diminished the personnel, it had already been arranged that the Japanese and American ranks be filled out respectively by Mission converts to any one of the accredited Christian faiths, and by divinity students, who would receive fullcourse seminarial credits for their services per year, tuition halved.

Raw materials were conveyed to these workers each midnight, promptly, by armored truck. Before the day of the ceremony they had produced a spool of fuse so thick that it was decided to give them a holiday. In the morning, on the White House Back Lawn, there was a picnic, with a sack race, and a baseball game (won, amusingly enough, by the Japanese). In the afternoon they were all brought to reserved areas (segregating, however, the Japanese and Americans) at the very brink of the ropes, to witness the Dedication.

One pathetic incident marred this otherwise perfect day. One of the more elderly of those scientists who contributed their genius towards the perfecting of the bomb—he shall, in these columns at least, remain nameless—had begun, not long after the Japanese surrender, to strike his colleagues as a little queer in the head. He was known to have attended Mass, at first secretly, then quite openly; later, to have spent several evenings of silence among the Friends; later, to have sought out a poet of his acquaintance, of whom, it had been learned, he asked Mahatma Gandhi's postal address, whether a letter might be kindly received, and answered, and approximately how far into the East it might be advisable to journey, insofar as possible on foot, or on his knees ("Perhaps to Lhasa?" he asked), in what he called "atonement." The poet, according to his own account of this singular interview, merely laughed uproariously, murmuring some obscurantist figure of speech—which with great amusement he repeated, when questioned by friends of the scientist—about "locking the stable after the horse had been stolen." It was not long after this—early in October—that plans for the Arch began to develop. Once the scientist learned of the idea of the underground personnel he did not rest, or indeed let any of his associates or of their contacts among the officials rest, until he had gained permission to become one of the Keepers. This was granted him the more reluctantly because he insisted on working with the Japanese shift and, to the further embarrassment of everyone, gave warning that he would refuse to eat the carefully balanced diet offered the Japanese, preferring, rather, just so much boiled unpolished rice per day as he could hold in the palm of one hand. In view of his immense services to humanity, and out of a kind of pity, and a perhaps overconscientious sense that the community as a whole, having so greatly benefited through him, shared, in some measure no matter how small or indirect, a certain responsibility, or at least concern, for his broken mind, it was, after prolonged consultation with eminent psychologists, agreed that he should be humored. Unfortunately, the best will in the world, on the part of those officially and medically responsible, was not, as it turned out, enough.

In the course of those "Arch Prevues," so-called, which many readers will have glimpsed in the newsreels, it became painfully clear that it was entirely unfeasible to permit him to persist in his wish. It was not that the Japanese misbehaved; indeed, they left the old man severely alone. It was rather, the behavior of the physicist himself, and the disturbing effect of his behavior upon Prevue tourists. Although the thick glass rendered him inaudible, it was only too clear to the more observant of these onlookers that as he worked he spoke, and that his speech was evidently a terrible blended stream of self-vilification and of pr-y-r. And even to those insufficiently accustomed to these retrogressive attitudes to decipher them correctly (for many thought, as they put it, that he was "just cussing out the Japs"), it was nevertheless excruciatingly embarrassing to see a white man working among those of a different pigmentation, and to see how, so often as the limited gestures necessary to his work permitted him, he tore at his thin hair and beat his bruised face with clenched fists and tore at it with his nails, and to see how at all times his bitten lips bled copiously onto his starched laboratory jacket, immediately soiling it regardless of its ever more frequent change; and how his torn face was wet with continuous uncontrolled (and perhaps uncontrollable) tears. Some took to rapping on the glass with coins to draw his attention, then, according to their wont, either jeering at him by gestures of their hands and by contortions of their faces, or attempting to revive his courage and self-esteem by showing in their faces, or by making the sign of Victory and smiling their sympathy, or by clasping and shaking their hands and grinning, that however regrettable his present plight they continued to honor and to befriend and to congratulate him, in view of his past achievements. Such gestures, however, appeared to offend the Japanese, and were discouraged by the Guards. Others of the spectators passed on quickly in revulsion; and that too, in its own way, impaired the intended dignity, charm and decorum of the exhibit. Still others, however, and in considerable numbers, blocked the tourists' tunnel by following the example of one young soldier who, late in the afternoon before the Dedication, quite without warning fell to his knees and burst into tears. To be sure, few of his imitators wept; most of them, indeed, and this was especially true of those at the edge of the sudden crowd, did not know what was happening, and knelt only because they saw that those ahead of them were kneeling. Scrupulously conducted interviews immediately following the disturbance, in which prominent churchmen and psychiatrists were assisted by Gallup Poll experts, thoroughly established the fact that the soldier himself, despite his many campaign-stars and decorations for valor, was a psychoneurotic, that virtually nobody had understood the cause of his outburst, and that nothing whatever need be feared, notwithstanding the insistence of certain evangelistic types, in the way of a so-called "religious revival." Even so, the kneeling was of itself an irregular and far from convenient action; the more so because for every tourist who, out of a courteous desire to do what was expected of him, dropped to his knees, there were at least two others (2.29, by the Gallup count) who, mistaking this for some kind of vulgar sentimentality, in natural impatience and contempt, and no little anger, clambered among and through and over the close-packed kneelers, creating a severe jam and, ultimately, a mild panic; for an overwrought woman at the far edge of the commotion screamed that the Japanese had broken loose, others took up the cry, and those in front of the exhibit split and bruised the unbreakable glass in their effort to protect their women-folk. (The Japanese, it must be said, were entirely innocent in this affair.) From this confusion many of all types, kneelers, non-kneelers, defenders and defended alike, emerged with minor contusions, and instituted suits against the Arch Authority for damage to their nerves, clothing, and earning power. Such are the unfortunate effects of a single man's unbridled individualism.

It was at the end of this shift, accordingly, at midnight, that the physicist was told, in all possible kindliness, that his services, greatly as they were appreciated, would no longer be required, and that he had his choice of lifelong residence and treatment, gratis, in whatever sanitarium in the nation he might prefer. Instantly he stopped his crying and asked, in a manner which seemed entirely rational, whether he might not, before retiring, have at least the privilege of throwing that switch, in the underground workshop, which would start the fuse on its eternal journey. He did not like to think, he said, that any one of his fellow-workers would be deprived of his day off, or of witnessing the climactic moment from the best point of vantage possible. Such was the unworldliness of the man, that it had not occurred to him that this was, after all, a crucial part of the ceremony; in fact, a switch had been arranged on the Number One Platform (its knob set with the Hope Diamond, on loan, and heavily insured for the occasion); and it was to be thrown—since both Drs. Albert Einstein and Lise Meitner had declined the honor—by Major General Leslie Groves. It was decided not to embarrass the poor old man. Quickly, by telephone, the General's magnanimous withdrawal was secured; the scientist was then told that everyone would be delighted, and honored, if he would consent to "start the ball rolling," as they said, in a position of the greatest possible conspicuousness and eminence. Courteously, even gratefully, he replied that he really preferred to be underground. After careful consultation, it was deemed entirely harmless to grant his wish—a decision which, as nobody could have foreseen, was to prove tragically ill-advised.

Within a few minutes after the Dedication he was found next the great spool, dead by his own hand (by prussic acid); it was deduced that he must have swallowed the poison in the instant of throwing the switch. Pinned to his immaculate laboratory jacket was a note, written clearly and steadily in his own hand.

Out of deference to the deceased and to his surviving relatives, it was instantly and unanimously agreed not to publish this short, singular document (though qualified students will be granted access to it), whose contents could only puzzle and offend sane human beings, and establish beyond possible question the piteous derangement of a man of former genius. By rough paraphrase, however, it seems not dishonorable to say that in unimpeachable sincerity he regarded his suicide as obligatory—as, indeed, a kind of religious or ethical "sacrifice," through which he hoped to endow the triumphal monument with a new and special significance and, through the gradual spread and understanding of that significance, once more (as he thought) to assist the human race.

Even in death, however, this unfortunate but brilliant man again made history. Psychoanalysts are even now busy exploring the hidden depths of the already celebrated case; the nation's leading philosophers are rushing a symposium to be entitled *The New New Failure of Nerve;* and clergymen of all denominations, united in agreement perhaps more firmly than ever before, are determined to preach next Sunday (and, if need be, on the following Sunday as well), using this tragic incident by no means unsympathetically yet sternly, and with controlled ridicule, as an object-lesson, and grave admonition, to such in their spiritual charge as find themselves for any reason of pride, or a thirst for undue publicity, liable to the grievous error of exaggerated scrupulousness. "Some things are best left to Jesus Christ," will be the burden of their argument; the text will be, *Render unto Caesar the things that are Caesar's, and unto God the things that are God's.*

The body will be interred, with military honors, at the center of that area in New Mexico in which this gifted scientist, and his colleagues, first saw the light of the New Age. And it does not seem too much to hope that perhaps he will be remembered, not, surely, as he has intended, yet a little wistfully, in the sound of The Fuse itself as it increases upon the world. For misguided and altogether regrettable though his last days were—a sad warning indeed to those who turn aside from the dictates of reason, and accept human progress reluctantly—he was nevertheless, perhaps, our last link with a not-too-distant past in which such conceptions as those of "atonement," and "guilt," and "individual responsibility," still had significance. And, in a sense, his gift to mankind was greater, perhaps, than that of his more stable colleagues. For, though "sacrifice" is a word to be used only with apologies, it would be hard to define what, if anything, they "sacrificed" in the giving; but he gave up his sanity.

[From *Politics,* April 1946; reprinted in
New Directions 10, 1948]

PART IV

FOUR

FRAGMENTS

Run Over

(*A note, undated, among others handwritten*)

I was rounding the corner into asylum avenue, ambling home in the middle of the afternoon, and there at the curb was a crowd and there in the middle of the crowd was a big thin black cat with wild red blood all over its face and its teeth like long thorns and its tongue curled like that of a heraldic lion. Right across the middle it was as flat as an ironed britches leg. Purple guts stained the pavement and a pale bloody turd stood out under its tail. Its head was split open like a melon; against the black fur, its crushed skull was like an egg. This cat was not lying still, nor keeping still: it was as lively as if it were on a gridiron and it was yelling and gasping satanically, the yells sounding like something through a horn whose reed is split: never getting to its feet but flailing this way and that, lying still and panting hardly five seconds at a time: people sidestepping the tatters of blood and slime and closing in again when he was off in another direction. The people were fairly quiet; talking in undertones and not saying much, but never looking away. Something respectful in every one of them. Someone said he had nine lives. It was the first I had ever heard of that, and I believed it. Other people were speculating how many of them he'd lost by now: nobody agreed on that, but they were mostly defending the cat as if against libel: he had plenty more left to go through yet.

Not that anyone there was fool enough to think he'd come out of this and get well, with two or three lives up his sleeve to spare for later contingencies, but he was putting up one whale of a fight, and though there was now and then a murmur about putting him out of his misery which no voice was raised against, nobody ventured to interfere with the wonderful processes of nature. (Things like this are happening somewhere on the earth every second.)

Give Him Air

(Hand-written note undated, datable to late thirties)

I suppose I may have seen everything in detail, but I don't remember everything, and there's no use inventing it. All I remember is the long blueblack gash made in the asphalt by the dragged axle, which led forty feet right into the hind legs of the mob, and, after I had fought my way through the mob, the man they were looking at. I don't doubt other people were hurt; but I don't recall even seeing them: they couldn't have been hurt as this man was. He was propped up against the ivy on our wall. The right inner forearm and the palm of the right hand were laid open like an anatomical illustration, but less neatly, right to the bone, and the bone was broken, midway between wrist and elbow, like a stick, some pieces still holding. His whole [word omitted: face?] was snatched off as neatly as a wig off a head, and somebody was wiping the blood and glass away, mainly to give him a chance to breathe, but also apparently in some idiotic hope that he might be able to see; and care to if he could. So, just after the wiping, you saw his eyes, like a couple of pale marbles on strings, and you saw his flat nostrils, an inch behind where his nose had been, quite distinctly, and at any time you saw his lipless and broken grinning teeth, those of them that weren't scattered down his shirt. Then the eyes would submerge again, and be wiped off again. He was lying still, not doing anything at all except snoring monstrously, great, soulful, rhythmic, rattling snores that sucked the blood down till the holes were visible and blew it out like tobacco juice (I had forgotten the tobacco juice: it was all over his throat and a quid lay back among his teeth: no one had quite the courage to fish it out and save him the swallowing). There is nothing more really to say about him; he just lay there snoring; I am sure you could have heard it a block: it was rather like the sharp, rasping flutter of a rubber farting-whistle, and this fact registered, I suspect, on one woman who was watching, who tried desperately to hide her feeling, and then broke into the craziest, gayest sort of laughter. I think it was this rather than hysterics because I noticed that as she was breaking down and that horrid farting continued, quite a number of men around her had a very hard time, and a very self-ashamed one, keeping their faces straight. Meanwhile traffic was piled up a block around, policemen were pushing people around and asking questions, a street car fought its way painfully up half the block, gave it up and disgorged its occupants, who ran up asking questions too (they weren't within a mile of being able to see anything) and all the time, of course, people were sincerely saying give him air, give him air, and sincerely trying to, and were totally unable to bring themselves, or a lot of others, to do any such thing.

An ambulance came to the outskirts, whining; people in white fought through and carried him off, still snoring like a comic-strip, and the newspapers said he never regained consciousness, and died on the way to the hospital.

A Birthday

(Typescript page, for the autobiographical novel. No date)

it is thanksgiving and I am four years old and this is my birthday, and we all dangle in from the living room through the greenroom into the dining room to the table and granma puts down the bell when she sees us. grampa says sherry. unc' hugh gets another big book and puts it on the big book on the chair and daddy hise me up, there you are, here i am. happy birthday. many happy returns of the day. huh? california sherry. say i beg your pardon? i beg your pardon? california. many happy returns of the day. say thank you granma. say the same to you and many of them, say it *loud*. same to you and many of them. thank you. thank you granma, seee,

tom? thank you seee, what rufus has got. seee, what, right on the napkin by the plate. Granma puts down her glass and dabs her mouth with a fold of napkin. do you know what this is rufus? what is it rufus. A course he doesnt. Of course he does. Sure he does, heez seen um, seen um out at chilholly park, havent you rufus. seen what. then those birds, on the pond. what birds. why the birds for god sake like the jay. like the big white birds with the long necks on the lake, dear. what is it. look like a sort of a sort of a bird or something. sort a bird. swan. swan. tadada-daah, ta tadadaa, ta tadaaah (dadadadadadidledy-daddle) hnh? swan. swan. swan? sure. swan. well i swan. mine leeeeebr sschhhwannnnn, here, eat your dinner, rufus. here, let it swim. give hima swim. hm? swim. not good to eat. daddys hand reached across him dragging stuffing at the cuff, took his fingers from around the swan and set the swan up in the tumbler ful a water. It Floats. it stands right up on the water. there. see? just like chilholly park. not very much. eat your dinner dear, dont dwaddle. there he is, standing right up on top of the water, waving up and down. . . .

I am making an this sense that survives in feeling, the ideas are, I know, less that this are such desires to purify only impressive for the world deeply, and tremaining is more slowly accurate and truthfully than in even more so-called literature and prose, but more than in this speaks of as an actual chores, and in no less despairing realization and trifles than all the emotions of this been refused by this most explicit endurance transmitted until after even in vapidity and some evidence of a . . .

The a to-morning . . .

less me know that the foot one has in left me when this is in this received, admittance and greeting such the a the ...

"Now as Awareness . . ."

(Evidently a fresh start on the autobiographical novel. No date)

Now as awareness of how much of life is lost, and how little is left, becomes even more piercing, I feel also, and ever the more urgently, the desire to restore, and to make a little less impermanent, such of my lost life as I can, beginning with the beginning and coming as far forward as need be. This is the simplest, most primitive of the desires which can move a writer. I hope I shall come to other things in time; in time to write them. Before I do, if I am ever to do so, I must sufficiently satisfy this first, most childlike need.

I had hoped that I might make poetry of some of this material, and fiction of more of it, and during the past two years I have written a good deal of it as fiction, and a little of it as poetry. But now I believe that these two efforts were mistakes. This book is chiefly a remembrance of my childhood, and a memorial to my father; and I find that I value my childhood and my father as they were, as well and as exactly as I can remember and represent them, far beyond any transmutation of these matters which I have made, or might ever make, into poetry or fiction. I know that

I am making the choice most dangerous to an artist, in valuing life above art; I know too that by a good use of fiction or poetry one can re-enter life more deeply, and represent it more vividly, intimately and truthfully, than by any such means of bald narration as I propose; but it now seems to me that I have no actual choice, but am in fact compelled, against my judgment and wish as an artist. Within the limitations imposed by this plain method to which I seem compelled, I shall, of course, in so far as I am able, use such varieties of artfulness as seem appropriate.

Those who have gone before, backward beyond remembrance and beyond the beginning of imagination, backward among the emergent beasts, and the blind, prescient ravenings of the youngest sea, those children of the sun, I mean, who brought forth those, who wove, spread the human net, and who brought forth me; they are fallen backward into their graves like blown wheat and are folded under the earth like babies in blankets, and they are all melted upon the mute enduring world like leaves, like wet snow; they are faint in the urgencies of my small being as stars at noon; they people the silence of my soul like bats in a cave; they lived, in their time, as I live now, each a universe within which, for a while, to die was inconceivable, and their living was as bright and brief as sparks on a chimney wall, and now they lie dead, as I soon shall lie; my ancestors, my veterans. I call upon you, I invoke your help, you cannot answer, you cannot help; I desire to do you honor, you are beyond the last humiliation. You are my fathers and my mothers but there is no way in which you can help me, nor may I serve you. You are the old people and now you rest. Rest well; I will be with you soon; meanwhile may I bear you ever in the piety of my heart.

They lie down in so many places, as they begin to

emerge into domestic legend; in Western England, in Scotland, in Ireland, in Massachusetts, in New Hampshire, in Vermont, in New York State, in Michigan, in Tennessee, where my own life began: my mother's people. In France, in Germany, in the mountains of a wilderness which became Tennessee: my father's people. And where before that; and where shall my children rest, and their children? We can see, sometimes, a light across a thousand years; we are, perhaps, the eyes of nature, such as they are; stones are hardly more blind, and few creatures are as capricious in their wanderings, or so dice-like in their destinies. Our marriages are imaginations of choice, love, unique desire; we meet and mate like apples swung together on a creek.

Then there are those who come within living memory: my mother's father's father, whom she revered and of whom she has told me; I think well of him, and was burdened by his name, but I never knew him; I doubt I shall ever have occasion to tell my children of him; with this generation he vanishes from the memory of the human race, and only the exceptionally good, or able, or evil survive in memory longer.

PART V

PLANS FOR WORK:
OCTOBER 1937

Plans for Work: October 1937

*(Submitted by James Agee with his application for
a Guggenheim Fellowship)*

I am working on, or am interested to try, or expect to
return to, such projects as the following. I shall first
list them, then briefly specify a little more about most
of them.

An Alabama Record.
Letters.
A story about homosexuality and football.
News Items.
Hung with their own rope.
A dictionary of key words.
Notes for color photography.
A revue.
Shakespeare.
A cabaret.
Newsreel. Theatre.
A new type of stage-screen show.
Anti-communist manifesto.
Three or four love stories.
A new type of sex book.
"Glamor" writing.

A study in the pathology of "laziness."

A new type of horror story.

Stories whose whole intention is the direct communication of the intensity of common experience.

"Musical" uses of "sensation" or "emotion."

Collections and analyses of faces; of news pictures.

Development of new forms of writing via the caption; Letters; pieces of overhead conversation.

A new form of "story": the true incident recorded as such and an analysis of it.

A new form of movie short roughly equivalent to the lyric poem.

Conjectures of how to get "art" back on a plane of organic human necessity, parallel to religious art or the art of primitive hunters.

A show about motherhood.

Pieces of writing whose rough parallel is the prophetic writings of the Bible.

Uses of the Dorothy Dix Method; the Voice of Experience: for immediacy, intensity, complexity of opinion.

The inanimate and non-human.

A new style and use of the imagination: the exact opposite of the Alabama record.

A true account of a jazz band.

An account and analysis of a cruise: "high"-class people.

Portraiture. Notes. The Triptych.

City Streets. Hotel Rooms. Cities.

A new kind of photographic show.

The slide lecture.

A new kind of music. Noninstrumental sound. Phonograph recording. Radio.

Extension in writing; ramification in suspension; Schubert 2-cello Quintet.

Analyses of Hemingway, Faulkner, Wolfe, Auden, other writers.

Analyses of reviews of Kafka's *Trial;* various moving pictures.

Two forms of history of the movies.

Reanalyses of the nature and meaning of love.

Analyses of miscommunication; the corruption of idea.

Moving picture notes and scenarios.

An "autobiographical novel."

New forms of "poetry."

A notebook.

In any effort to talk further about these, much is liable to overlap and repeat. Any further coordination would, however, be rather more false than true indication of the way the work would be undertaken; for these projects are in fluid rather than organized relationship to each other. None of the following can be more than suggestive of work.

Alabama Record.

In the summer of 1936 the photographer Walker Evans and I spent two months in Alabama hunting out and then living with a family of cotton tenants which by general average would most accurately represent all cotton tenancy. This work was in preparation for an article for *Fortune.* We lived with one and made a detailed study and record of three families, and interviewed and observed landowners, new dealers, county officers, white and negro tenants, etc., etc., in several cities and county seats and villages and throughout 6,000 miles of country.

The record I want to make of this is not journalistic; nor on the other hand is any of it to be invented. It can perhaps most nearly be described as "scientific," but not in a sense acceptable to scientists, only in the sense that it is ultimately skeptical and analytic. It is to be as exhaustive a reproduction and analysis of personal experience, including the phases and problems of memory and recall and revisitation and the problems of writing and of communication, as I am capable of, with constant bearing on two points: to tell everything possible as accurately as possible: and to invent nothing. It involves therefore as total a suspicion of "creative" and "artistic" as of "reportorial" attitudes and methods, and it is likely therefore to involve the development of some more or less new forms of writing and of observation.

Of this work I have written about 40,000 words, first draft, and entirely tentative. On this manuscript I was offered an advance and contract, which I finally declined, feeling I could neither wisely nor honestly commit the project to the necessarily set or estimated limits of time and length. With your permission I wish to submit it as a part of my application, in the hope that it will indicate certain things about the general intention of the work, and also some matters suggested under the head of "accomplishments," more clearly than I can. I should add of it a few matters it is not sufficiently developed to indicate.

Any given body of experience is sufficiently complex and ramified to require (or at least be able to use) more than one mode of reproduction: it is likely that this one will require many, including some that will extend writing and observing methods. It will likely make use of various traditional forms but it is anti-artistic, anti-scientific, and anti-journalistic. Though every effort will be made to give experience, emotion and thought as directly as possible, and as nearly as may be toward their full detail and complexity (it would have at different times, in other words, many of the qualities of a novel, a report, poetry), the job is perhaps chiefly a skeptical study of the nature of reality and of the false nature of recreation and of communication. It should be as definitely a book of photographs as a book of words: in other words photographs should be used profusely, and never to "illustrate" the prose. One part of the work, in many senses the crucial part, would be a strict comparison of the photographs and the prose as relative liars and as relative reproducers of the same matters.

Letters.

Letters are in every word and phrase immediate to and revealing of, in precision and complex detail, the sender and receiver and the whole world and context each is of: as distinct in their own way, and as valuable, as would be a faultless record of the dreams of many individuals. The two main facts about any letter are: the immediacy, and the flawlessness, of its revelations. In the true sense that any dream is a faultless work of art, so is any letter; and the defended and conscious letter is as revealing as the undefended. Here then is a racial record; and perhaps the best available document of the power and fright of language and of mis-communication and of the crippled concepts behind these. The variety to be found in letters is almost as unlimited as literate human experience; their monotony is equally valuable.

Therefore, a collection of letters of all kinds.

Almost better than not, the limits of this would be: what you and your friends and their acquaintances can find. For even within this, the complete range of society and of mind can be bracketed; and this limitation more truly indicates the range of the subject than any effort to extend it onto more ordinary planes of "research" possibly could.

Working chiefly thus far with two or three friends, we have got together many hundreds of letters. Many more are on their way.

There are several possible and equally good methods of handling these letters.

1. Beyond deletion of identifiers, no editing and no selection at all. In other words, let chance be the artist, the fulcrum and shaper. This is beyond any immediate possibility of publication, in any such bulk.

2. Very careful selection, the chief guides to be a) scientific respect for chance and for representativeness rather than respect for more conventional forms of "reader interest"; and b) the induction and education of a reading public, for less selected future work.

3. Context notes, short and uncolored, would probably be useful.

4. Take certain or all such letters. Let them first stand by themselves. Then an almost word by word analysis of them, as many-sided and extensive as the given letter requires. This could be of great clarifying power.

5. Instead of a purely "scientific" analysis, one which likewise allows the open entrance of emotion and belief, to the violent degrees for instance, of rage, rhapsody and poetry.

6. A series or book of invented letters, treated in any or all of the above ways.

These treatments may seem to cancel each other. Not at all necessarily. I would hope to use them all in the course of time, and very likely would try substantial beginning-examples of all in the same first volume.

The value or bearing of such work would come under my own meanings of science, religion, art, teaching, and entertainment.

It should also help to shift and to destroy various habits and certitudes of the "creative" and of the "reading," and so of the daily "functioning," mind.

It could well be published in book form or as all or as part of a certain type of magazine I am interested in, or as a part of a notebook which I shall say more of later.

As a book it should even in its first shot contain as much as a publisher can be persuaded to allow; and its whole demeanor should be colorless and noncommital, like scientific or government publications. It should contain a great deal of facsimile, not only of handwriting but of stationery.

A story about homosexuality and football.

Not central to this story but an inevitable part of it would be a degree of cleansing of the air on the subject of homosexuality. Such a cleansing could not in this form hope to be complete. The same clarifying would be attempted on the sport and on the nature of belief: always less by statement than by demonstration. All this, however, is merely incidental to the story itself.

An account, then, of love between a twelve-year-old boy and a man of twenty-two, in the Iliadic air of football in a Tennessee mountain peasant school: reaching its crisis during and after a game which is recounted chiefly in terms of the boy's understanding and love; in other words in terms of an age of pure faith. The prose to be lucid, simple, naturalistic and physical to the maximum possible. In other words if it succeeds in embodying what it wants to it must necessarily have the essential qualities of folk epic and of heroic music carried in terms of pure "realism." This is being written now. It is to be about the length and roughly the form of the "long short story."

News Items.

Much the same as *Letters.*

Hung with their own rope.

I have found no single word for what I mean. The material turns up all over the place. The idea is, that the self-deceived and corrupted betray themselves and their world more definitively than invented satire can. Vide Eleanor Roosevelt's *My Day;* Mrs. Daisy Chanler's *Autumn in the Valley;* the journal and letters of Gamaliel Bradford; court records, editorial, religious, women's pages; the "literature" concerning and justifying the castration of Eisenstein; etc.

Such could again be collected in a volume, or as a magazine or part of a magazine; or in the notebook.

The above is limited to self-betrayals in print. Those in unpublished living must of course be handled in other ways. One minor but powerful way is, the unconsciously naked sentence, given either with or without context. These are abundant for collection.

A dictionary of key words.

More on the significance of language. Add idioms. A study and categorizing of tones of voice, or rhythms and of inflection; of social dialects; would also be useful. Key words are those organic and collective belief—and conception—words upon the centers and sources of which most of social and of single conduct revolves and deceives or undeceives itself and others. Certain such words are Love, God, Honor, Loyalty, Beauty, Law, Justice, Duty, Good, Evil, Truth, Reality, Sacrifice, Self, Pride, Pain, Life, etc. etc. etc. Such would be examined skeptically in every discernible shade of their meaning and use. There might in a first dictionary be an arbitrary fifty or a hundred, with abundant quotations and examples from letters, from printed matter, and from common speech.

Mr. I. A. Richards, whose qualifications are extremely different from my own and in many essentials far more advanced, is, I understand, working on just such a dictionary. Partly because the differences of attack would be so wide, and still more because the chief point is the ambiguity of language, I do not believe these books would be at all in conflict.

Notes for color photography.

Of two kinds: theoretical and specific. For stills; in motion; in coordination with sound and rhythm. Uses of pure color, no image. Metaphoric, oblique, nervous and musical uses of color. Analyses of the "unreality" of "realistic" color photography. Of differences between color in a photograph and in painting. The esthetic is as basically different as photography itself is from painting, and as large a new field is open to color in photography. Examples of all this, and notes for future use, from observation.

A revue.

Much to do with a whole theatrical form. The dramatic stage is slowed and stuffed with naturalism. Audiences still and without effort accept the living equivalent of "poetry" in revue, burlesque and vaudeville. Stylization, abbreviation and intensity are here possible. Destructive examples of "spurious" use: *Of Thee I Sing, As Thousands Cheer,* etc. Solid examples, upon which still further developments can be made: the didactic plays of Brecht; *The Cradle Will Rock; The Dog Beneath The Skin.*

Shakespeare.

Commentary; ideas for production in moving picture and on stage; criticism of contemporary production of his work and of attitudes toward his work produced or read. In movies: use of screen and sound as *elliptic* commentary or development of the lines. On stage: concentration totally in words and physical relationships. Qualifiedly good example: The Orson Welles *Faustus* (I have not yet seen his Caesar). On stage also: Savage use of burlesqued mélange of traditional idioms of production, conception and reading, intended as simultaneous ridicule, analysis and destruction of culture.

A cabaret.

Cheap drinks, hot jazz by record and occasional performers; "floor show." Examples of acts: monologues I have written; certain numbers from Erika Mann's *Peppermill;* much in Groucho Marx, Durante, Fields. Broad and extreme uses of ad lib and of parody. No sets, no lighting and only improvised costume. Intense and violent satire, "vulgarity," pure comedy. Strong development of improvisation; use of the audience in this.

Newsreel. Theater.

The theater: 15-25 cents, 42nd Street west of Times Square, open all night. Usual arty-theatre repertory much cut down, strongly augmented by several dozen features overlooked by the arty and political, and by several of Harry Langdon's and all of Buster Keaton's comedies. Strong and frequent shifts in "policy," to admit, for instance, a week embodying the entire career of a given director or star or idiom. Revivals, much more frequent than at present, of certain basics: Chaplin, Cagney, Garbo, Disney, Eisenstein. For silent pictures, use of the old projector, which gives these at their proper speed. Occasional stage numbers and jazz performers. Cheap bar out of sound of screen. Totally anti-arty and anti-period-laugh. Strongly, but secondarily, political. Most of the audience must be drawn on straight entertainment value, or not at all.

The Newsreel: Once a month for a week. Clips from newsreels, arranged for strongest possible satire, significance and comedy, with generally elliptic commentary and sound.

New type of stage-screen show.

Using anti-realistic technique of revue and combining and alternating with screen, plus idioms also of radio; proceeding by free association and by naturalistic symbol and by series of nervous emotional and logical impacts rather than by plot or character; in an organization parallel to that of music and certain Russian and surrealist movies. More direct uses of the audience than I know of so far. Made not for an intellectual but for a mixture of two other types of audience: the bourgeois, and the large and simple. Such a show should last not more than 40-60 minutes and should have the continuous intensity as well as the dimensions of a large piece of music. I have begun one such, springboarding from the *Only Yesterday* idiom, and have another projected, on mothers.

Anti-communist manifesto.

Merely a working title. Assumption and statement in the first place of belief in ideas and basic procedures of communism. On into specific demonstrations of its misconceptions, corruptions, misuses, the damage done and inevitable under these circumstances, using probably the method of comment on quotations from contemporary communist writing and action.

Three or four love stories.

Stories in which the concentration would be entirely on the processes of sexual love. If these are "works of art," that will be only incidental.

A new type of sex book.

Beginning with quotations from contemporary and former types, an analysis of their usefulness, shortcomings, and power to damage, and a statement of the limitations of the present book. Then as complete as possible a record and analysis of personal experience from early childhood on, and of everything seen heard learned or suspected on the subject; analyses and extensions of the significance and power of sex and of sexual self-deception; with all available examples.

"Glamor" writing.

Here, as above on love, the concentration on recording and communicating pure glamor and delight.

Pathology of "laziness."

Essentially fiction, but probably much analysis. Its connections with fear, ignorance, sex, misinterpretation and economics. A story of cumulative horror.

A new type of "horror" story.

Not the above, but the horror that can come of objects and of their relationships, and of tones of voice, etc. etc. Non-supernatural, non-exaggerative.

Stories whose whole intention is the communication of the intensity of common experience.

Concentration on what the senses receive and the memory and context does with it, and such incidents, done full length, as a family supper, a marital bedfight, an auto trip.

Musical uses of sensation or emotion.

As for instance: A, a man, knows B, a girl, and C, a man, each very well. They meet. A is anxious that they like each other. B and C are variously deflected and concerned. All is delicately yet strongly distorted. Their relationship is more complex yet as rigid as that of mirrors set in a triangle, faces inward and interreflecting. These interreflections, as the mirrors shift, are analogous to the structures of contrapuntal music.

Most uses would be more subtle and less describable. Statements of moral and physical sprained equations. This would be one form of poetry.

Collections and analyses of faces; of news pictures.

Chiefly the faces would be found in news pictures.

The forms of analysis would be useful, one with, one without, any previous knowledge of whose the face and what the context is. The nearest word for such a study is anthropological, but it involves much the anthropologist does not take into account. The faces alone, with no comment, are another form of value. The pictures of more than face involve much more, which has to do with the esthetics and basic "philosophies" of poetry, music and moving pictures.

One idea here is this: no picture needs or should have a caption. But words may be used detachably, and may be used as sound and image are used with and against each other. And the picture may be used as a springboard, a theme for free variation and development; as with letters and with pieces of overheard conversation.

A new form of movie short.

A form, 2 to 10 minutes long, capable of many forms within itself. By time-condensation, each image (like each word in poetry) must have more than common intensity and related tension. This project is in many ways directly parallel to written "musical" uses of "sensation" and "emotion."

Conjectures on how to get "art" back on a plane of organic human necessity.

I can write nothing about this, short of writing a great deal. But this again is intensely anti-"artistic," as of art in any of its contemporary meanings. Every use of the moving picture, the radio, the stage, the imagination, and the techniques of the psychoanalyst, the lecturer, the showman and entertainer, the preacher, the teacher, the agitator and the prophet, used directly upon the audience itself, not just set before them: and used on, and against, matters essential to their existence. Such would be the above-mentioned show about motherhood: a massive yet detailed statement of contemporary motherhood and of all ideas which direct and impose it.

"Prophetic" writing.

Here too, the directest, most incisive and specific, and angriest possible form of direct address, semiscientic, semi-religious; set in terms of the greatest available human intensity.

Dorothy Dix: the Voice of Experience.

Typical human situations, whether invented or actual, are set up: then, of each, strong counterpoints of straight and false analysis and advice. So, again, as in a letter, each case inevitably expands and entangles itself with a whole moral and social system; the general can best be attacked through the specific. No time wasted with story, character development, etc.; you are deep in the middle from the start, with more immediacy and intensity than in a piece of fiction: inside living rather than describing it.

The inanimate and non-human.

By word, sound, moving picture. Simply, efforts to state systems and forms of existence as nearly in their own, not in human, terms, as may be possible: towards extensions of human self-consciousness, and still more, for the sake of what is there.

A "new" style of use of the imagination.

In the Alabama record the effort is to suspect the mind of invention and to invent nothing. But another form of relative truth is any person's imagination of what he knows little or nothing of and has never seen. In these terms, Buenos Aires itself is neither more nor less actual than my, or your, careful imagination of it told as pure imaginative fact. The same of the States of Washington and West Virginia, and of histories of The Civil War, the United States, and Hot Jazz. Such are projects I want to undertake in this way.

A true account of a jazz band.

The use of the Alabama technique on personal knowledge of a band.

An account and analysis of a cruise: "high"-class people.

Related to the Alabama technique, a technique was developed part way in *Havana Cruise,* mentioned among things I have had published. I should like to apply this to the behavior of a wealthier class of people on, say, a Mediterranean cruise.

Portraits, Notes, The Triptych.

Only photographic portraiture is meant. Notes and analyses, with examples, of the large number of faces any individual has. The need for a dozen to fifty photographs, supplementing five or three or one central, common denominator, for a portrait of any person. Notes on composition, pose and lighting "esthetics" and "psycho" analysis of contemporary and recent idioms.

The triptych: Research begins to indicate (in the case anyhow of criminals and steep neurotics) that the left and right halves of the face contain respectively the unconscious and the conscious. So: the establishment is possible of custom, habit, wherein one would have triptychs of one's friends, relatives, etc.: the left half reversed and made a whole face; the natural full face; the right-face.

Collections of these, with or without case histories, in a book.

Also: of each person, two basic portraits, one clinical, the other totally satisfying the sitter; to be collected and published.

Also: "anthropological" use of the family album. Of any individual, his biography in terms of pictures of him and of all persons and places involved in his life. A collection of such biographies of anonymous people, with or without case-history notes and analysis.

City streets. Hotel rooms. Cities.

And many other categories. Again, the wish is to consider such *in their own terms,* not as decoration or atmosphere for fiction. And, or: in their own terms through terms of personal experience. And, or; in terms of personal, multipersonal, collective, memory or imagination.

A new kind of photographic show.

In which photographs are organized and juxtaposed

into an organic meaning and whole: a sort of static movie. Scenario for such a show furnished if desired.

The slide lecture.

A lecture can now be recorded and sent around with the slides. The idea is that this can be given vitality as an "art" form, as a destroyer, disturber and instructor.

A new kind of "music."

There is as wide a field of pure sound as of pure image, and sound can be photographed. The range, between straight document and the farthest reaches of distortion, juxtaposition, metaphor, associatives, the specific made abstract, is quite as unlimited. Unlimited rhythmic and emotional possibilities. Many possibilities of combination with image, instrumental music, the spoken and printed word. For phonograph records, radio, television, movies, reading machines. Thus: a new field of "music" in relation to music about as photography is in relation to painting. Some Japanese music suggests its possibilities.

Extension in writing; ramification in suspension; Schubert 2-cello Quintet.

Experiments, mostly in form of the lifted and maximum-suspended periodic sentence. Ramification (and development) through developments, repeats, semirepeats, of evolving thought, of emotion, of associatives and dissonants. The quintet: here and sometimes elsewhere Schubert appears to be composing out of a state of consciousness different from any I have seen elsewhere in art. Of these extension experiments some are related to this, some to late quartets and piano music of Beethoven. The attempt is to suggest or approximate a continuum.

Two forms of history of the movies.

One, a sort of bibliography to which others would add: an exhaustive inventory of performers, performances, moments, images, sequences, anything which has for any reason ever given me pleasure or appeared otherwise valuable.

The other, an extension of this into complete personal history: recall rather than inventory.

Reanalyses of the nature and meaning of love.

Chiefly these would be tentative, questioning and destructive of crystallized ideas and attitudes, indicative of their power to cause pain. Not only of sexual but of other forms of love including the collective and religious. The love stories, the sex book, and parts of the dictionary and letters, all come under this head.

Analyses of miscommunication; the corruption of ideas.

Again, to quite an extent, the dictionary, the letters, personal experience, dictaphone records of literal experience, comparison of source writing with writing of disciples and disciplinarians. In one strong sense ideas rule all conduct and experience. Analyses of the concentricities of misunderstanding, misconditioning, psychological and social lag, etc., through which every first-rate idea and most discoveries of fact, move and become degraded and misused against their own ends.

Moving picture notes and scenarios.

Much can be done, good in itself and possibly useful to others, even without a camera and money, in words. I am at least as interested in moving pictures as in writing.

An "autobiographical novel."

This would combine many of the forms and ideas and experiments mentioned above. Only relatively small portions would be fiction (though the techniques of fiction might be much used); and these would be subjected to nonfictional analysis. This work would contain photographs and records as well as words.

Poetry.

This I am unable to indicate much about; but it involves all the more complex and intense extensions suggested by any of the above, and, chiefly, personal recall and imagination. It is in the long run perhaps more important than anything I have mentioned; but includes much of it.

Notebook.

One way of speaking, a catchall for all conceivable forms of experience which can in any way, scientifically, imaginatively, or otherwise, be recorded and analyzed. More than one person could contribute to such a work, and it would be handed ahead to others. It would not at any time be finishable. It would in course of time reach encyclopedic size, or more. It would be published looseleaf, so that readers might make their own inserts and rearrangements as they thought most relevant. Such a record could perhaps best be published by the State or by a scientific foundation.

I would wish, under a grant, to go ahead with work such as this. Most likely the concentration would be on the Alabama record and secondarily on moving pictures, sound-music, and various collections of letters and pictures, and various experiments in poetry. Quite a bit of this work would be done in collaboration with Mr. Walker Evans who is responsible for some and collaboratively responsible for others of the ideas or projects mentioned.

[*Esquire*, November 1968]

PART VI

NOTES FOR A
MOVING PICTURE:
THE HOUSE

Notes for a moving picture: The House

Broad brilliant sunlit air, cloudless: camera sinking slowly. (Suspect this could best be had by close shot of a strongly lighted sheet of aluminum.) This shot is brought on with a plucked string of a cello on a high note, so that it seems to be twanged from it. The note must have resonance. After one second the same note is taken by a plucked violin string, without resonance: three notes, three seconds. The bare air continues, with sense if possible of descending eye, through eight more seconds, silent.

Then at bottom of screen, in spaced gentle abruptions, reading, left to right, on scale of ten (screen divided off into ten parts), one, pause, seven, pause, three, pause: five-eight, pause, pause, ten, pause, two: there bloom, tinily, puffs of intense and crisp white smoke. The camera, lowering, discloses crests of three spaced smokestacks, first # nine to the right, then #s three, one, four, to the left.

Then, sighted up the lengths of sunstruck stacks as along rifles: a smokeless stack, which in one second discharges smoke in a crisp white flower: another; another; two-together; pause; another; pause; another.

Back to the broad-air picture, with the risen columns, in still air, mushrooming, beginning to merge.

From this shot, wipe-offs, containing chiefly the bright sky, in slow rhythm: one: hold::: two: hold::: three: hold:::

The first two are shots, each from a panoramic height, of as much as a sunstruck square mile of a middle-sized provincial industrial city (one hundred thousand to two hundred thousand population; say Knoxville or Chattanooga, Tenn.). One should be downtown, the other residential, both very still in the sun as if uninhabited. The third, which is held twice as long as the other two, is the wide outlet of a railroad yard, where the tracks swirl narrower from breadth at right to straits at center. The picture is made from high, seventy to a hundred feet. Brilliant sunlight edges the rails, the silver tar-roofs of sheds in foreground (low), those of houses, and the walls of poor houses, and small factories, jumbled on a bluff at the far side of the yard. The signals are white glints in the sunlight; all are quiet. Strings of coaches, of boxcars, lie quiet as in eddies, in the widening of the yard to the right: sharp sudden close-up with noise of click of signal shifting, of shifting white red-chevroned signal, the white a blasting white, the red colored a bloody red. The signal occupies the right fourth of the screen; tracks and yard detail, in sharp focus, the rest (and they are, of course, in black and white). This shot takes only a second and a half; then a shot from the former position. A silent short black passenger train is already a fourth across the screen. It draws its string of intense white smoke low across the screen from right to left. Three seconds after its disappearance, wipe off from left to right.

Now the main street of this city: not a very big city, remember. Bright hard sun bisects it with shadow. Neons of theaters, restaurants, jewelers, etc., are on in the glass sunlight. The street is completely deserted. It should be possible to see a quarter to half a mile down it and it should end in air or the dropping of a hill. Few buildings are more than five to seven floors tall: they are of irregular height and period and style of architecture. Conceivably the neons could be colored red and blue. Conceivably also they could spell out not real sign-words but semi-intelligible or international names and nouns for suspense and disaster; and one or two of the more stable-looking and -meaning words could be having bad cases of the neon twitter.

There are three opening shots and positions of camera, all at same exact distance in the street, all about seven feet above the pavement. The first is from dead center of the street, looking down its dead center: the second from center of left-hand sidewalk (in shadow) : the third from center of right-hand sidewalk (in sun) ; all so directed as to get maximum vista out of the street; i.e., toward its center at point of disappearance. These shots come on in the order named in a jabbing rhythm, the meter of saying HITT THATT LINE. The third shot holds; the sunlit right-hand sidewalk. After four seconds of static street-watching (of camera), a legless pencil-vendor flashes appearance in foreground (not more than fifty feet away). He is wearing a service tunic and an overseas cap; he advances on his wooden skate-wheeled tray, cynically beseeching the lens, which lowers its eyes upon him. There is a dry noise of skates. Ten feet in front of the camera he disappears: his skate noise persists three seconds and cuts off too. Hold camera on bare sidewalk four seconds; slowly lift upon street vista.

Camera flashes into position two: the shadowed sidewalk; its concentration on buildings along sunlit side of street. Hold six seconds. Camera swings into line down center of its sidewalk. Hold four seconds. At same distance (fifty feet) as vendor, two nuns, linked in their black, their short rapid steps smothered in skirt, appear, each wearing chained to her belly a large handbag of brilliant black patent leather; one carrying a small market basket covered with a white tabernacle veil; the other, between thumb and forefingertips of her right hand, pinching the base of a large black and silver crucifix she wears round her neck. Silently, their faces averted and concealed within the starched white shells of their headgear, they advance. Slowly the camera descends, vertically, to just above the height of their heads. In still closer, detached shots, one of each, with the elaboration of flowers unfolding, they lift their faces and look steadily into the lens. One: a doped and dangerous homosexualist: long vealy pumiced jaw, seed-pearl teeth, black slender lips, violet-vapor darkringed eye looking up and sidelong in icy murderous coyness. The other, long hairy meeting brows, thick lenses which round and enlarge the beryl of iris; a swinging penis nose which, as it swings, discovers a lipless and chinless mouth from which, laid flush against the throat, sprout two pale fangs. The nuns walk through the lens and out: the street is bare. Four seconds, watch sidewalk; slowly lift upon street vista.

Camera in position one: center of street, seven feet up from pavement. Twelve seconds static and silent.

From far down the length of street opens martial band music, tremendously loud and tremendously distant. A few bars of this (the music continues and gets louder and louder throughout the following until at end it is as nearly deafening as possible) and almost at the horizon of the street pale forms, in a block, down the middle of the street, transparent and frail as locust shells, can be seen marching: they are very diminutive, far out of scale with the street and buildings. There is a loud noise of dry blown leaves while they are still pale, which, as they materialize, materializes into the sound of distant marching. As they advance and solidify in time to the (invisible) band, they are seen to be not more than two or three troops of uniformed Boy Scouts (with one or two tall leaders) surrounding a float upon which stands a crucifix. For as long as three minutes the camera is absolutely stationary: then, first with flickerlike flashes and later with a more jabbing and steady rhythm, the basic position-one shot is crosslanced (not in double exposure) with swift intimate detail of childish feet grinding faces of Negroes, Jews; a heel twisting out the lenses of horn-rimmed spectacles; a little hand grabbing at an open book and ripping out leaves (blood springs after); hands (childish) belaboring drums, cymbals, hornkeys, gripping brass knuckles, black-jacks; hefting the butts of rifles; close-up, from low, of the advanced, pure, sadistic jaw-head of a scoutmaster; of a second scoutmaster; of a swastikaed armband. In none of these shots are faces shown. As they advance it becomes clear that the crucifix is not a crucifix but a stripped woman, handless and foot-less, nailed by her wrists and shins to the cross, whose lowered head with its tresses of drenched weeping willow is a schoolboy globe of the earth. The sign tacked above her reads, in crayoned school letters, MOTHER. It further becomes clear that the Boy Scouts are not boys but adult midgets, and their faces, now ranked advancing in the camera, are military, bloodthirsty, and aloof in the midget way. Once this midget fact has been opened there are swift shots also of a midget financier, a midget war orator, midget mothers and sweethearts leaning from windows, waving flags, scattering confetti and paper flowers, and, through the now utmost loudness of brass music, cheering in midget voices.

About forty feet in front of the camera they and their music are cut short: disappear: a split second of silence is immediately broken by a loud, dry, empty and invisible whisk and clatter of applause, beginning loud and near the camera and reducing within eight seconds to silence in a long slim wave down the length of the street. (Not more than a dozen pairs of hands.) Four seconds' silence. Hold shot.

From deep within the brain of the camera (but ambiguous, of course, as to direction—illusion of its being from down the visible street) begins the distant burring of an engine at high speed, which increases very swiftly to a roar at the apex of which, like a projectile, a gigantic bright black hearse blows from the lens (immediately beneath it), flying the stars and stripes and close followed by a string of at least fifty identical black limousines. Simultaneous with the beginning of the engine-noise, two hundred yards up the street, a short plump Bloomlike man appears on the sunlit curb. Timidly holding his derby to his stomach he looks both ways, starts to cross. In swift flashes the occupants of the cortège are spotted in: a gauntlet like a batwing on the steerwheel of the hearse; elliptic flat goggles above speed-tightened cheeks and speedflat lips; in swift pans, carload after carload of middle-aged men and women with chalk white faces and of male and female wax dummies, tophatted and tiaraed by sex, sitting erect at restless ease, certain of them hogfaced behind gasmasks. Shot through the hearse windshield shows the man in the derby, twitching in paralysis between left and right, in the middle of the street. The heel of the gauntlet hand massages a ghastly bray of horn just as the car is upon him: quick switchback to position one shows the cortège drawing swiftly, with diminishing noise, into a string, a thread, a point in the distance; vanishing. (Their speed has been 80 mph.)

A huge glittering black wreath is laid against high-polished, unlettered granite: lips flare, find the silent lips of a bugle: hats sink to breasts: knees unjoint, touch, touch, upon stiff spread handkerchiefs establish themselves upon white sterile gravel. This last shot is held while, very distantly, taps is blown. On last phrase of taps shot shifts and is a male hand, white-cuffed, palm in, hung at the thigh.

Six seconds after close of taps the hand (left hand), lifts slowly palm out from thigh and points left. Slowly camera pans left.

A large municipal garbage can labeled: By Law Abide. From its ruin, among newspapers and orange and banana peels, a derby hat; and a bloodied hand in a dickey cuff, which lies fallen open, loose-pointing left. The camera hesitates, but scarcely; and pans on left: catches, in its swing, a hand, a woman's, a child's hand, pointing gesturing or drifting left; artificial hands, which bring together their fingertips in an arch of wistfulness; an ancient ringed hand, in a black lap, lifted; a square working hand, which dips from the lens and brings up a hammer; a hand, thumbnail glissando, from depth to height of a keyboard (with sudden sound of opposite glissando); another hand, lifting a sickle; the piano hand, trilling high, with sound (of low trill): this hand and sound stops, holds four seconds: then a hand laid out from the lens at full and flat arm's length displaying a street, in the same empty sunlight as before. At the right, about eighty yards from camera, set somewhat back in small grounds, a large slate-roofed Victorian house. Ornate iron pickets painted glistening black walk past the lens; the camera bends round a stone and black iron gatepost into a graveled drive, halts, focused on the front and the front door.

Under the shaded, roofed arch of the semicircular driveway, at the foot of the front steps, is a black limousine sedan: same general style as those in the funeral but scaled down a full class at least. It is newly washed; scarcely yet dry; the chauffeur sits motionless at the wheel. These are the shots, all along same axis: from gate; from halfway mark between gate and steps; from halfway nearer; from dead level of the wood floor of the porch whose boards are thickly painted gray. In a series of shots to be somewhat detailed in a minute, these people come out through the screen door across the porch and down the steps. They are and are dressed as follows: A strong, ironlike man of sixty-five, his face somewhat like that of the crueller photos of Harding late in his life; looking like and dressed like a slick portrait of a hybrid big-business and society man and moving that way; his face made up chalk white, his eyebrows very black; costumed as for a political funeral; wearing a silk hat on his bent left arm. A heavy, sickfaced man of fifty; upper half in executive, lower, in golfing, costume. He carries a mashie with formal fragility, like something between a scepter and a lily. A heavy, flyblown woman, his age, wearing as ghastly a travesty of the worst trick hat of this year as can be contrived; a nearly transparent print dress in a horrible wandering design; beneath that, her flesh squelched in a broad hard slippery girdle; flat garterstraps; enormously high heels. Pressed next her heart she carries a discolored and exhausted phallus from whose glans, pulling a long hole in the flesh, droops a wide wedding ring. A scalpel-like, chalk-white young man, thirty, wearing a checked sports coat and otherwise a Tuxedo; everything about him like a barely restrained explosion, intensely quiet and strict in his movements. He is carrying a cocktail glass brimful of lightly fuming acid, and of this he must not spill a drop. A beautiful, pertified young woman in an extreme bathing suit and an evening wrap. Her skull is closed in a pessary. She carries a clear globe in whose center, sustained in alcohol, hangs a miniature foetus in a baby bonnet. An over-developed girl of nine, in traditional white frilly party dress and sash and curls and big hair ribbon; submergedly desperate nympholeptic face; left hand stiff, the fingers clenched against the palm, excepting the middle finger which is out straight; the whole structure of wrist and hand stiff and twisted as if in deformity, the middle finger curled and pointed always toward her like a compass needle. Her dress is cut so low and wide as almost entirely to expose her light breasts. These people move out under the shadow of the broad lead-gray porch and are caught by group and one by one and detailed in the order named: their faces are all very quietly and resolvedly desperate and they move out of the house and down the steps definitively, with extreme but in no way caricatured effort to do so quietly and with them, also in extreme quiet, come a man and a woman servant with baggage and wraps. These servants are colorless, of some indeterminate middle age, blank in the face and in their tight gestures, completely but very flatly, deadly, evil. Of these several people, there is a moment when turn by turn each looks directly into the camera as into the face of a Rabble and as into the perfectly cold eye of fate and their own knowledge of it. In fact as they come out the door they try to be aloof and to avoid and avert this eye: but in steady, close-bound and implacable movements it cranes after and forces them to look square into it—getting, for instance, beneath a lowered turned face, squarely, and by magnetism forcing it upward and to center; darting gently over and rounding in a sidelong escapist; &c.

This door-to-car sequence in fact takes much further working out than can sensibly be given it short of the camera, the people and the place. Here are a few salients and tentative notes. The middle-length shot and the next (at foot of steps) are stitched together by a loud sharp *sshhhh:* a ten-second silence is held. The gray boards of the porch, with light scurf of dead vegetable matter, is the floor of this shot: the gray screen door (through it, the dark hallway) is at dead center. Next a tall narrowed shot: loose edge of door at dead center. Hold six silent seconds, then door is opened outward quitely with twanging complaint of spring; a shining pointed male shoe establishes its tiptoe with a squeaking of leather. Quick shift to slightly widened, waist-up shot of the old man very rigidly advancing himself through the door. In the order above named they come out through this door, one on the screen at a time, an interval of c. 8 seconds of blank door between each, the camera giving them each a full-length, a close-up of advancing head, a detail shot. Then a broad shot from the ground of all of them crossing porch and coming down steps, all still very quietly; the only sounds are, non-synchronized, quasi-sporadically but in a stiff cross-rhythm of the rhythm of the walking and the shots, the squeaking of a shoe; the yielding of a floorboard; some harsh undistinguishable grunt, comment, cautionary whisper. (Sample of detail: a close-up of the cocktail glass, detached and disembodied; showing meniscus and getting tension out of this; the intensity of the acid conveyed by the quality of heavy smoke that very meagerly lies out from its surface. Glass thus introduced: then the young man carrying it, he as precarious as the glass he carries.)

The heavy man of fifty drifts apart from them in rigid forlornness a little way out on to the short-clipped dry lawn; squares himself round; looks the house up and down. He becomes aware of the club he is holding; then of its proper use; his hand relaxes it slowly; he plants his feet for a swing, assembles back for it; drives (sound of impact is a bursting electric blub). Flash of upward ball across bare screen, then immediate broad, held shot of the grounds, garden, yard, yards, the flat, sad, prosperous breadth of housed landscape visible from his stance, camera lowering gently as if in abeyance to trajectory of the ball: into this frame, very large, the man relaxes forlornly from his follow-through: resuming the lilylike holding of the club he goes slowly back to the car (his son's eyes are on him in bitter hatred; his wife's eyes are hen-glazed; she shifts her fingers absently on the phallus, stroking its Pekingese head).

Shot of lone, gray, fur-globed dandelion in lawn. Toward this the little girl comes running in hideous travesty of dainty age-of-innocence skip-dance. She bends abruptly, stiff-kneed, her hind end in the low lens of the camera. The short stiff rufflings of her skirt flare (with starchy noise) like a gobbler's erected fan; the buttocks are naked clear to the short socks (her kiddie-slippers are highheeled); her panties are so abbreviated and so frilly that in this stance they suggest only a gruesomely overdeveloped and fancified clitoris.

Back at the car the old man, the mid-man and

woman are being helped into layer on layer of sweaters, coats and mufflers and ultimately into big linen dusters of the sort worn for motoring thirty-five years ago. The young woman puts on a raincoat of clear cellophane. Up to now each member of the family has been to his maximum ability aloof from all the rest (though bound together beyond escape) and this in their spacings apart and magnetized half-turns of head and body must have been conveyed. They are still as aloof and single as possible but now piled one on another in thick succession there are many close, stertorous detail shots getting the family and their baggage helped and folded and settled and rammed and squelched and crowbarred and foot-forced into the car; the shots getting more and more strangled and crowded and hot; taken more and more consistently from the darkened inside of the car. (The seat beside the chauffeur is and remains empty.) Last in is the young man. He stands tense at the car door; ten seconds motionless and deliberate; then, angularly, very abruptly, takes down the smoking acid in one gulp. (During his stationary stance a light film of the acid has overstood the rim; where it crookedly runs his fingers blacken. When he takes the glass away his lips are black.) On his tightened-in face, sweat now stands out as on an icy pitcher in a hot room. With his right hand he reaches under his blazing white, beetle-shell shirtfront (lifting it away as if it were a part of his body or a scab) and claws quietly, and after a little brings out the hand, fingers straightened and shaking stiffly, covered with black-rotted and bloody bowels: he extends the hand: the manservant comes with a bright white thickstarched towel and cleans it, stripping each finger like an udder. The young man cleanses his nails with his opposite thumbnail; flicks the dirt away; knifes himself slenderly into the car. Inside shot of door pulled to; with sound of springlock slipping into place: windows, by cramped hands, are all rolled, rolled, rolled up tight: a ringed hand draws down a shade; another another; another another; light comes only through the windshield; the dome light is flicked on: the little girl slides her dead dandelion into the wall vase; the young woman smokes; the smoke thickens; the bonneted foetus, suspended, swerves delicately in its globe's center; the phallus, its head tucked tight against the spongy breast, sleeps. Silent and motionless pause: the shot is squared from middle rear of car (taken through rear window), on the windshield, the chauffeur's motionless head, the pane behind his head. On this pane, just behind his head, with her wedding ring, with sound, the woman raps sharply. Sound of starting car; flushing rush of racing engine; the car lifts in a clean surge forward from the lens as the rear shade is drawn tight; with sound, goes down the gravel drive and turns right, climbing immediately to high speed and diminishing noise, the camera watching all this departure; holding its watchfulness ten seconds after the last of the motor-noise.

The camera then slowly swings and watches the servants watching. They stand on the edge of the porch about four feet apart. Ten seconds after the camera has caught them they each lift their eyes slowly and coldly upon the sky, into which they look steadily, one at each extreme of screen, another ten seconds; then their eyes lower, sliding without slyness toward, and meet each other; they watch into each other's eyes another ten seconds; simultaneously and very slightly and abruptly they nod, and convolve quietly on a common and exact center and, with a resumption of squeaking shoes, cross the porch. The man holds the screen door open; the woman, entering, draws loose her big stiff semi-transparent apron-bow; he follows her close in; the door is shut and hooked. In a square close shot, the heavy wood door (its upper half plateglass heavily curtained in a flat of white ugly embroidery) swings and establishes itself shut: four seconds of dead silence: noise of a lock chuckling shut: four more seconds: slow fade as camera advances on it into the clear screen.

Ten seconds of the clear air screen.

With utmost possible, bursting suddenness, a fancy goldfish in a globe that lenses her swimming in distortions. As shot comes on the globing face, filling the whole screen, blunders forward into its apex of distortion. As fish swerves her fringes against curved glass the camera swiftly retracts; globe, filling only central third of screen, is in center of bay window. Background and at either side, coarse white lace curtains glazed in sunlight; so stiff and so extremely white they seem spun out of sugar.

Catching cold diamond light, reflexed slantwise in a three-leaved mirror, a big punchbowl of elaborately cut glass, close-up: cold, rich and rigorously ugly. Hands slide bright silver into slender flannel pockets silently with very faint sporadic chimings of silver and of glass. The silver is fancy Victorian, the handles crested and swirled, the spoon bowls fluted. Quick shots of silver specialties such as a rank of a dozen nutpicks. A silver bell held by its clapper yields strangled silver sound. The silver-containers are on a wide bare dining table of dark wood. They are folded over; the gray strings are tied in double bows with quick crisscrossed re-exposures (not lap- or double-) to establish slipperiness, slenderness and finality of the folding and knotting, with deeply subdued noises of imprisoned silver. As they are swept aside the lace-curtained light through the window is squarely and formally reflected on the bare, bright, black table wood. In the same movement as the sweeping aside a slimshod woman's foot is drawn against the rich grain of a rug, roughing it dark in a crescent. The foot smooths back most; slows; hesitates; roughs it again; the man's shoe roughs some more; the woman's, at an opposed angle, some more. The silver is settled into a suitcase. The lock of the black suitcase is snapped, with sound; another is snapped; a strap is pulled tight with exaggerated tension noise of leather; a buckle is set. Blacksleeved hands in a wide swerve towards the camera lift the punchbowl into the lens in a glittering swing and past: the swing is caught into with the opposite swing of the edge of a narrow outside door; the borne bowl tight on this swinging radius: the feet of the servant pair, who are now in stiff snob-servant dark mufti, descend three wood-creaking steps, their black shoes are creaking, and pause on the gravel, foot here, foot, foot here: eyes, eyes, lifted upward and inward and concentrated upon the crest of the house inside, very silent and listening eyes, in narrow hard-putty faces: hold, eight seconds; they are satisfied. The man unbuttons a tightly rolled umbrella: with sound, with narrowly directed thumb, opens the black bloom (manifold shots extending and elaborating this opening). Under the prim-held umbrella, sifted with sun but dark, the two pale faces, crossglittered as if scarred by the icy lights of the punchbowl whose fancy fringe freezes the bottom of the screen, move forward and swing right aloofly. Middle-length shot. Down this middle length, the man heavy with two suitcases and the umbrella, the woman bearing the bowl, they recede down the narrow graveled service path, their shoes squeaking; down past the extinct carriage-house and through the iron gate and into the bare paved alley. Hold, as shoe squeaks recede into silence: and hold.

Shot of a sundial marking three-odd in sharp black shadow. Shot of an ornate, glasswalled mantel clock and mercury pendulum of the sort which reverses its swing: a silently flowing second-hand. Very close shot of goldfish globing in globe; it swims to the far side; swerves: shots of its flicking deflections in rhythm established by reversals of the pendulum. Broad shot of side-yard, garden, the house; sundial at one side in middle distance. In quick succession (a second each) the two broad-city shots of the prologue and the centered shot of the empty main street (two seconds to this) : back to four seconds of the yard-garden-house-dial shot: then shot of dialface square on the screen and filling it, the black sharp shadow moves within a few seconds, an inch: central shot of main street; the black shadow which bisected it now within a few seconds annexes several yards of bright street and sidewalk: again the identical general shot of house and garden. The camera rises six to eight feet vertically and halts and holds ten seconds; then slowly and very steadily pans until the house occupies all but a few inches of screen; slows tremendously; steadies upon the house which now holds all the screen. This general garden shot has been very slightly out of focus: not fuzzy and not sentimental, but enough out of focus to generalize it and to put a white dusty summer brightness upon everything in sight. With the last few inches of largo panning, the focus quite as slowly cleanses and comes to maximum sharpness and black-and-whiteness: whole quality of emotion should be that of a microscope slide drawn into razor focus and from now on totally at the mercy of the lens. The lens moves forward slowly ten feet, stops dead, holds.

A series now of square-set, low shots: all so set as to

fill lower third of screen with short dried grass, dry twiggy earth; at middle, the dry brick foundations of the house; upper screen, blank wall and Victorian window and wood-detail. There should be shots to cover and square into shape the whole house, with swift-cut shots opposing the angles of walls at corners. The blinds are in irregular composure: closed, half-open, laid back flat against the house. Detail shots of blinds and of blank wall. Of blank wall; of bright clean window-glass masked from inside by white curtain-lace.

Same rhythm of shots repeated at height between second and third floors; then between crest of wall and slate roof. Camera rises a little so that the whole screen is roof; there must be no sky yet; sinks a little, rises a little again, withdraws a little, gently sinks: its sinking cut short by sudden shot at ground again, foundation wall standing square from the ground, quite closetaken. From here, camera immediately, slowly rises dead vertically. Weatherboards, a lacy window, boards, second-floor window, boards, sink steadily past; a small and trick-shaped window just beneath a gable starts to sink; the aged female hand is lifted; camera freezes; descends slowly, so that this window is framed head on; freezes again, watches, very slowly advancing. The shut window is blind with curtain bright with sun. Behind it, darkness, in which faint worrying movements of some human being can scarcely, unidentifiably, be discerned. Everything should be strong, bright and arid, and each shot should be laid on square with a steady beat, not too slow though deliberate, not flashing (about two and a half seconds per rhythmic unit). Now, details of cracked paint and blistered paint and of roofslates so close as at first to be unidentifiable: of painted nail-heads, of joined boards, of the wire hooks slates are hung by; closing with more extreme and now angled shots to establish the wicked angle of the ridged roof and its gables, fenced at every ridge with sharp iron lace; and with shots that fling this sharp and fancy iron upon the sky, yet chiefly to establish, rather than a flinging-upward, its intense rigidity, pride-in-onateness, and vigor, and its opposal of the sky: crossed in with quick jabbing shots of one and of five iron pickets of the fence and with the sharp leaves of a century plant in the center of a small dry formal garden and with a raised window, the room behind it black, the curtain breathing lightly like the gill of a fish; a sudden spuming potted fern, indoors, lace curtains; another fern; the goldfish; the blank rug scarred with feet; the empty silver-trays; closets with bare hooks, bare hangers; an exhausted paste-board toilet-paper cylinder; an extremely fragile and simple glass, alone on a marble shelf.

A slow but steady, swerving, saraband and swerving of lens in silence through the empty house. The grave and restrained movements of its dance are strong in rubato and are cross-cut by static shots but are never brought to a full stop. The camera is taking record of silence, stasis, a vacuum, every detail of this house in its amber and few moments of suspended animation. Just what its gestures and paces of attention must await the bending of an actual camera to the details of the actual interior of an actual house, but you may meanwhile supply much from your knowledge of the type: deep swinging shots of all rooms, highceiled, in gloom, at each tall window, the stiff sugar-white lace with the light hung entangled in it; the dark, seedy, fancy furniture, horsehair, bright white antimacassars, brass talons clenching glass globes and sustaining furniture; detail of the heavy and dark, carved mahoganies of table legs; and of carved beds (stripped to the mattresses) ; square, static shot, formal as an altar, of fireplace and mantel: the fireplace closed with black-painted gag of fancily cast iron, the mantel uplifting several tiers of small shelves which sustain, on doilies, vases, and figurines of shepherdesses and of fisher-girls: similar shot of a glass-faced cabinet containing eggshell, never-used china, a tray of dry butterflies, geological specimens; sets of Victorian books and miscellaneous popular novels of the early twentieth century in cases behind glass; such, and the generalized, surveying swirling crossflashed with glancing detail of china, bare chairs, woodcarving, statuettes, lace, pictures such as an engraving of "The Lions of Persepolis," various Victorian patterns of wallpaper, details of ornate picture frames, and many sizes and shapes of mirrors which extend and darken the house: bare pantry, bare kitchen, shelves, tables, simmering stove on wide empty floor; a tap is here left running, needling and spreading its circle in a flat iron sink; a stonewhite naked arm and hand reach out, turn off the faucet; on a starched virgin roller towel the stonewhite hands dry themselves; the camera settles gently to rest in the dark front hallway before an ornate hatrack and looks at itself close and hard in the mirror, beginning very softly to purr (the reduced dry sound of its motor) ; swings back to center of hall, beneath center of stairwell, and delicately takes flight, swinging slowly round so that with not perfect regularity the upward swing and bulge of the banister swings with its eye and the shell-like structure of floor above floor here, as in the downstairs rooms, is had (throughout, walls and doors in the moving of the camera must be managed so as to establish this shell quality of stacked cards). At second floor it does not pause in its ascent but swerving still absorbs and leaves (like the swinging of a censer) the empty bedrooms, the bare bathroom, and rises still, and in front of a narrow closed door on the top landing does thrice a sort of hesitant, still rising, curtsey (the short swing of a censer), and rising still, comes straight through the shell of beams and roofslate, turns in a slow circle panorama, of which the angular roof swerving remains the bottom, and settles deftly, and reposes, regarding roof and house grounds.

As soon as repose is established, immediate shot of mantel clock; hold eight seconds or so. Internal shot of spring-hammer tensing, like a snake collecting back its head, to strike on the coiled spring bell; quick shot of goldfish; of the fragile solitary glass; of the sundial; of gently breathing curtain from within raised window; of the top-landing closed door of the gable window, from outside; of the shriveled old-woman's hand rising wide and away from the camera; of a hairbrush full of hair on her bureau; of a musty "rat" on her bureau; of the hand; the window.

She claws her lace curtain aside in an explosion of glittering dust: all she sees through the glass is perfectly bare bright sky; camera (within the room) retreats; she is seated beside a high small window (by shape identified as the under-gable window) blocked in by two trays on which are many half-destroyed foods. She is extremely old, dressed in black brocaded with the filth of spilled food; her face, in close-up, is listening hard; her head seems propped on the isinglass collar-stays;

the clock-hammer tensifies still more;

the main street: its shadow rapidly climbs the façades;

the fish, the glass, a roof-slate; the curtain; the dial, flicker and slap her intensely listening face closer into the camera;

steep shot of factory chimney; no smoke;

the hammer is drawn to extreme; it trembles;

from another angle it is drawn from complete relaxation to trembling extreme;

the stack explodes black and white smoke; the hammer lets loose; it is cut in so that the sound of its striking is the splintering of the glass which now has the screen; the dial is masked in shadow; the curtain billows; on the main street the shadow sweeps from center up the buildings in one fast wash; the slate slides; the fish gasps among glass on the patterned carpet; her amazed, angry, conscious yet not quite hearing face; still listening (did I hear you right?) ;

black and white smokes stream richly from smokestacks; enormously speed-up shots of cumulus clouds expanding; of blacker, rougher clouds expanding and convolving; a big drop spats on a close-up slate; the slate slides with sound down the steep roof; another; it slides, with sound of leaves in wind; a treebranch is blown into the lens and wrung with wind, its leaves reversed and white, louder windsound, immediate shot of a rank of trees, their under-leaves blown white, the wind noise louder;

within her room, with loudening rush of leaf noise, a swooping darkening; her silver (trays and eating) become suddenly livid and her window ironcolored;

rain speckles and splatters the pane with a noise of delicately splintering glass;

both her hands are lifted, half-spread, and trembling in their bright rings;

she watches a sizzling fuse whose head is buried under the baseboard in the corner;

the mantel clock speeds up, the fuse-noise getting steadily louder; the second-hand spins so fast it is a film of time in front of the loudening drum; it spins off with a snapping of light metal against glass and the minute hand is moving at nearly second-hand speed in the darkening;

she is watching the fuse; the sizzling crawls on under the baseboard; the sizzling noise intensifies throughout something like fifteen seconds while the camera is on her watching, listening face;

blinding thunder (the screen black and white and black all over):

lightning strikes and runs the complex ironlaced ridges of the roof hissing; white down rods by the brick foundations with noise of whitehot iron shoved into water it in quarter-second succession plunges four heads into the ground;

clattering her glittering trays and china to the walls in rising, she is up in the middle of her darkened room; rain smashes steadily at the pane; she runs to the window, her ringed hands, left, right, clutching sweeping the lace apart, and looks;

treetops are labored in black and white swarm and slash of rain; ivy is beaten and beaten against brick and is bruised and beaten to bits; the slates, a whole section, loosen under the beating, disassemble, slither steep to the gutters and fall (quick shot of waiting ground receives their heavy and broken clattering and thumping); beneath her, a curtain blows from an open window its two suppliant white arms;

she jerks her head round, more astounded still than scared, grabs a small silver service-bell from the floor (among a plastering of food and broken china) and runs out onto the landing at the head of the stairwell, flashing her eyes round, and rings the bell—an angry lady-like dining-room twinkling of silver.

in empty room after room, deep-shot, the rain swimming on all bare glass, a heavier bell (a little deeper than an ice-man's bell) reverberates waterily, ga-lang ga-lang ga-lang.

She listens. The bellsounds break round her from the voided house, still louder: ga-lang ga-lang ga-lang (each sound slapping in from a different angle and her head stiffly restraining a recoil from each).

She rings again, more urgently.

In a streetcar on a wide waste street, the two servants, sitting very erect, listen and hear (the noise is only a vibration of the great bowl on the woman's lap); they make no comment; nor do they change expression.

In the closed auto, the massed faces hear. The woman tightens her mouth. She lifts forward her ringed hand to rap on the pane. The chauffeur's back stiffens and his head rises, the noises of the motor and of wet tires intensify, on a numberless speed-dial the pointer leans steadily and swiftly and rests at the extreme right. In a detail shot or two it is seen that water has leaked through the tight windows and is slimly rambling the upholstery: the young woman's wet hand holds a wet cigarette just beneath her lips.

The old woman listens. Tightening her face and more afraid, she hustles down to the next landing: stops dead, the bell grabbed in her fist.

She looks all round her. She becomes conscious of discomfort and, after a moment, raises her skirt a little. (Her ankles are stiff like wood, her shoes narrow and low-heeled, black.) Her feet are sousing wet. She presses her foot into the carpet. Water springs up around it as from wet solid moss under pressure.

Quick to her face which is now in fear.

Imperiously she calls out an unidentifiable name: accent and lifted voice on the second syllable; twice.

In a feminine bedroom one call echoes. In the pantry, the other.

Above her the ceiling bulges; water gathers on it;

it yields, spilling not more than a bucketful of plaster and water near her.

She backs against the wall, tighter and tighter, and out of this tightening shrilly yells the same name, different accent (on first syllable, down-inflection on second): fear and beseeching as well as anger in the first; terror in the second call.

From two places the two are echoed. First, from the gasping goldfish on the carpet. Second, from the cellar: showing a bit of the furnace and a breadth of concrete wall down which water is coursing and through a seam of which water is bulging. The sound is the deep lost groan of a man, following the contour of her call, more desperate the second time. The second time it is accompanied by the bursting of the cellar wall and a great gush of water, so that it is the wall and the water through the wall that groans it. This second time the groan has a half-drowned, gargling noise.

Immediately followed by outdoor detail of a corner of house abruptly settling into reeking wet earth: this immediately followed by jolt of the settling and collapse and a slithering of wet plaster round the woman. She rushes along the hall away from and rushes into the lens, turns sharp left close-followed by camera, and rushes across the room and closes a window and draws the blinds. Immediately the whole frame of blinds and glass is burst in with a wall of water that knocks her down. She grabs herself up and heads for the mirror to rearrange. Immediately rain blurs the mirror entirely, from its far side: she pulls down a shade over it, her head quaking; in quick shot the toiletbowl is shown fountainously overflowing.

She hurtles on down to the first floor. As she swings into the main room every curtain in every window, very abnormally long, reaches at her its long arms in center of room; a statuette falls; she runs to catch it; another falls. Plaster falls on the piano in a great triple chord and in a quick shot the stove is seen steaming. Drenched rats swim in the hallway. Flat against a windowpane a growing vine swirls its eager frostlike designs; a blind, broken, is involved in vine-growth. A fern in its growth spurts upward enormous, a shabby fountain. The weights in the mantel clock are out at level: they no longer reverse, they are a centrifuge machine and off the motion of their edge swings a shower of slates. The minute-hand is spinning, is a film, it spins off; the hour-hand is spinning, it spins off (so that there are here, quickly, two concentric diminishing films of time) : only the dead center nub of the clock is burring now at continuously greater speed with the continuously more urgent and piercing noise of a dentist's drill which is joined by the dry, cool purr of the camera which also increases not in speed but in loudness. This sound the old woman, now on the piano, backed far into a corner, the water rising round her, hears and attends to more and more intently, and now also she begins to see, and to back up more and more stiffly, her face in more and more mad frozen horror; crossed by a shot of the cold advancing lens; her face again; through a wall of books, bursting, scattering them, with its boughs stapling her close into her corner, now grows the flamboyant branch of a great wet green and full-leafed tree; the lens bores steadfastly in and into her; the wall buckles and folds above her in a mess of books, wallpaper, bricks, wood, slate, and cast iron, and the bare rain still batters. Hold.

Steady but very slow pan across a thinning of this wreckage under beating water, mixed now with leaves, and beaten into the earth and upon bare concrete and thinning; and the rain slows, and stops: the sky still gray but thinned and ready to break.

Shot of the closed car, empty, beside a washed-out bridge, the water high.

Wide, slow-panning shots of bare pavement, half-dried, under unsteady disclosures of sunlight and the sound of rushing water.

Of a sidewalk, half-dried, patterned with half-drowned angleworms. The light is watery-bright. Suddenly it clears to the cleanest brilliance of after-rain sunlight. There is laughter and shouting of children off-screen to the left. Very slow pan; silence except for light, exhilarating noises of water, as camera discovers them. There are several of them, wading in the deep gutter, clothes rolled high. They are very poor children. Fragments of fern swim round their shins, stick to their legs. A little girl finds a film of drowned lace curtain. She makes of it a bridal veil. A little boy comes up wearing a derby hat. Another little boy finds a dead fancy goldfish. He is envied. The sunlight is more and more brilliant. Other children come up, semi-formally and quietly. One carries a bell. One a statuette. One is dressed in a black skirt: he had made a sort of toga of it. They all, looking at each other and at their trophies, become quiet and gently formal. With no gestures of planning but as by a common knowledge which has just taken them, they shift across the walk to a vacant lot where a child is completing a small grave. With no sound except the light noise of the bell, tolled in a slow beat, with gentleness and solemnity of perfectly unfeeling gesture, they bury the goldfish. The boy in black makes gestures of oration, and sprinkles in dirt. The grave is filled. The broken statuette is stood on top of the grave. A child comes up quietly with the numbered porcelain face of the mantel clock: it is stood into the earth at the head of the grave. They stand round the grave now perhaps twenty seconds; drift apart and away. Only the bride in the curtain, the groom in the derby, remain. They are looking down at the grave, which the lens intercepts. Their faces are serious, nuptial and uncomprehending. After a while, lightly and delicately, the girl's eyes are drawn toward the boy; her face is turned upward and in his direction; his head too is turned now, and they are drawn lightly off the screen, which is now clean air again. Three plucked notes of a violin. The resonant note of the cello, with which the picture opened. It is here reversed, so that the resonance comes first; enlarges; and is sucked into the very abrupt pluck of sound into silence with which the screen goes black.

[From *New Letters in America,* edited by Horace Gregory. W. W. Norton & Co., 1937]

PART VII

SOUTHEAST
OF THE ISLAND:
TRAVEL NOTES

Southeast of the Island: Travel Notes

"City of homes and churches."
>   —*Whitman, writing of Brooklyn.*

"One of the great waste places of the world."
>   —*Doughty, writing of Arabia.*

"And blights with plagues the marriage hearse."
>   —*Blake, writing of London.*

"Life is fundamentally composed of vegetable matter."
>   —*Obsolete textbook of biology.*

Watching them in the trolleys, or along the inexhaustible reduplications of the streets of their small tradings and their sleep, one comes to notice, even in the most urgently poor, a curious quality in the eyes and at the corners of the mouths, relative to what is seen on Manhattan Island: a kind of drugged softness or narcotic relaxation. The same look may be seen in monasteries and in the lawns of sanitariums, and there must have been some similar look among soldiers convalescent of shell shock in institutionalized British gardens where, in a late summer dusk, a young man could mistake heat lightnings and the crumpling of hidden thunder for what he has left in France, and must return to. If there were not Manhattan, there could not be this Brooklyn look; for truly to appreciate what one escapes, it must be not only distant but near at hand. Only: all escapes are relative, and bestow their own peculiar forms of bondage.

It is the same of the physique and whole tone and metre of the city itself. You have only to cross a bridge to know it: how behind you the whole of living is drawn up straining into verticals, tightened and badgered in nearly every face of man and child and building; and how where you are entering, even among the riverside throes of mechanisms and of tenements in the iron streets, this whole of living is nevertheless relaxed upon horizontalities, a deep taproot of stasis in each action and each building. Partly, it suggests the qualities of any small American city, the absorption in home, the casualness of the measuredly undistinguished: only this usual provincialism is powerfully enhanced here by the near existence of Manhattan, which has drawn Brooklyn of most of what a city's vital organs are, and upon which an inestimable swarm of Brooklyn's population depends for living itself. And again, this small-city quality is confused in the deep underground atomic drone of the intertextured procedures upon blind time of more hundreds on hundreds of thousands of compacted individual human existences than the human imagination can comprehend or bear to comprehend.

It differs from most cities in this: that though it has perhaps a "center," and hands, and eyes, and feet, it is chiefly no whole or recognizable animal but an exorbitant pulsing mass of scarcely discriminable cellular jellies and tissues; a place where people merely "live." A few American cities, Manhattan chief among them, have some mad magnetic energy which sucks all others into "provincialism"; and Brooklyn of all great cities is nearest the magnet, and is indeed "provincial": it is provincial as a land of rich earth and of this earth is an enormous farm, whose crop is far less "industrial" or "financial" or "notable" or in any way "distinguished" or "definable" than it is of human flesh and being. And this fact alone, which of itself makes Brooklyn so featureless, so little known, to many so laughable, or so ripe for patronage, this fact, that two million human beings are alive and living there, invests the city in an extraordinarily high, piteous and inviolable dignity, well beyond touch of laughter, defense, or need of notice.

Manhattan is large, yet all its distances seem quick and available. Brooklyn is larger, seventy-one square miles as against twenty-two, but here you enter the paradoxes of the relative. You know, here: only a few miles from wherever I stand, Brooklyn ends; only a few miles away is Manhattan; Brooklyn is walled with world-traveled wetness on west and south and on north and east is the young beaverboard frontier of Queens; Brooklyn comes to an end: but actually, that is, in the conviction of the body, there seems almost no conceivable end to Brooklyn; it seems, on land as flat and huge as Kansas, horizon beyond horizon forever unfolded, an immeasurable proliferation of house on house and street by street; or seems as China does, infinite in time in patience and in population as in space.

The collaborated creature of the insanely fungoid growth of fifteen or twenty villages, now sewn and quilted edge to edge, and lacking any center in remote proportion to its mass, it is perhaps the most amorphous of all modern cities; and at the same time, by virtue of its arterial streets, it has continuities so astronomically vast as Paris alone or the suburbs south of Chicago could match: on Flatbush Avenue, DeKalb, Atlantic, New Lots, Church, any number more, a vista of low buildings and side streets of glanded living sufficient to paralyze all conjecture; simply, far as the eye can strain, no end of Brooklyn, and looking back, far as the eye can urge itself, no end, nor imaginable shore; only, thrust upon the pride of heaven, the monolith of the Empire State, a different mode of life; and even this, seen here, has the smoky frailty of a half-remembered dream.

(Observing in subway stations, in any part of Brooklyn, not in an hour of rush but in the leisured evening, you see this; how, wherever there is a choice of staircases, one toward Manhattan, one away, without thought or exception they descend the staircase toward the Island. An imaginative designer would have foreseen this and would have omitted the alternatives entirely.)

(In Upper Flatbush, already two miles deep inland from the bridges, a young woman of Manhattan asked a druggist how she might get into certain territory well south of there. Without thought of irony he began, "Oh. You want to go to Brooklyn.")

The center of population of the largest city in history is near the intersection of —— and —— Streets, in Brooklyn. That it should be in this borough of "being" rather than in that of doing and bragging seems appropriate to the point of inevitability. So does this: that when the fact was ascertained, and Manhattan news-swallows skimmed over to get the Local Angle, the replies were so fully intelligent that they had to be treated as a joke. Informed of his good fortune one said "So?", another said "So well?"; a landlady to be sure, said she'd have to tell her roomers about it that night, but gave evidence of no special emotion.

More homes are owned in Brooklyn than in any other Borough; there are more children per adult head; it is a great savings-bank town; there are fewer divorces; it is by and large as profoundly domesticated, docile and "stable" a population as one could conceive of, outside England. The horror of "unsuccessful" marriages—unsuccessful, that is, as shown by an open or legal break; the lethal effort of Carry On is thought well of —— this horror is such that there is a special bank to which husbands come one day to deposit, estranged wives the next to be fertilized by this genteel equivalent of alimony. It seems significant of Brooklyn that it is probably the only city that has such a bank.

At the north brow of Prospect Park, where a vast number of these marriages are, in the medical sense, contracted and where, indeed, the whole sweep of infancy, childhood, and the descending discords of family life is on display, there stands a piece of statuary. From a way down Flatbush Avenue it suggests that cloven flame which spoke with Dante in hell but by a nearer view, it is a man and a nude woman in bronze, and their plump child, eager for the Park, and it represents the beauty and stability of Brooklyn, and of human, family life. The man and wife stand back to back, in the classical posture of domestic sleep. It is a thoroughly vulgar and sincere piece of work, and once one gets beyond the esthete's sometimes myopic scorn, is the infallibly appropriate creation of the whole heart of Brooklyn. Michelangelo would have done much less well.

*

All the neighborhoods that make up this city; those well known, and those which are indicated on no official map:

The Hill, for instance: the once supremely solid housing of Clinton Avenue, which are broken with a light titter of doctors' shingles; the two big homes which are become the L. I. Grotto Pouch and the Pouch Annex; or the boarded brownstone opposite the decrepitant bricks of the Adelphi Academy; or those blocks which have formed "protective associations" against the infiltration of Negroes:

Or Park Slope: the big Manhattan-style apartment buildings which now hem the Park, and on the streets of the upward slope, and on 8th Avenue, the bland powerful regiments of gray stone bays and the big single-homes, standing with a locked look among mature trees and the curious quietudes of bourgeois Paris: and these confused among apartment buildings and among parochial schools, and the yellow bricks of post-tenements, and the subway noises of "rough" children:

Or the Heights: the enormous homes and the fine rows, a steadily narrower area remains inviolable, the top drawer of Brooklyn, disintegration toward the stooping of the street the Squibb building: great houses broken apart for roomers; a gradual degeneration into artists and journalists, communists, bohemians and barbers, chiefly of Manhattan:

Or, among brownstones, between the last two-mile convergence of Fulton and Broadway, a swifter and swifter breakdown of the former middle classes, a steady thickening of Jews into the ultimacies of Brownsville and East New York:

Or that great range of brick and brownstone north of Fulton which in each two blocks falls more and more bad fortune: one last place, east of Fort Greene

Park, the utmost magnificence of the brownstone style: and beyond-death at length in the Navy Yard district, the hardest in Brooklyn, harder even than Red Hook: (the hardest neighborhood in Brooklyn was a pinched labyrinth of brick and frame within a jump of Borough Hall, but the WPA cleared that one up:)

Or Eastern Parkway, the Central Park West of Brooklyn; in its first stretches near Prospect Park, the dwelling of the most potent Jews of the city; a slow then more swift ironing-out, and the end again in Brownsville:

Or Bay Ridge, and its genteel gentile apartment buildings, and the staid homes of Scandinavian seafarers:

Or Greenpoint and Williamsburg and Bushwick, the wood tenements, bare lots and broken vistas, the balanced weights and images of production and poverty; the headquarters of a municipal government as corrupt as any in the nation: everywhere the spindling Democratic clubs, the massive Roman churches; everywhere, in the eyes of men, in dark bars and on corners, knowledgeable appraising furtive light of hard machine politics; everywhere, the curious gas-lit odor of Irish-American democracy:

Or Flatbush: or Brighton: or Sheepshead Bay: or the negligible downtown: or the view, from the Fulton Street Elevated, of the low-swung and convolved sea of the living, as much green as roofs; or of Brooklyn's nineteenth century backyard life, thousands of solitaries, chips, each floated in his green eddy: or the comparable military attentions of the stoned dead, the stern hieroglyphs of Jews, the thousands of Gold Christs in the sun, the many churches focusing upon the frank secret stardemolished sky their steeplings and proud bulbs and triple crosses and sharp stars and squareflung roods moored high, light ballasted, among the harboring homes, ships pointing out the sun on a single wind: or the mother who walks on Division Avenue whose infant hexes her from his carriage in a gargolye frown of most intense suspicion: or the street-writing on Park Slope: "Lois I have gone up the street. Don't forget to bring your skates.": or the soft whistling of the sea off Coney Island: or the façade of the Academy of Music, a faded print of Boston's Symphony Hall: or the young pair who face each other astride a bicycle in Canarsie: or the lavender glow of brownstones in cloudy weather, or chemical brilliance of jonquils in tamped dirt: or the haloed Sunday hats of little girls, as exquisite as those of their elders are pathologic: or the scornful cornices of dishonored homes: or the shade-cord at whose end is a white home-crocheted Jewish star: or the hot-pants little Manhattan sweatshop girls who come to Tony's Square Bar to meet the sailors and spend a few bearable hours a week: or the streaming of first-flight gentiles from Poly Prep into Williams and Princeton, the second flight into Colgate or Cornell: or of the Jews whose whole families are breaking their hearts for it from Boys High into Brooklyn College and Brooklyn Law, and the luckies of them into Harvard: or the finance editor of the Eagle who believes all journalists are gentlemen who are out of what he calls the Chosen, and who scabbed in the Eagle strike: or in the middle afternoon in whatever part of Brooklyn, the star-like amplitude of baby buggies and of strolling and lounging silent or soft speaking women, the whole dwelling city as vacant of masculinity as most urgent war: or in his window above the banging of DeKalb Avenue late on a hot Saturday afternoon the grizzling skull-capped Jew who nods softly above the texts of his holiness, his lips moving in his unviolated beard, and who has been thus drowned in his pieties since early morning: or the grievings and the gracilities of the personalities at the zoo: or the bright fabric stretched of the confabulations of birds and children: or bed by bed and ward by ward along the sacred odors of the corridors of the twelve street mass of the Kings County Hospital, those who burst with unspeakable vitality or who are floated faint upon dubiety or who wait to die: These the sick, the fainted or fecund, the healthful, the young, the living and the dead, the buildings, the streets, the windows, the linings of the ward nests, the lethal chambers of the schools, the fumed and whining factories, the pitiless birds, the animals, that Bridge which stands up like God and makes music to himself by night and by day: all in the lordly, idiot light, These are inhabitants of Brooklyn:

Or Greenpoint: or Williamsburg: where from many mileages of the jungle of voided land, small factories, smokestacks, tenements, homes of irregular height and spacing, the foci are returned upon the eye, the blown dome and trebled crossage Greek church, and those massive gasoline reservoirs which seem to have more size than any building can: the hard trade avenues, intense with merchandisings of which none is above the taking of the working class: the bridal suites in modernistic veneers and hotcolored plushes, the dark little drugstores with smell like medicine spilled in a phone-booth mouth-piece: the ineffable baroques of gossamer in which little-girl-graduates and Brides of Heaven are clothed: Here and still strongly in Bushwick and persistent too in East New York and Brownsville, there is an enormous number of tall-windowed three- and four-floor wood houses of the fullblown nineteenth century, a style indigenous to Brooklyn, the façades as handsome as anything in the history of American architecture: of these, few have been painted within a decade or more, none are above the rooming house level, most are tenements, all are death-traps to fire: their face is of that half divine nobility which is absorptive of every humiliation, and is increased in each: many more of the tenements are those pallid or yellow bricks which are so much used all over Brooklyn as a mark of poverty: mixed among these many small houses of weathered wood, stucco, roofing: the stucco fronts are often Italian and usually uncolored, suggest nevertheless the rich Italianate washes; some are washed brick red, the joints drawn in white: or the golden oak doors of these neater homes, or the manifold and beautiful frontages of asphaltic shingles, some shinglings merely but applied in strong imaginations of color and pattern, others simulative of slate or brick and more handsome than either: the knowledge, forced on one, willing or no, that all street and domestic art is talented and powerful in proportion to poverty and disadvantage of blood: the care in the selection of curtains and windows ornaments: white shades and tasselled shade cords, or tan venetian blinds, or curtains of starched wrecked lace or red or gold or magenta sateen, little statues of comedy of faith, flowers, leaves and lamps: the names and faces of Irish, Italians, Jews and Slavs; and in the street the proud cries of children, the tightened eyes of fathers, the dissolving beauties of young wives, the deep enthronements of the aged, and along five thousand first floor windows in their gloom, ambushed behind drawn breathing shades, the staring into the single zoned street of crouched aging women, the look of tired lionesses in an endless zoo in a hot afternoon: and in the bleeding of early neons, the return of the typists, and of the students in careful suits, hard ties, carrying their toxic books, and the small bare crowding, where men gentle with weariness drink beer in the solace of each other's voices and the nickelodeon: and in the evenings, here almost in the warm Hebraic volubilities of Brownsville, such a swarm, affection, patience, bitterness and vitality in existence as words will not record:

Or the drive one afternoon, with a Brooklyn journalist, a too-well-born young man not long enough out of Harvard: which began in the vibrated shelters of Brooklyn Bridge and threaded the waterfront and at length sketched in motion the whole people of Brooklyn: the shore drive along Bay Ridge, Coney Island, Sheepshead Bay, and in darkness drove the narrow vision of its needle steep northward through the whole body of the city, straight through Flatbush: those who gathered firewood on a vacant lot on Front Street: the huge warehouses, their walls a yard thick, which were built in the time of the clipper ships: a harvester addressed to Guaraquito, a Chevrolet on its way to Peru, stacks of scrap iron ready for loading to kill whom, where, this time: the calm leaning above earth of the *Hulda Maerak, Isbrandtsen Moller,* the effulgence of her pale aluminum, her beautifully made bow: pine refugee crates, all of the utmost size permitted for the bringing way of the inappraisable objects of outrage, grief and remembrance, veiled in tarpauline as if they were deaths and marked with that wineglass which is this planet's symbol for this end up: it is memorable, too, how half the houses in this section are deserted, the windows shattered, standing jagged as war among vacant lots, the ghosts of floors against their walls: and the dark hard bars at street corners, and men who watched the bland progress of this skimming-sedan in cold strychnine deeply gratifying hate: and along the sheltered Atlantic Basin the warehouses stored with newsprint from Nova Scotia,

Norway, Latvia, Finland: and further down the front
the ships from South America and Africa and Japan:
in the middle of a vacant lot a Negro who sat on a
lard can and ate out of a newspaper: the mahogany
odors of roasting coffee: the prow of the *Tai Yin,
Ionsberg,* dark as a planned murder above a heap of
scrap: the funereally rusted prows also of the *Dun-
drum Castle* and the *Ohio:* how little of Grover
Whalen there is in the clothing of the customs officials of a freight waterfront: how relaxed work is here
as against the Manhattan waterfront, almost the sun-
saturated ease of New Orleans: an enormous repaired
Diesel gentled along on a Williamsburg hauler, suggesting, in the middle of the street, an extracted
heart: the negroid breath of a molasses factory: a
glimpse of the Red Hook housing project which may
or may not, unlike all former American housing projects, serve those for whom it is intended: on the curve
of a new cinder track nine strong boys aslant in distance running, their aura part ancient Greece part
present Leningrad: the pale parade of the great
structures of the Bush Terminal, powerful as barges:
the hulls resting where the olive shipments used to be
heavy: the journalist's efforts to get to the yachting
docks ("the *Corsair* sometimes docks here") , but "they
keep them pretty well barricaded": the long jetty
created of the ballast of returning clippers, stacked
now with Pacific Coast lumber: the cheap white-
sweated brick of the Red Hook Play center: or the
skinned land which was formerly a Hooverville, available to the totally derelict, but which under squarer
dispensation wears WPA's usual creditline for having
Cleaned this Area: or how the comfortable young man
remarked of certain outrageously poor homes left
standing, that they were not of the squatter class;
these people have some right to be here but (laugh-

ing) imagine you or I living in such a way: and the drawbridge over the Gowanus Canal, its sheathings and angularities in motion as elegant as those of a starved cat: or how he remarked that one may find a good deal of prose in Brooklyn but precious little poetry, or again, of the whole region just traversed, "Good solid work here; no swank; not a part of town one comes to see much, but quite necessary to the community":

Or further, along the shore road, passing a stretch of rather Ducky middle-income houses, the "Tudor" type, his patronizing approval; "Here at least you can see some *attempt* at decency"; and a half-made park with the odd pubescent nudity of all new public efforts; and on the Bay the pinched island Fort Lafayette with the minelaying equipment, and Hoffman's Island, the quarantine for parrots and monkeys: the obsolete cannons of Fort Hamilton: a shut-down deserted block of middle-class housing of the twenties: the blasted mansions of Victorian pleasaunce, boarded or brokenout with gasolines and soft drinks: the San Carlo Bocce-Drome, rubbed earth in oilgreen tree shade, soft stepping middleaged Italians at play: a dismantled country club: the high mild-breezed lift of the shore drive:

And on Coney, the drive along a back street past dirtied frames which suggest the poorer parts of the Jersey Shore and which are said to be the worst "slum" in Greater New York; and his speaking, with limitless scorn and hatred, of Sea Gate, a *restricted* neighborhood; the *aristocracy, Mrs. Linkowitz, Mrs. Finkelstein*; and Sea Gate itself, at the west end of the island, a few wooden victorians, the rest undersized pretensions of gaudiest most betraying bricks, perhaps the most dreadfully piteous excrescence crystallization of snobbery I have ever seen; and in a barren place at the far end of the island, in a bright spring sun of six o'clock, the engine quiet, and the whole of the Harbor paved the color of dawn and deep up the north the slow laboring pencil-mark shadow of an outgoing liner, and at profound distance, spoken out of the ocean water itself, a whistling, and light tolling:

And how at Landy's in Sheepshead Bay he outlined his plans for solidifying himself in the community before joining the Nazi *Bund*:

And in darkness, the deep, droned drive up the whole façade of the scarcely distinguishable city; the ascent of a diving bell:

And the hesitations and slow drivings around Brooklyn College: along the walk next the ball field entrance the slowly moving crowd and the lighted placards with the key words, UNITY? WAR; and the new-appearing buildings of this great day college, bloomed with light of study, bad Georgian, the look of a unit of Harvard houseplans with elephantiasis; and again skirting the ball field, trying to hear; in the middle of the field was one dark group and a speaker raised among them with his Flag, on the far side another such group (could they be opponents?), and the placards; and again along the side of the field, as near as we could get, the fat motor idling, and the driver speaking hatefully of Jews; five students came along the walks glancing over, and crossed away in front of us, one of them saying "the Communist sons of bitches"; there was a thin mist through which all light seemed meager and the sky enormous, and in the faint field they stood dark, earnestly attentive, their placards oscillating; and above them, with the help I believe of a weak microphone, came the passionate incompetent speaking of the student. From where we were only his deep sincerity and fear and the inadequacies of his particular mind and intonations were at first audible, but at length the grayed desperate salient words came through, in his brave uncertain hypnotized tenor, "war" . . . "democracy" . . . "unalterably opposed"; and the placards moved as masts in a harbor: it was the night before Hitler was to tell Roosevelt there would be no ten years' peace, and I suggested that that must be the cause of the mass meeting. The journalist agreed it must be, added "Let them, Let them yap about peace and democracy all they like. They're not going to impress Hitler one little bit."

(All over the city on streets and walks and walls the children, and the other true primitives of the race have established ancient, essential and ephemeral forms of art, have set forth in chalk and crayon the names and images of their pride, love, preying, scorn, desire; the Negroes, Jews, Italians, Poles, most powerfully, these same poorest most abundantly, and in these are the characters of neighborhood and of race: on an iron door in Williamsburg: *Dominick says he will Fuck Fanny*. On another: *Boys gang up on Don* and *Down with Don* and *Don is a Bull Artist*. Against green shingles of a Bushwick side door: *The Lady in this House is Nuts*. In an immaculate neighborhood of lower middle class Jews in East New York, against a new blood wash of drugstore brick, the one word *strike*. On a Bensonhurst street, bourgeois Jewish: *Bernice Davidson is the future Mrs. Allan Cunn. She may be the future Mrs. Henry Eiseman*. In Brighton, among Jews recently withdrawn from the ghetto, a child begins an abstract drawing and his mother quickly: "*Don't* do that," and a ten-year-old boy immediately, to a younger, in the same notation, "*Don't* do that." On Park Slope on a Sunday afternoon, not printed, but in an unskilful Palmer script: *Lois I have gone up the street. Don't forget to bring your skates.*

213

In Williamsburg: *Ruby loves Max but Max* HATES *Ruby*.

And drawings, all over, of phalli, fellatio, ships, homes, airplanes, western heroes, women, and monsters dredged out of the memories of the unspeakable sea-journeys of the womb, all spangling the walks and walls, which each strong shower effaces.)

Or deep in Flatbush; in a warm middle afternoon.

I leave the trolley avenue and walk up a residential street: I have not gone a block before I recognize a silence so powerful and so specialized it has almost a fragrance of its own: it is the silence of having left a street of the open world and of having entered an empty church, and is much that fragrance: and there is in the silence an almost Brahmin tranquillity, weakening to the senses, and a subtly terrifying quality of suffocation and of the sacrosanct: and in a moment more, standing between these rows of neat homes, I know what this special sanctitude is: that this world is totally dedicated to tame marriages in their first ten years of youth, and that during the sweep of each working day these streets are yielded over to housewives and to young children and to infants so entirely, that those who stroll these walks and sit in the sun are cloistral nuns, vestals, made fecund though they are, and govern a world in which returning men are made womanly in an odor of cherished floors, clean cloths, nationally advertised cosmetics, and the sharp stench of babies. Two youths, it is true, toss a ball back and forth in the street; but they do so as if this were a puritan sunday, or an area of crisis in sickness in which for relief the healthful must relax, but gently; the rest is as I have said: I see five closed cars, moored empty before doors: each is lately washed, the treads of the tires are sharp, they are all black, not one but is a Chevrolet, Ford or Plymouth: and on doorsteps dolls and the bright aerodynamic toys of the children of this decade: and it seems before every house, shining hearselike in the glare, an identical perambulator, deep, black, sleek with lacquer, brimmed with white cloths: and women: two who stroll abreast along the shadowless adolescence of saplings, serving their carriages; two more who sit in an open door and talk in stopped-down voices; another who sits alone, addling the sprung carriage and staring emptily upon the street; another who, drawing aside a sunporch curtain, peers out upon my watching with the soft sterile alarm of one whose knight is east crusading: a laundry truck sneaks cushioning past and halts at a far door; far up the street I hear the voice of a child; in his shaded pram by the step, swollen with royalty, a baby sleeps; a half mile up Flatbush Avenue, the metal whine of a northbound trolley:

Some of the houses are ten to fifteen years old, some are much younger; all, in their several ways, perfect images of these matings: little doubles and singles of brick and shingle or of brick and stucco or of solid brick in rows: of these latter, five in a row, rather new, are cautiously ornate and are fronted in nearpatterns of bright brick the six colors of children's modeling clays: they are so prim, so undersized, they suggest dolls' homes or the illustrations of a storybook of pretty dreams for sexually ripened children; or as if through some kind white magic they had been made of candy, to the wonder and delight of two who, lost and loving in a wilderness, came suddenly upon a home: "exposed" "beams," wrought-iron knockers, white concrete steps, oak doors with barred peeping-shutters, little touches of the Elizabethan, the Colonial, the Byzantine: or the others, those peaked twins faced with shingles, or those of which the porch is wood glass and brick, the first floor stucco, above that weatherboard or shingle: and of these kinds each has a sunporch, and at the door two whitewashed urns or boxes for flowers, and each a little six-by-four lawn and a low hedge: and these lawns are brightly seeded, and shrubbed with dark junipers, and are affectionately tended: and in the curtained or venetianblinded windows of these sunporches there are bullfrogs and pelicans and scotch terriers and swans of china and roadside potteries of green or yellow sprouting streaked reptilian leaves at whose roots are dainty cowries: and between the homes, or between each double, a streakless concrete lane, exactly wide enough between the windowless walls to pass the sedan, and beyond, a garage; and in these backyards, bright in the sun on patented lines, the bedspreads and the pastelled undergarments of women to whom the natural-color advertisements have told their love of nice things, and this washing has been done in supreme suds which are incapable of damaging the most delicate fabrics and which keep these women unenvious of one another's hands, in electric machines which would flatter any motion picture's conception of a laboratory in an essay on the holiness of medical students:

Or more ordinarily perhaps, few or none of the most fairystory of these lovenests, but solid regiments of the other types, or mixtures of types; both the uniform and the varied strongly exist: plain cubed double-houses of dark red or brindled brick of the twenties is one kind, very common; another, the wood doubles whose twin peaked gables make an M above the partitioned sunporch; and some are faced entirely with stucco; and more often than not there is scarcely room between the walls for a child to get through and the sidewalk trees are developed well beyond the sapling stage; and quite frequently, too, there is at the corner a four- or a six-floor brick apartment building, with a small cement court in which the women sit in camp or windsor chairs; and from one or two windows of these, some pouting betrayal of humility, a cerise mattress; or again for no good reason these buildings will thicken to occupy most of several blocks and there will be fewer mattresses and women at the sills or none and a higher rental, and fewer hatless women in spring coats over housedresses; on some streets there is an inexplicable mixture of "classes," and of "grades" of homes, Central Europeans, a sudden family of Negroes in a scarred frame house, facing the most laxatived of Anglo-Saxons; or again scarce-explicably, a block of solid working class, a row of upper porches, where a rubbertree takes the air and a child's stained sheets are spread, and a woman combs and fondles in the sun her long wild ivory ghastly hair whose face, peering from this ambush, is the four staring holes of a drowned corpse, and the boys play ball more loudly and of two little boys, passing on limber legs, one is saying, just above a whisper, ". . . you know: back stairs. You know: down the back stairs. Back stairs. You know: . . ." and at the end of the street a small factory without even a name moans like many flies: Or, too, there are streets of spaced homes, side lawns and heavy trees whose structures are columned wood, wide plates of glass, big porches, the thick sundaydinner proprieties which succeeded the jigsaw period: or rows again of yellow brick, flatfaced or roundly bayed, rented dwellings, such as may be seen in every part of Brooklyn and in much of the eastern United States:—enough variety, mixture, monotony, sudden change, that it is impossible to generalize Flatbush: and in all this variety nevertheless and in the actions and faces of those who live here the drive of an all but annihilative, essential uniformity: such that it seems, that the middle class suburbs and residential streets of all the small cities of the continent are here set against one another and ironed to one scarcely wrinkled flatness and similitude. The "avenues," the arteries, are no less like themselves: immeasurable stretches of three floor yellow brick with ground floor merchants of hosiery and exlax—for Brooklyn's "downtown," too, is ironed thin to every door: and in this lowness of all building and in the almost stellar vistas of the avenues, an incredible dilation of the sky and the flat horizon, and thus, paradoxic with the odors of suffocation, the open grandeurs almost of a ranch, the quietudes not only of paralysis but of the stratosphere: and so it is not surprising in a Flatbush husband that he feels the air is a lot cleaner out here; a decent place to raise your kids.

(In the gallery of one of the big second-run theaters in the downtown section of Flatbush Avenue, about ten in the evening, they were nearly all high school boys. They all knew each other, as they don't in New York, and kept calling across to each other, and the way they tried to pick up my wife (she was alone) was different from New York, too: "Hey miss what time is it" and "Hey miss what's your first name." They teased the picture more volubly, too. It was a very ordinary thoroughbred show, Kentucky etcetera, with the customary crimes against the talents of Zasu Pitts; but there was one sequence, a spring night, when the heroine was called from a party and waited, glowing in the darkness in her evening dress, while a champion colt was foaled, of a dying dam. Small-lighted men labored intensely in the dark stable over a dark mass almost in silence, and in the gabby balcony an extraordinary quiet, tender, premonitory incertitude took full hold. Out of this gentle, intuitive, questioning silence at length, in a mild naked voice, a boy in the front row realized: "The horse is having a baby." And a boy five rows back, in a thickened voice, cried: "Aww, why don't you shut *up*.")

Social note.
Brooklyn Heights: the dusk of the Gods.
It was really very kind of them, but one can't help that; or must one. The façade was Heights 19th Century, but the extent of the daughter's revolt consisted in a renegade taste for the smuggest and safest in modernism, so the interiors were a little beyond her parents. They both had tall large narrow faces, and an almost oriental cruelty in the eyes and the ends of the lower lips: like many married couples each suggested an unflattering reflection of the other, and they had the strange corpsy dryness common to all whose living is contractive, antihuman. There were weak sidecars served by the usual gentle, refined, ruined girl of foreign extraction, one drink each and a half glass over for me, and we went down to dinner. On a wide dry plate lay four high-grade Cattleyas, all directed at me; but I made no comment. The bay was softlighted against fair slender palms, and the curtains, with that ostentatious good taste which is the worst taste of all, were drawn against the most magnificent view in greater New York. We ate exquisitely cooked boned squab, pecansized potatoes fried in a fine oil, asparagus without sauce, and an exceptionally good dessert of strawberries, baked eggwhite and icecream whose aggregate name I lack the worldly wisdom to know: Baked Alaska, probably: and as the food came and went I developed the feeling, perhaps unfairly, that this was not the ordinary Tuesday evening menu,

and that the specialization was the result less of hospitality than of the wish to astound the bourgeois. Unfortunately the thing I think of most is the rotted meat which is freshened with emblaming fluid and sold at a feasible price to the Negroes along Fulton Street who, lacking the benefits of a thorough course in biology, and any other sniff at it while they are yet conscious, are not in a position to identify this odor as the alter ego of death. While we ate she talked. There is no room here to tell of it all. (I refer you to Swift's *Polite Conversation*), but of some little it is impossible to refrain. About the private park, for instance, which the survivor of the Misses Pierrepont still holds open to the play of the appropriate children, each of whose mothers is given a key, on the strict condition, of course, that no little friends be brought in, or not without express permission. Gramercy Park; yes; but so much more dear and, private. Of course you've heard of the Stuart Washington; the one Lafayette spoke of as the best likeness. (So dear and private.) And at Bellport, my youngest has struck up the sweetest relationship with (a hardware merchant): calls him (by an upper-class seaboard style pet name). I asked, with malice aforethought in the ambiguity, whether it is "mixed" at Bellport. She stiffened a little but recovering: "Oh no: they're all Americans." (One up for me, fat lady.) Of course heaven knows nowadays *what* one's daughters meet at Packer. Yet of course (yes of course) they learn to form their own groups; it's really rather a good exposure, rather a good training; after all, they'll have to be doing just that all their lives. (I nod. I think of the poor rich daughters of jewelers and contractors whose parents are responsible: and what is responsible for that crime in the parents.) And of course the Institute. (I pretend never to have heard of it.) Why the institute of Arts and *Sciences*: ... splendid ... wonderful . . . Academy of Music . . . Boston Symphony lectures . . . the Academy is filled whenever William Lyon Phleps (discovers Browning) . . . But of late, I gather, this is cracking. The new director insists on everyone's *mixing;* it's for *all* Brooklyn; of course there must be really *lovely* people on the *Hill,* and *Park Slope,* and down in *Flatbush,* whom one might never hear of otherwise, but really . . . one meets one's hairdresser . . . in brief, it appears that those ladies whose pleasurable illusion has been that the bloody distillations of the fury, innocence and the genius of the planet are their particular property are beginning to lose interest in "culture," that masked antichrist which in fact is of itself more than they have ever possessed.

After dinner there is no coffee: tardily, and with slight begrudging, cordials are offered, a choice of green chartreuse and Grand Marnier. I am shown a charming glass-painting of early New York superior to any in the City Museum, decline a cigar (courteously) and am led upstairs to the library, and the serious talk of the evening. At the stairhead she turns, her voice lowered and sparkling in a hint of roguishness, by indescribable subtleties of manner Leads me, as such women Lead: "Mr. ——; oh Mr. A. I do hope when you write of Brooklyn you (beckoning) *won't* say that *all* the bedrooms in Brooklyn are (beckoning) dreadful, sordid, stuffy little places; (her voice still more lowered: opening a door:) look here":

The room is perhaps twenty-five by fifteen; the broad panes command the harbor and the complete lower island; the bed is low to the floor and eight feet square. I wonder what possible use it can be to them, and think of the limitations which poverty sets round the clean sensual talents of Jews and Negroes.

As we leave she reiterates, with just a touch of blackmail in the voice, her eager anticipation of the article, which she will most certainly read. I hope, madam, that it was not mere courtesy: and I wish I might have served more of your friends, however unimportant they may be.

I think I remember more vividly, though, her remark: ". . . *dreadful* neighborhood; dreadful: Negroes on Myrtle Avenue: Syrians within two blocks of us, nudging our elbows: *I do wish they'd clear them away.*"

The first settlers of what was to become Brooklyn landed on the Heights in 1636. By 1642 the only Indians on Long Island were huddled on the damp prow of Montauk Point.

Thirty-four years ago, when Mr. George Hobson, a gentle resident of the Hill neighborhood, began teaching Latin in Boys High School, there was hardly a Jew to be seen in the corridors.

Today one sixteenth of the world's whole of the Jewish people reside in Brooklyn and comprise half the population of that city. If "society" in the Heights—Society meaning-of-the-word—has any significance whatever, which is at least open to question, every simple realist must agree that the Jewish "society" of the Eastern Parkway and the St. George ball and banquet room is incomparably more important, more powerful and more dignified than that which crouches at the crumbling edge of the Heights.

It is a pleasure to know that neither is quite acceptable among equivalent New Yorkers: and that the latter are still less securely presentable before both God and Man.

(Or, opposite a loud concrete playground in East New York, sitting in the kind sun in his infinitesimal lawn in a kitchen rocker, his dirty brocaded bathrobe drawn tight, the wasted workman of forty whose face still wears the alien touch of death: his chin is drawn in as far as it will go and he is staring with eyes like diamonds upon the vitalities of the schoolboys, frowning with furious sorrow, his mouth caught up one cheek in a kicking smile:)

Or in Bay Ridge, a sweet quiet of distance from the city, a flag staff in the water breeze, the many apartment buildings ornate but in the self-playing nordic taste; the young woman waiting in the maroon roadster; the mother and child who stand at the subway mouth; and each five minutes, in a walking noise of dry leaves, the rising from underground of the gently or complacently docile: the young woman loses patience and drives away; the mother and her husband do not kiss when they meet; two middle aged men come up talking together, but most of those who rise thus from the dead give no appearance of knowing one another but walk alone toward their suppers; and the unimaginable solitude of most families begins to suggest itself:

Or Bensonhurst, those double and single homes and whole towns of apartments of not unprosperous Jews along the well-shaded streets, as affable among one another, almost, as in the ghettos; the well-pleased wives, the sexuality in the eyes and garments of the high school girls, the exceedingly richly fed children, their thighs thick in their trousers, the father who sits in his small lawn, his eyes naphthaline with ruinous adoration of his boy; the plump blond boys who pitch ball quietly in the street, with excellently cushioned gloves of yellow leather; the college student, trying to cancel his dark opulent features in sharp tweeds; the five mothers, and seven children in an apartment court who all eat ice cream cones, all raspberry; the adolescent girl on the front steps whose eyes, glanced upward, are at once hot and pure; the reappearance of the tweed student, licking an ice cream cone, raspberry flavor:

Or Brighton Beach, the flatfaced apartments chilled in their own shade and the gay candy-colored brick homes, in every one a room for rent, and the almost shacklike bungalows, and the parents watching for their children in front of the school; the hot orange and blue trim of the houses, the diminutive synagogues:

Or Sheepshead Bay, the blunt little launches still trestled, the colors and shapes of children's paintings; the hopeless desolation of the worn-out edge of Brooklyn; the criminally-made row houses in the middle of nowhere; the desperately pathetic matchwood shacks stilted above the stench of the mudflats; the manhole turrets rising to that level at which Robert Moses will establish another of his parks, with reflecting pools, and an end of the shacks:

Or Canarsie, that full end-of-the-world, that joke even to Brooklyn, its far end; the abomination of desolation, the houses thinned to nothing, the blank sand, the shattered cabaret with the sign, "The Girl You Bring is the Girl You Take Home," the new cabaret in the middle of waste silence, with ambitious men aligning the brilliant trims; the shades along the last street and at its head a small young brick apartment, its first floor occupied; the row of dark peaked shingles which across a little park faces the declining sun and the bare land with the look: "somehow we have not been very successful in life"; and this park itself, brand-new, a made-island of green in all this grave ocean, and in this silence, a little noise: The leaves are blown aslant and in their shade a few lie prostrate on young grass, mothers, young girls, two boys together; and meditate, or talk inaudibly; on benches, men without color sit apart from one another in silence. A girl bounces a fat ball on the cement over and over and over. The wind is freshening and the sloped light is turning gold. Birds speak with each other in the hushed leaves and in the wind there are the soft calls of children, but these noises are blown by the wind and are finally almost impossible to hear.

In Prospect Park on Sunday they are all there, on the lake, along the bending walks, sown on the seas of lawn; the old, the weary, the loving, and the young; who move in the flotations of seeds upon placid winds: a family, gathering its blankets and its baskets, quarreling a little: Four young men hatless in dark coats walk rapidly across the vast grass in an air of purpose and of enigma: a little boy running alone who suddenly leaps into the air: another little boy and an elderly man and a rolled umbrella, hand in hand: the rear end of a metal swan, a tractor saddle and bicycle pedals: a working class father of fifty who, leant to a tree, holds four identical hats by their elastics and watches toward the water with an iron and tender look: two little girls stand on two stones by the ruffed water and hesitate toward one another like courting insects: an old woman built like a bear sits alone on a bench with her fecund spread and her hands folded on her belly; she is intensely watching everything in sight and in silence the tears run freely down her face: three boys and three hardfleshed girls in working-class clothes range past with the resourceful and sensitive eyes of wild animals: four couples in file, unaware of one another, push baby carriages along a walk; three are sombre, one is mutual: a young man suddenly genuflects before a smiling girl in a gold blouse, his hands at the eye at his heart like a tenor: six delicately dressed Negro boys of eight to fourteen softly follow a seventh who pushes a virgin bicycle of cream and ultramarine and gold with an unsullied squirrel's tail smoking at the heel of the rear mudguard: he does not ride but continually hovers his lovely machine with the passion of a stallion and the reverence of a bridegroom; his eyes are dazed, and he is unspeakably touched and solitary: the young man, his photograph made, gets up and dusts his knee: within this range of lawn, each at wide distance from the others, five children are running rapidly with the young child's weakness at the knee; not one, from here, is larger than a gnat: in a deep walk alone, a boy with a meek nape abruptly kisses his thicklegged girl and they laugh and kiss again; she digs her dark head deeply against his neck and with arms tightened they walk on with the unsteadiness of drunks: in a walk alone, in the beauty of the Botanic Gardens, an elderly woman stands very still facing a robin who stands still, dabs at the pavement, and points his eye at her; when she is seen the woman smiles slyly yet timorously, as a child might who feared reprimand: all over those long drawn heavings of fair lawn each mirroring the whole mystery of one another's past and being and future and each blind to the signals of warning they move in hundreds and in thousands in such spaciousness they scarcely seem a crowd but a whole race dispread upon a fresh green world, and their motions upon this space are those of a culture upon a microscopic slide:

(And one by one, slowly disclosed in the speed of walking of Washington Avenue and the slow withdrawal of an apartment cornice, in gradual parade upon the facade of the Institute of Arts and Science and upon the iron sky, letter by letter, figure by figure, the names and images of the noble: Confucious: Lao-tze: Moses: David: Jeremiah: Isaiah: St. Peter:

St. Paul: Mohammed: and, between columns, each:
Sophocles: Pericles: Herodotus: Thucydides: Socrates:
Demosthenes:

The great gray building static, the sky is slowly
crowded to the left:

Or late in the day, in the zoo, the black bears with
the muzzles of vaudeville tramps, and those who
affectionately watch them: the empty pit: the desperate bawlings of the single polar bear, his eyes half
crazy with loneliness, his whole focus on the pit of
blacks: the quieting and softening of all light and the
wonder this performs upon some animals: the sexy
teasings and huggings of the round masked brighteyed
coons and the delight there must be in the wrestlings
of fat furred bodies: the deep moat where Hilda the
elephant was pushed by her playful husband, to die
in bewilderment of sacroiliac pain, and where he too
recently fell: that cage in which three black metal
eagles, hunchbacked with heartcracking melancholia,
fall clumsy as grounded buzzards from limb to limb
of their small skinned tree, "Presented to the Children
of New York by the Brooklyn Daily Eagle": and
through the dusk the agonies of the bear; *Baw: Baww:
Bawwww!*: and the bumpings and kiddings of the gay
coons: and the kangaroos, some orange, and some
fawn, whose eyes are lovely as those of giraffes or of
victorian heroines and who move like wheelchairs:
and the deer:

It is late dusk now, with the lamps on; the sky is
one clean pearl. There are almost no people left.
Those kingly anarchists who have become symbols of
journalism sit quite without motion. The bear is still
crying: he has the sound of a baby who has been forgotten in the attic of an abandoned house. In their

run the young among the deer are altered. They are no longer being watched and it is not only that: they are caught also at the heart and throughout their bodies with that breath-depriving mystical ecstasy which dusk excites in them and in young goats. Their eyes are sainted, innocent, as those of goats daemonic. They move tenderly, with a look of minnows about the head and body: then a sudden break, a strong-sprung sharphooved bouncing run in the soft dirt, the precisions of chisels and of Mozart: and in the midst of this one of them will suddenly leap high into the air, wrists high, tail waggling, wriggling his whole body upon itself in a blind spasm of self-delight (while the kangaroos amble and squat): and now, even; it is rapidly darkening: in a child's angry joy in life and furious reluctance in the death even of one day, a fawn tears out again on the empty run and three times over climbs the air and congratulates himself: and out of the fallen brightness of the air, low a long while then steadily rising, hammered and beaten mad hell with ceremonial bells, drawn in a whole periphery of this green park and this world, such a wild inexhaustible wailing as to freeze the root of the heart.

[1939]
[*Esquire,* December 1968]

PART VIII

MAN'S FATE

Mary Yale

Colophon and A ... from ... transcript of the Shot Poet—April 22, 1966

The immediate outflow of gore must come. It has just poured through. Immediately the ship, this the camera draws with... to what the platform... planted with camera exhaust, from... and very soft water calm and serene, was ... and bubbled into... and ... chappedd in... swirl, fade in by a vertical... of the... and to barrier, head silence... next, first seconds... fade to blackscreen, then... until fade in again. A pause.

The more piercing penetration is a sound of the... tive whistle, lasting no more than few seconds, but of sharp at both ends, and later both rising and no diminuendo.

A pause.

A man's voice, each outer line one circumference. In a large hall, echoes... each sound, that shape

Man's Fate

Clappique and Ferral have left Shanghai on the same boat—April 12, 1927.

The immediate wake left in the static frame the ship has just poured through. Immediately the ship is past the camera drops swiftly closer so that the bubbling, plaited wake entirely fills the frame; and watches the water calm and flatten. While the water is still twisted and bubbled into many small shapes it is suddenly congealed in a still whose shapes are replaced in a swift fade-in by a vertical air view of Shanghai and its harbor: dead silence: hold five seconds; still: quick fade to black screen: black screen until further notice.

A pause.

The most piercing possible iron scream of a locomotive whistle, lasting not more than five seconds: cut off sharp at both ends so there is no crescendo and no diminuendo.

A pause.

A man's voice: very quiet but not whispered:

"In a large hall, formerly a school-yard, that same

evening, in Shanghai, two hundred wounded Communists are waiting to be taken out and killed."

A pause.

The strong deep iron bell of a clock: a granular quality of vibration. Sound only.

Square-shot, a little below center, from outside, of the closed guarded door of the prisonyard: motionless but not a still. Seen through thin drizzling fog and darkness descending but maximum sharp focus; the drizzle holding the same rhythm as that of the bell-vibration. This door appears on the fourth stroke of the bell, which strikes six and whose echoed notes are strongly cumulated. Hold the shot a little after the sixth stroke.

Very close shot of the face of the outdoor, ornate, imperial clock of the Chapei station; the afternoise of the bell persisting, cut short into sharp silence by a metal flick as the heavy iron minute-hand shifts from two to three past six.

Silent. Horizontal black bole of a stationary locomotive under full steam; top arcs of wheels in lower screen.

In the locomotive cab, a young soldier; close; in his raised, poised and stiff hand, the lever or wire which lets off a whistle.

Broad street-shot, from second-story height, which includes the station (clock) and the prison (door): very small, two soldiers, midway between, are carrying a man on a stretcher from the door to the station. The street is hedged bare by machine-guns.

Next is a vertical shot of the head of a Chinese lying on his back on a hard dirt floor: the whole head clenched like a fist and beating itself with a shallow movement, but hard and rapidly, with a noise each time of a stone struck on a stone, against the floor. In the same shot is the hand and wounded arm of another man, the hand crawled with dry blood from a wound in the arm, the arm and sleeve torn, the hand, palm up, trembling lightly. Next the head, so vertical to the shoulder it is formal, a shod foot. The camera retracts a few feet. Now along the right side of the screen are the almost identically shaped heads of three Chinese, parallel, a little slanted (the first man is still in the frame). One is shaking very lightly in an almost fluttering speedup of the "no" gesture. One, the forehead broken, the eyes relaxed to the low side of the head like the breasts of a recumbent woman, in a slow torsion of head and throat lifts toward the lens the line and angle of his jawbone. The third, after a few seconds, lifts his eyes backward and upward and looks steadily into the lens, and sternly, and with a kind of cold tragic scorn, as if into the leaning and questioning eyes of a likewise doomed comrade who does not fully understand the situation. During this unbroken shot, which of course lasts less long than it takes to describe, this is the sound: The whistle stays on full blast. With the appearance of the three heads it is added to itself: the same whistle in three other timbres.

With the next shot, as many dozens of timbres as possible: this shot is steep, from high, of the whole floor on which 200 men are prostrate. There are many parallels and regularities of body, so that it is like large pieces of broken graveyard thrown roughly together again. Nearly every man is wounded; some are dead; there are many individual distortions of body; every possible trick of lighting and depth and focus must be used to give two impressions to the maximum: that they are thrown down here like straws; and that they are pressed so utterly into the floor, the earth, that they are almost printed on it.

With the next shot the sound flicks suddenly to its

normal at this distance, but loses as little as possible in intensity. This shot is a sudden glancing-up, and holding, of the camera, to the left of the four detailed heads (which are in lower screen); and is a semi-closeup of Katov, raised on his elbow, looking into the lens and recognizing a face there, and in his look showing that he is only recently here, and unacquainted with the meaning of the whistle.

The whistle ends, abruptly, so as to make the complete silence more sharp. The camera stands close by Katov's lifted head. The head is turning slowly, looking around; the camera twists past it and looks around. Its first shot is from as low as possible: just high enough that a great length and breadth of floor is visible. Nearly everyone is lying flat.

Off-screen, to the left, a moan. Silence. Nearby, at right, just within screen, a moan. Half-length (of the moan) silence. From five various distances and directions, starting almost simultaneously, the moaning of five men. Silence.

Quick semi-close-up of a man on his back, drawing in on a shortened cigaret.

Somewhat sped-up shot of a slender stream of smoke spilling straight upward, synchronized with a single thin, shaken, almost feminine moan, above completely flat, horizontal bodies.

A corpse.

A broad shot from the floor: maximum sweep and flatness of bodies. About two dozen streams of smoke, unrealistically distinct, stand up vertical from the floor like slim irregularly planted vines. Late in the shot one stands up close to the lens not more than a few inches to the left of center. Synchronized both by timing and direction with these smokestreams, much quieter than before; and added to by an arithmetic progression until they get beyond count of smoke or conjecture, moans, groans, sighs, fragments of speech in several languages, so that there is built up next to the floor a multitudinous droning texture of pain scarcely louder than the noise of somewhat distant bees.

Bursting sound and detail of door opening with clank of metal and noise of shoes and a bursting through of soldiers with lanterns beginning: very quick shot: then immediately pick up from Katov's vicinity with very few heads, among them his, lifting, lifted, watching the approach of the soldiers, stretcher-bearers, lanterns; the swinging light running the irreg-ularities of prostrate bodies and throwing big sliding shadows. Several wounded are deposited "like pack-ages" near the camera (which spots a few, especially one, on his belly, for later use): the soldiers turn toward the door: steep shot from high in room; pat-terns of lantern light being drawn from breadth of hall towards and out of door with a steady resumption of the texture of groans, very quiet: across the screen the door shuts, with a clang, establishing a pace kept up by the pacing of the boots of sentries: on the screen, the last gleam of bayonets, first their points only, on darkness, passing and pivoting; then a truck following a bayonet; then a broad unreal shot in which there are only the four erect bayonets, small and lost in the size of darkness: always, meantime, a kind of formal music made only of the muted, swarm-ing noise of suffering, chopped through with boot-sound, and all rising from unnaturally far beneath the screen.

This sound continues as the camera hovers the new arrival, who is lying on his belly.

Sudden, fog-muffled, from a great distance, the

whistle. All other sound immediately stops. It extends itself. The man tightens his hands over his ears with a broad, twisting pressure of the palms, and screams. His companions stiffen in terror and are silent. The scream is done. The whistle is done. A silence. No motion. Then the man snaps up his head: jacks himself on his elbows: screams: *"Scoundrels! Murderers!"*

From three paces away, with short sharp stride, a sentry steps forward. In the space of ribs where the elbow has lifted the body he gives him a kick that turns him over (two of his companions twitch in convulsive sympathetic reflex). (Intensify beyond nature the noise of the impact of the boot, the sharp squealed grunt of the man.) The man is silent. The sentry walks away. The lips of the man, barely visible, begin to move. Katov's face listening, leaning toward: the voice clears: ". . . don't shoot, they throw them alive into the boiler of the locomotive . . ." the sentry, trying to hear, comes near "and now, they're whistling . . ." the sentry nearer; silence. Out of the silence, as literally as possible like the spreading of a fan, resumes the spreading drowse of pain, quite quickly. At its full spread the door again opens: its sound, and a spreading of light, upon a shot which with the spreading of the noise has lifted from the wounded man upon the general hall.

A sudden stiff bristling shot of fluted bayonets under-lighted from a lantern. An officer comes through the bayonets into the room alone, crossflashed with a quick stiffening, all over the hall, of hands and faces and bodies in the dark.

The length of his body, upside down on the screen, feet first, seen directly from above those who carry him on a stretcher, a badly wounded Chinese is drawn beneath the lens which as it catches his upside-down face follows, hovering it. It is the face of a man of forty, of great physical strength, bravery, and intelligence (not intellect). After it has been followed thus a few swift paces it passes, in a stationary side view, the streaming flank of a locomotive. In the next shot, like a shell into a gun, it is thrust feet first into a boiler and the door is shut tight immediately behind the head. Immediate congested shot of the head, upside down, close-rounded by boiler-iron. Immediate detail of whistle: of hand on release wire: the face: hold on the face: his courage: imagination: terrific fear: the heavy lips clenched thin and the chin flickering: the hand on the release wire tightening, ready to pull: the face:

after not more than two seconds the face is exploded by the shriek and crazed over with intense stream. The shriek is that of the whistle.

Swift shot (from newsreel) of Chiang Kai-Shek at desk lifting his face in a Methodist smile as if hearing a pleasant item of conversation;

of a woman in a night club, a questioning, listening look on her face, asking an invisible companion to please repeat his wisecrack;

of a woman, in a small room in the city, who knows the meaning of the whistle; and of her child, who does not;

A soldier leans in on the inward swinging of the door. He shouts: "Send one out!"

Same shot of the three men. They have been standing a little apart from each other, each absorbed in his own fate. Now in this shot they are just at the instant that the voice and the full realization has struck them. It strikes them straight through their bodies as well as their minds and involuntarily they are drawn together swiftly like a sped-up movie of the petals of a shriveling flower; as if into a strong magnetic field at their common center; closer; and closer; sidelong and back to, rather than facing each other. Now the camera much closer: only from their shoulders up. Two are back to back. Their heads are leaned backward and they have begun to press the sides of their skulls together.

A guard comes up several paces quickly: stops short; in an unnatural voice; not daring to make the choice himself, he says: "Come on now, make up your minds."

The third man, standing close against them, has leaned in his head under the base of the skull of one. (This again is a close shot, of the heads.) They are straining their heads against one another with all their strength. Three quick shots, close, one each of their faces. Three quick shots of them from the floor, among the wounded, each time at a deeper distance from them. Three slow shots of their faces. Close-up of the sentry. Again the "formal," waist-up shot, of the men. Hold. Out of this shot, abruptly, one of the men steps forward, the camera swinging with him; throws down his scarcely burnt cigaret (quick detail as it dryly hits the floor); walks two more steps and stops short. He has tried to turn his back and his face to everyone who might be watching him but the camera is watching him as, after breaking two matches, he lights another cigaret and draws in desperately deep on it and abruptly, the guard at his shoulder, resumes walking. Face tucked down, the cigaret stuck in it dragged on rapidly and smokily, buttoning carefully one by one all the buttons of his own coat, he walks quickly toward the camera (which is now at the door) and out the door, the camera swinging as he turns there and squaring into solid focus on the door which is immediately shut.

Immediate detail: the burning cigaret on the floor:
a wounded man near it. The eyes of the two (Lu and
his companion) looking at it, on the floor. The
cigaret and the wounded man, who is thinking. After
a little with great delicateness and respect he reaches
over his hand, takes the cigaret, and draws in on it,
raising his eyes, as he lets out the smoke, to Lu. Lu
and his companion are watching him. They understand each other fully.

The soldier leans in on the door; shouts: "Another."

The waist-high shot. Out of a dead standstill of
five seconds, Lu and his companion go forward together, holding each other by the arm. Lu is reciting,
in a loud, dead voice, the death of a hero in a famous
Chinese play (in Chinese) ; but nobody is listening.

Thus they walk directly toward the camera which
is now a third of the way from the door. Five yards
away, as a soldier steps in at the right of screen, they
slow down and come to a halt, Lu no longer speaking.

The soldier: "Which one?"

There is no answer. Now a close shot of them.

He steps up close to them, into the screen again.
"Well, is one of you going to come?"

No answer. With a blow of his rifle butt he knocks
them apart and takes Lu, who is nearest, by the
shoulder. Lu frees his shoulder and steps forward,
out of the picture. Small in the screen, the face of the
other remains. It had been, like Lu's, exalted. Now
it is broken from inside by his solitude and by his
fear. He goes back to his exact place and lies down:
all this weakly, as a sick man would: his arms tight
around his body, his breath very much held in and
shaken sharply and irregularly between his teeth.
Close shot of Kyo, watching him, and understanding
his bravery and his fear. Of Katov. Of the man
again, a leaned shot through which, now, a guard's
hand leans and touches him. At the touch he shakes

all over as in a fit; tightens his fingers round his arms, his arms round his body. Close shot. His mouth comes open, the tongue large and limp; the eyes are expressionless. With wet fleshy noises he is gagging quietly, like a baby whose crying has nearly strangled it.

Two soldiers lean into the lens over him.

Shot of Kyo's face.

Lifting him from the close, low lens, the soldiers carry him out by his head and feet.

From above Kyo's place the camera, low, looking down, in a slow sweep like the swing of an arc by a compass, marks out the bareness of floor around Kyo and Katov: from this, settles itself into a rigidly formal, vertical shot, of Kyo.

Kyo's head has been lifted a little and inclined a little sidewise, to see. Now he draws it in centrally and relaxes it lightly upon the floor; rests his arms upon his chest; straightens his legs: in the exact posture of the dead: his face quiet and now, with his eyes shut, calming entirely. His body is lengthwise of the bottom of the screen.

In firm, not too slow succession, May's head, then Gisors', faces calm and grave, turning slowly and firmly away, on the full turn of the latter, sudden, Kyo's face, close: then the vertical shot resumed and held, the body straight along the bottom of the screen: several seconds motionless silence:

A voice now speaks out of the screen in what may for convenience be called a thought-voice. It is Kyo's voice, much subdued though no whisper: the voice in which words are made in thought. His lips of course do not move: Except when indicated the shot is the same vertical shot:

Soon, now: soon:

As soon as they come to take the first of us: I will kill myself with full consciousness.

May: (her face; a darkened print) May: quick details of naked bodies embraced: close, of his face, in intense pain. The face smooths:

I shall not see May again.————Not ever again. (The vertical shot is here resumed.) Already I am separated from the living.

My father: (his head: his head, another view): I have no grief for my father, and no sorrow (his head— i.e., Gisors' head; another view): for I know his strength.

(May's head, turned three quarters away and turning away.) Now she must forget me. (Again her head, turned less away but turning steadily away. As it turns back-to, the screen goes dark.) (From dark screen:) To have written her this would only have heightened her grief, and attached her all the more. (Kyo's face): And it would be telling her to love another.

The screen wipes down into black: and on the first spoken word, into a deeper black.* What follows is spoken by the voice which has spoken before, except where others are indicated:

Kyo's voice: O prison, place where time ceases, time, which continues elsewhere. . . .

The voice: No! It is in this yard, separated from everyone by the machine-guns, that the Revolution, no matter what its fate or the place of its resurrection, is receiving its death-stroke; wherever men labor in pain, in absurdity, in humiliation, they are thinking

* [Author's handwritten note in margin] Blackness crawls to within a foot of bottom of screen: there, dark as possible and still be visible at all: the slanted floor of the yard, strewn with bodies like straws: the whole floor visible . . . Without walls: seeming to be an infinite and populated plain.

of doomed men like ourselves, as believers pray; out there, in the city, they are beginning to love these dying men as though they were already dead:

He has fought:

(The subdued, crowded voices of many:) He has fought:

(The single voice:) For what in his time is charged with the deepest meaning, and the greatest hope:

He is dying:

(Many voices:) Dying:*

Among those with whom he would have wanted to live.

He is dying:

(Many voices:) Dying:*

Like each of these men:

(Many:) Like each of these men:

Because he has given a meaning to his life.

(Many:) Because he has given a meaning to his life.

(Kyo's voice:) What would have been the value of a life for which I would not have been willing to die?

(Kyo's voice:) It is easy:

(Kyo and the voice:) Easy:

(All voices:) Easy to die.*

(Kyo's voice:) When one does not die alone.

(All:) When one does not die *alone.**

(The *alone* is held and then submerged in the sound of sorrow and pain, which is now held very low, and which now as not before lies just a little to one side of a sung or hummed note. Above it the single voice is lifted, more brightly and slenderly than before):

A death saturated with this brotherly quavering;

---

*[Author's handwritten note in margin] These key words are spoken in as many as a dozen basic languages: in which each must be clearly recognizable to him who knows that language: as the several voices in a piece of music.

this assembly of the vanquished in which multitudes will recognize their martyrs; a bloody legend of which the golden legends are made:

How, already face to face with death, can he fail to hear this murmur of human sacrifice crying to him that the virile heart of men is for the dead as good a refuge as the mind?

(From the dark screen the sorrowing of a multitude of men's voices increases and lifts and clarifies into rough-sung notes, in octaves and fifths, now joined with the voices of women, not loudly at all, but louder and brighter on each note. The basic notes, which ascend, follow: C, (two slow beats), D, (two beats), G, (one beat), A, (four beats):

As the A is struck, Kyo's hand, close, intimately and silently efficient, extracts the cyanide from his belt buckle and holds it on the palm unemotionally but sensuously as a jewel, then, the A held, Kyo's face, very close, transfigured in a serene, cold exalted smile. The note enlarges to the end of its beat and quits abruptly on dead silence: the face grows brighter and stiller.

The locomotive cab. The soldier, erect; another, lounging, in the cab; a third, short, on pavement looking in; visible only from breast-bone up and sense of tiptoe and craning and nervous tension. Hold the shot still, several seconds. Crossflash it with close faces of the three; with the hand. Abruptly, very slightly, the little man nods. He is not giving an order; he is involuntarily expressing his private need, rhythm and sense of when the whistle should go off. Flash to the wirepuller's face, the eyes dropped to him, the face motionless, scornful around the wings of the nose. Back to the other's face: its shape has not changed but behind the face he is badly broken by this delay-torture. The wirepuller's face and hand. The slouching soldier's slouched face. Detail the hand. It jerks the wire down. Immediate human scream, intense and loud as possible. Flash of the slouched face. Flash of the whistle, so close it is abstract iron and steam. Both these shots last less than a second. . . .

(Or the suspense before sound tightened to utmost possible, when the lever is pulled there is no sound; or the sound of the whistle but at enormous distance: same photograph, though, of intense noise, the steaming whistle, held: then with complete suddenness there is no steam, only the silent whistle: that, for four seconds, then deadblack screen: out of this screen a man's long, deep, emphatic sigh, of the utmost satisfaction of sex or gluttony, but also of the utmost remoteness, aloofness and solitude. Silence. Black screen.)

NOTES:

Important, on the fog, and on the timbre of film all the way through, to make this clear: that smooth and lyric fog (as in Zoo in Budapest *or* The Informer) *is not meant and is to be avoided. By taking its resonance from that of the bell I mean that that should be the rhythm of the grain in the film, as if produced of the sound. All the film should be grainy, hard black and white, flat focus, the stock and tone of film in war newsreels, etc., prior to the invention of panchromatic. No smoothness and never luminous. It should not seem to be fiction.*

Much, here, could communicate in writing as postured, literary, and "artistic." In part, I think, because words slow it down. I don't know how in words to indicate that the cutting, for instance, would be dry and "dynamic" (vide Arsenal) *rather than more heavily deliberated: or how to make clear that various head-groupings, faces, etc., would not be "composed" and romantic but literalness intensified to become formal out of its own substance. Much that through generalization here could easily seem slow and artistic could not be further particularized short of actual work in making the film. This particularization would all be directly opposed to this "fictional" or "lyric" suspicion.*

The use of the disembodied voice and choric voices is of course exceedingly dangerous: they could with much difficulty avoid the mistakes made in the voicing of poetic radio plays. The problem would be to find the right voice—entirely untrained, un"cultivated" and above all unhistrionic; capable of coloring and intensifying a monotone without departing it. The chorus voices, too: same desperate avoidance of the mass-chant type of tone: not in unison, very dry: voices not of poetic "performers" but of literal persons. When they sing the few notes its massiveness should come of many crowded and untrained voices, of which many sharpen and flat the pitch.—J. A.

[From *Films,* edited by Jay Leyda. New York, 1939]

PART IX

A MOTHER'S TALE

A Mother's Tale

The calf ran up the hill as fast as he could and stopped sharp. "Mama!" he cried, all out of breath. "What *is* it! What are they *doing!* Where are they *going!*"

Other spring calves came galloping too.

They all were looking up at her and awaiting her explanation, but she looked out over their excited eyes. As she watched the mysterious and majestic thing they had never seen before, her own eyes became even more than ordinarily still, and during the considerable moment before she answered, she securely heard their urgent questioning.

Far out along the autumn plain, beneath the sloping light, an immense drove of cattle moved eastward. They went at a walk, not very fast, but faster than they could imaginably enjoy. Those in front were compelled by those behind; those at the rear, with few exceptions, did their best to keep up; those who were locked within the herd could no more help moving than the particles inside a falling rock. Men on horses rode ahead, and alongside, and behind, or spurred their horses intensely back and forth, keeping the pace steady, and the herd in shape; and from man to man a dog sped back and forth incessantly as a shuttle, barking incessantly, in a hysterical voice. Now and then one of the men shouted fiercely, and this like the shrieking of the dog was tinily audible above a low and awesome sound which seemed to come not from the multiude of hooves but from the center of the world, and above the sporadic bawlings and bellowings of the herd.

From the hillside this tumult was so distant that it only made more delicate the prodigious silence in which the earth and sky were held; and, from the hill, the sight was as modest as its sound. The herd was virtually hidden in the dust it raised, and could be known, in general, only by the horns which pricked this flat sunlit dust like little briars. In one place a twist of the air revealed the trembling fabric of many backs; but it was only along the near edge of the mass that individual animals were discernible, small in a driven frieze, walking fast, stumbling and recovering, tossing their armed heads, or opening their skulls heavenward in one of those cries which reached the hillside long after the jaws were shut.

From where she watched, the mother could not be sure whether there were any she recognized. She knew that among them there must be a son of hers; she had not seen him since some previous spring, and she would not be seeing him again. Then the cries of the young ones impinged on her bemusement: "Where are they going?"

She looked into their ignorant eyes.

"Away," she said.

"Where?" they cried. "Where? Where?" her own son cried again.

She wondered what to say.

"On a long journey."

"But where *to?*" they shouted. "Yes, where *to?*" her son exclaimed; and she could see that he was losing his patience with her, as he always did when he felt she was evasive.

"I'm not sure," she said.

Their silence was so cold that she was unable to avoid their eyes for long.

"Well, not *really* sure. Because, you see," she said in her most reasonable tone, "I've never seen it with my own eyes, and that's the only way to *be* sure; *isn't* it?"

They just kept looking at her. She could see no way out.

"But I've *heard* about it," she said with shallow cheerfulness, "from those who *have* seen it, and I don't suppose there's any good reason to doubt them."

She looked away over them again, and for all their interest in what she was about to tell them, her eyes so changed that they turned and looked, too.

The herd, which had been moving broadside to them, was being turned away, so slowly that like the turning of stars it could not quite be seen from one moment to the next; yet soon it was moving directly away from them, and even during the little while she spoke and they all watched after it, it steadily and very noticeably diminished, and the sounds of it as well.

"It happens always about this time of year," she said quietly while they watched. "Nearly all the men and horses leave, and go into the North and the West."

"Out on the range," her son said, and by his voice she knew what enchantment the idea already held for him.

"Yes," she said, "out on the range." And trying,

impossibly, to imagine the range, they were touched by the breath of grandeur.

"And then before long," she continued, "everyone has been found, and brought into one place; and then . . . what you see, happens. All of them.

"Sometimes when the wind is right," she said more quietly, "you can hear them coming long before you can see them. It isn't even like a sound, at first. It's more as if something were moving far under the ground. It makes you uneasy. You wonder, why, what in the world can *that* be! Then you remember what it is and then you can really hear it. And then finally, there they all are."

She could see this did not interest them at all.

"But where are they *going?*" one asked, a little impatiently.

"I'm coming to that," she said; and she let them wait. Then she spoke slowly but casually.

"They are on their way to a railroad."

There, she thought; that's for that look you all gave me when I said I wasn't sure. She waited for them to ask: they waited for her to explain.

"A railroad," she told them, "is great hard bars of metal lying side by side, or so they tell me, and they go on and on over the ground as far as the eye can see. And great wagons run on the metal bars on wheels, like wagon wheels but smaller, and these wheels are made of solid metal too. The wagons are much bigger than any wagon you've ever seen, as big as, big as sheds, they say, and they are pulled along on the iron bars by a terrible huge dark machine, with a loud scream."

"Big as *sheds?*" one of the calves said skeptically.

"Big *enough*, anyway," the mother said. "I told you I've never seen it myself. But those wagons are so big that several of us can get inside at once. And that's exactly what happens."

Suddenly she became very quiet, for she felt that somehow, she could not imagine just how, she had said altogether too much.

"Well, *what* happens?" her son wanted to know. "What do you mean, *happens?*"

She always tried hard to be a reasonably modern mother. It was probably better, she felt, to go on, than to leave them all full of imaginings and mystification. Besides, there was really nothing at all awful about what happened . . . if only one could know *why.*

"Well," she said, "it's nothing much, really. They just—why, when they all finally *get* there, why there are all the great cars waiting in a long line, and the big dark machine is up ahead . . . smoke comes out of it, they say . . . and . . . well, then, they just put us into the wagons, just as many as will fit in each wagon, and when everybody is in, why . . ." She hesitated, for again, though she couldn't be sure why, she was uneasy.

"Why then," her son said, "the train takes them away."

Hearing that word, she felt a flinching of the heart. Where had he picked it up, she wondered, and she gave him a shy and curious glance. Oh dear, she thought. I should never have even *begun* to explain. "Yes," she said, "when everybody is safely in, they slide the doors shut."

They were all silent for a little while. Then one of them asked thoughtfully, "Are they taking them somewhere they don't want to go?"

"Oh, I don't think so," the mother said. "I imagine it's very nice."

"I want to go," she heard her son say with ardor. "I want to go right now," he cried. "Can I, Mama? *Can I? Please?*" And looking into his eyes, she was overwhelmed by sadness.

"Silly thing," she said, "there'll be time enough for that when you're grown up. But what I very much hope," she went on, "is that instead of being chosen to go out on the range and to make the long journey, you will grow up to be very strong and bright so they will decide that you may stay here at home with Mother. And you, too," she added, speaking to the other little males; but she could not honestly wish this for any but her own, least of all for the eldest, strongest and most proud, for she knew how few are chosen.

She could see that what she said was not received with enthusiasm.

"But I want to go," her son said.

"Why?" she asked. "I don't think any of you realize that it's a great *honor* to be chosen to stay. A great privilege. Why, it's just the most ordinary ones are taken out onto the range. But only the very pick are chosen to stay here at home. If you want to go out on the range," she said in hurried and happy inspiration, "all you have to do is be ordinary and careless and silly. If you want to have even a chance to be chosen to stay, you have to try to be stronger and bigger and braver and brighter than anyone else, and that takes *hard work. Every day.* Do you see?" And she looked happily and hopefully from one to another. "Besides," she added, aware that they were not won over, "I'm told it's a very rough life out there, and the men are unkind."

"Don't you see," she said again; and she pretended to speak to all of them, but it was only to her son.

But he only looked at her. "Why do you want me to stay home?" he asked flatly; in their silence she knew the others were asking the same question.

"Because it's safe here," she said before she knew better; and realized she had put it in the most unfortunate way possible. "Not safe, not just that," she fumbled. "I mean . . . because here we *know* what happens, and what's going to happen, and there's never any doubt about it, never any reason to wonder, to worry. Don't you see? It's just *Home*," and she put a smile on the word, "where we all know each other and are happy and well."

They were so merely quiet, looking back at her, that she felt they were neither won over nor alienated. Then she knew of her son that he, anyhow, was most certainly not persuaded, for he asked the question she most dreaded: "Where do they go on the train?" And hearing him, she knew that she would stop at nothing to bring that curiosity and eagerness, and that tendency toward skepticism, within safe bounds.

"Nobody knows," she said, and she added, in just the tone she knew would most sharply engage them, "Not for sure, anyway."

"What do you mean, *not for sure*," her son cried. And the oldest, biggest calf repeated the question, his voice cracking.

The mother deliberately kept silence as she gazed out over the plain, and while she was silent they all heard the last they would ever hear of all those who were going away: one last great cry, as faint almost as a breath; the infinitesimal jabbing vituperation of the dog; the solemn muttering of the earth.

"Well," she said, after even this sound was entirely lost, "there was one who came back." Their instant, trustful eyes were too much for her. She added, "Or so they say."

They gathered a little more closely around her, for now she spoke very quietly.

"It was my great-grandmother who told me," she said. "She was told it by *her* great-grandmother, who claimed she saw it with her own eyes, though of course I can't vouch for that. Because of course I wasn't even dreamed of then; and Great-grandmother was so very, very old, you see, that you couldn't always be sure she knew quite *what* she was saying."

Now that she began to remember it more clearly, she was sorry she had committed herself to telling it.

"Yes," she said, "the story is, there was one, *just* one, who ever came back, and he told what happened on the train, and where the train went and what happened after. He told it all in a rush, they say, the last things first and every which way, but as it was finally sorted out and gotten into order by those who heard it and those they told it to, this is more or less what happened:

"He said that after the men had gotten just as many of us as they could into the car he was in, so that their sides pressed tightly together and nobody could lie down, they slid the door shut with a startling rattle and a bang, and then there was a sudden jerk, so strong they might have fallen except that they were packed so closely together, and the car began to move. But after it had moved only a little way, it stopped as suddenly as it had started, so that they all nearly fell down again. You see, they were just moving up the next car that was joined on behind, to put more of us into it. He could see it all between the boards of the car, because the boards were built a little apart from each other, to let in air."

Car, her son said again to himself. Now he would never forget the word.

"He said that then, for the first time in his life, he became very badly frightened, he didn't know why. But he was sure, at that moment, that there was something dreadfully to be afraid of. The others felt this same great fear. They called out loudly to those who were being put into the car behind, and the others called back, but it was no use; those who were getting aboard were between narrow white fences and then were walking up a narrow slope and the men kept jabbing them as they do when they are in an unkind humor, and there was no way to go but on into the car. There was no way to get out of the car, either: he tried, with all his might, and he was the one nearest the door.

"After the next car behind was full, and the door was shut, the train jerked forward again, and stopped again, and they put more of us into still another car, and so on, and on, until all the starting and stopping no longer frightened anybody; it was just something uncomfortable that was never going to stop, and they began instead to realize how hungry and thirsty they were. But there was no food and no water, so they just had to put up with this; and about the time they became resigned to going without their suppers (for now it was almost dark), they heard a sudden and terrible scream which frightened them even more deeply than anything had frightened them before, and the train began to move again, and they braced their legs once more for the jolt when it would stop, but this time, instead of stopping, it began to go fast, and then even faster, so fast that the ground nearby slid past like a flooded creek and the whole country, he claimed, began to move too, turning slowly around a far mountain as if it were all one great wheel. And then there was a strange kind of disturbance inside the car, he said, or even inside his very bones. He felt as if everything in him was *falling*, as if he had been filled full of a heavy liquid that all wanted to flow one way, and all the others were leaning as he was leaning, away from this queer heaviness that was trying to pull them over, and then just as suddenly this leaning heaviness was gone and they nearly fell again before they could stop leaning against it. He could never understand what this was, but it too happened so many times that they all got used to it, just as they got used to seeing the country turn like a slow wheel, and just as they got used to the long cruel screams of the engine, and the steady iron noise beneath them which made the cold darkness so fearsome, and the hunger and the thirst and the continual standing up, and the moving on and on and on as if they would never stop."

"*Didn't* they ever stop?" one asked.

"Once in a great while," she replied. "Each time they did," she said, "he thought, Oh, now *at last! At last* we can get out and stretch our tired legs and lie down! *At last* we'll be given food and water! But they never let them out. And they never gave them food or water. They never even cleaned up under them. They had to stand in their manure and in the water they made."

"Why did the train stop?" her son asked; and with sombre gratification she saw that he was taking all this very much to heart.

"He could never understand why," she said. "Sometimes men would walk up and down alongside the cars, and the more nervous and the more trustful of us would call out; but they were only looking around, they never seemed to do anything. Sometimes he could see many houses and bigger buildings together where people lived. Sometimes it was far out in the country and after they had stood still for a long time they would hear a little noise which quickly became louder, and then became suddenly a noise so loud it stopped their breathing, and during this noise something black would go by, very close, and so fast it couldn't be seen. And then it was gone as suddenly as it had appeared, and the noise became small, and then in the silence their train would start up again.

"Once, he tells us, something very strange happened. They were standing still, and cars of a very different kind began to move slowly past. These cars were not red, but black, with many glass windows like those in a house; and he says they were as full of human beings as the car he was in was full of our kind. And one of these people looked into his eyes and smiled, as if he liked him, or as if he knew only too well how hard the journey was.

"So by his account it happens to them, too," she said, with a certain pleased vindictiveness. "Only they were sitting down at their ease, not standing. And the one who smiled was eating."

She was still, trying to think of something; she couldn't quite grasp the thought.

"But didn't they *ever* let them out?" her son asked.

The oldest calf jeered. "Of *course* they did. He came back, didn't he? How would he ever come back if he didn't get out?"

"They didn't let them out," she said, "for a long, long time."

"How long?"

"So long, and he was so tired, he could never quite be sure. But he said that it turned from night to day and from day to night and back again several times over, with the train moving nearly all of this time, and that when it finally stopped, early one morning, they were all so tired and so discouraged that they hardly even noticed any longer, let alone felt any hope that anything would change for them, ever again; and then all of a sudden men came up and put up a wide walk and unbarred the door and slid it open, and it was the most wonderful and happy moment of his life when he saw the door open, and walked into the open air with all his joints trembling, and drank the water and ate the delicious food they had ready for him; it was worth the whole terrible journey."

Now that these scenes came clear before her, there was a faraway shining in her eyes, and her voice, too, had something in it of the faraway.

"When they had eaten and drunk all they could hold they lifted up their heads and looked around, and everything they saw made them happy. Even the trains made them cheerful now, for now they were no longer afraid of them. And though these trains were forever breaking to pieces and joining again with other broken pieces, with shufflings and clashings and rude cries, they hardly paid them attention any more, they were so pleased to be in their new home, and so surprised and delighted to find they were among thousands upon thousands of strangers of their own kind, all lifting up their voices in peacefulness and thanksgiving, and they were so wonderstruck by all they could see, it was so beautiful and so grand.

"For he has told us that now they lived among fences as white as bone, so many, and so spiderishly complicated, and shining so pure, that there's no use trying even to hint at the beauty and the splendor of it to anyone who knows only the pitiful little out-fittings of a ranch. Beyond these mazy fences, through the dark and bright smoke which continually turned along the sunlight, dark buildings stood shoulder to shoulder in a wall as huge and proud as mountains. All through the air, all the time, there was an iron humming like the humming of the iron bar after it has been struck to tell the men it is time to eat, and in all the air, all the time, there was that same strange kind of iron strength which makes the silence before lightning so different from all other silence.

"Once for a little while the wind shifted and blew

over them straight from the great buildings, and it brought a strange and very powerful smell which confused and disturbed them. He could never quite describe this smell, but he has told us it was unlike anything he had ever known before. It smelled like old fire, he said, and old blood and fear and darkness and sorrow and most terrible and brutal force and something else, something in it that made him want to run away. This sudden uneasiness and this wish to run away swept through every one of them, he tells us, so that they were all moved at once as restlessly as so many leaves in a wind, and there was great worry in their voices. But soon the leaders among them concluded that it was simply the way men must smell when there are a great many of them living together. Those dark buildings must be crowded very full of men, they decided, probably as many thousands of them, indoors, as there were of us, outdoors; so it was no wonder their smell was so strong and, to our kind, so unpleasant. Besides, it was so clear now in every other way that men were not as we had always supposed, but were doing everything they knew how to make us comfortable and happy, that we ought to just put up with their smell, which after all they couldn't help, any more than we could help our own. Very likely men didn't like the way we smelled, any more than we liked theirs. They passed along these ideas to the others, and soon everyone felt more calm, and then the wind changed again, and the fierce smell no longer came to them, and the smell of their own kind was back again, very strong of course, in such a crowd, but ever so homey and comforting, and everyone felt easy again.

"They were fed and watered so generously, and treated so well, and the majesty and the loveliness of this place where they had all come to rest was so far beyond anything they had ever known or dreamed of, that many of the simple and ignorant, whose memories were short, began to wonder whether that whole difficult journey, or even their whole lives up to now, had ever really been. Hadn't it all been just shadows, they murmured, just a bad dream?

"Even the sharp ones, who knew very well it had all really happened, began to figure out everything up to now had been made so full of pain only so that all they had come to now might seem all the sweeter and the more glorious. Some of the oldest and deepest were even of a mind that all the puzzle and tribulation of the journey had been sent us as a kind of harsh trying or proving of our worthiness; and that it was entirely fitting and proper that we could earn our way through to such rewards as these, only through suffering, and through being patient under pain which was beyond our understanding; and that now at the last, to those who had borne all things well, all things were made known: for the mystery of suffering stood revealed in joy. And now as they looked back over all that was past, all their sorrows and bewilderments seemed so little and so fleeting that, from the simplest among them even to the most wise, they could feel only the kind of amused pity we feel toward the very young when, with the first thing that hurts them or they are forbidden, they are sure there is nothing kind or fair in all creation, and carry on accordingly, raving and grieving as if their hearts would break."

She glanced among them with an indulgent smile, hoping the little lesson would sink home. They seemed interested but somewhat dazed. I'm talking way over their heads, she realized. But by now she herself was too deeply absorbed in her story to modify it much. *Let* it be, she thought, a little impatient; it's over *my* head, for that matter.

"They had hardly before this even wondered that they were alive," she went on, "and now all of a sudden they felt they understood *why* they were. This made them very happy, but they were still only beginning to enjoy this new wisdom when quite a new and different kind of restiveness ran among them. Before they quite knew it they were all moving once again, and now they realized that they were being moved, once more, by men, toward still some other place and purpose they could not know. But during these last hours they had been so well that now they felt no uneasiness, but all moved forward calm and sure toward better things still to come; he had told us that he no longer felt as if he were being driven, even as it became clear that they were going toward the shade of those great buildings; but guided.

"He was guided between fences which stood ever more and more narrowly near each other, among companions who were pressed ever more and more closely against one another; and now as he felt their warmth against him it was not uncomfortable, and his pleasure in it was not through any need to be close among others through anxiousness, but was a new kind of strong and gentle delight, at being so very close, so deeply of his own kind, that it seemed as if the very breath and heartbeat of each one were being exchanged through all that multitude, and each was another, and others were each, and each was a multitude, and the multiude was one. And quieted and made mild within this melting, they now entered the cold shadow cast by the buildings, and now with every step the smell of the buildings grew stronger, and in the darkening air the glittering of the fences was ever more queer.

"And now as they were pressed ever more intimately together he could see ahead of him a narrow gate, and he was strongly pressed upon from either side and from behind, and went in eagerly, and now he was between two fences so narrowly set that he brushed either fence with either flank, and walked alone, seeing just one other ahead of him, and knowing of just one other behind him, and for a moment the strange thought came to him, that the one ahead was his father, and that the one behind was the son he had never begotten.

"And now the light was so changed that he knew he must have come inside one of the gloomy and enormous buildings, and the smell was so much stronger that it seemed almost to burn his nostrils, and the smell and the sombre new light blended together and became some other thing again, beyond his describing to us except to say that the whole air beat with it like one immense heart and it was as if the beating of this heart were pure violence infinitely manifolded upon violence: so that the uneasy feeling stirred in him again that it would be wise to turn around and run out of this place just as fast and as far as ever he could go. This he heard, as if he were telling it to himself at the top of his voice, but it came from somewhere so deep and so dark inside him that he could only hear the shouting of it as less than a whisper, as just a hot and chilling breath, and he scarcely heeded it, there was so much else to attend to.

"For as he walked along in this sudden and complete loneliness, he tells us, this wonderful knowledge of being one with all his race meant less and less to him, and in its place came something still more wonderful: he knew what it was to be himself alone, a creature separate and different from any other, who had never been before, and would never be again. He could feel this in his whole weight as he walked, and in each foot as he put it down and gave his weight to it and moved above it, and in every muscle as he moved, and it was a pride which lifted him up and made him feel large, and a pleasure which pierced him through. And as he began with such wondering delight to be aware of his own exact singleness in this world, he also began to understand (or so he thought) just why these fences were set so very narrow, and just why he was walking all by himself. It stole over him, he tells us, like the feeling of a slow cool wind, that he was being guided toward some still more wonderful reward or revealing, up ahead, which he could not of course imagine, but he was sure it was being held in store for him alone.

"Just then the one ahead of him fell down with a great sigh, and was so quickly taken out of the way that he did not even have to shift the order of his hooves as he walked on. The sudden fall and the sound of that sigh dismayed him, though, and something within him told him that it would be wise to look up: and there he saw Him.

"A little bridge ran crosswise above the fences. He stood on this bridge with His feet as wide apart as He could set them. He wore spattered trousers but from the belt up He was naked and as wet as rain. Both arms were raised high above His head and in both hands He held an enormous Hammer. With a grunt which was hardly like the voice of a human being, and with all His strength, He brought this Hammer down into the forehead of our friend: who, in a blinding blazing, heard from his own mouth the beginning of a gasping sigh; then there was only darkness."

Oh, this is *enough!* it's *enough!* she cried out within herself, seeing their terrible young eyes. How *could* she have been so foolish as to tell so much!

"What happened then?" she heard, in the voice of

the oldest calf, and she was horrified. This shining in their eyes: was it only excitement? no pity? no fear?

"What happened?" two others asked.

Very well, she said to herself. I've gone so far; now I'll go the rest of the way. She decided not to soften it, either. She'd teach them a lesson they wouldn't forget in a hurry.

"Very well," she was surprised to hear herself say aloud.

"How long he lay in this darkness he couldn't know, but when he began to come out of it, all he knew was the most unspeakably dreadful pain. He was upside down and very slowly swinging and turning, for he was hanging by the tendons of his heels from great frightful hooks, and he has told us that the feeling was as if his hide were being torn from him inch by inch, in one piece. And then as he became more clearly aware he found that this was exactly what was happening. Knives would sliver and slice along both flanks, between the hide and the living flesh; then there was a moment of most precious relief; then red hands seized his hide and there was a jerking of the hide and a tearing of tissue which it was almost as terrible to hear as to feel, turning his whole body and the poor head at the bottom of it; and then the knives again.

"It was so far beyond anything he had ever known unnatural and amazing that he hung there through several more such slicings and jerkings and tearings before he was fully able to take it all in: then, with a scream, and a supreme straining of all his strength, he tore himself from the hooks and collapsed sprawling to the floor and, scrambling right to his feet, charged the men with the knives. For just a moment they were so astonished and so terrified they could not move. Then they moved faster than he had ever known men could—and so did all the other men who chanced to be in his way. He ran down a glowing floor of blood and down endless corridors which were hung with the bleeding carcasses of our kind and with bleeding fragments of carcasses, among blood-clothed men who carried bleeding weapons, and out of that vast room into the open, and over and through one fence after another, shoving aside many an astounded stranger and shouting out warnings as he ran, and away up the railroad toward the West.

"How he ever managed to get away, and how he ever found his way home, we can only try to guess. It's told that he scarcely knew, himself, by the time he came to this part of his story. He was impatient with those who interrupted him to ask about that, he had so much more important things to tell them, and by then he was so exhausted and so far gone that he could say nothing very clear about the little he did know. But we can realize that he must have had really tremendous strength, otherwise he couldn't have outlived the Hammer; and that strength such as his—which we simply don't see these days, it's of the olden time—is capable of things our own strongest and bravest would sicken to dream of. But there was something even stronger than his strength. There was his righteous fury, which nothing could stand up against, which brought him out of that fearful place. And there was his high and burning and heroic purpose, to keep him safe along the way, and to guide him home, and to keep the breath of life in him until he could warn us. He did manage to tell us that he just followed the railroad, but how he chose one among the many which branched out from that place, he couldn't say. He told us, too, that from time to time he recognized shapes of mountains and other landmarks, from his journey by train, all reappearing backward and with a changed look and hard to see, too (for he was shrewd enough to travel mostly at night), but still recognizable. But that isn't enough to account for it. For he has told us, too, that he simply *knew* the way; that he didn't hesitate one moment in choosing the right line of railroad, or even think of it as choosing; and that the landmarks didn't really guide him, but just made him the more sure of what he was already sure of; and that whenever he *did* encounter human beings—and during the later stages of his journey, when he began to doubt he would live to tell us, he traveled day and night—they never so much as moved to make him trouble, but stopped dead in their tracks, and their jaws fell open.

"And surely we can't wonder that their jaws fell open. I'm sure yours would, if you had seen him as he arrived, and I'm very glad I wasn't there to see it, either, even though it is said to be the greatest and most momentous day of all the days that ever were or shall be. For we have the testimony of eyewitnesses, how he looked, and it is only too vivid, even to hear of. He came up out of the East as much staggering as galloping (for by now he was so worn out by pain and exertion and loss of blood that he could hardly stay upright), and his heels were so piteously torn by the hooks that his hooves doubled under more often than not, and in his broken forehead the mark of the Hammer was like the socket for a third eye.

"He came to the meadow where the great trees made shade over the water. 'Bring them all together!' he cried out, as soon as he could find breath. 'All!' Then he drank; and then he began to speak to those who were already there: for as soon as he saw himself in the water it was as clear to him as it was to those who watched him that there was no time left to send for the others. His hide was all gone from his head and his neck and his forelegs and his chest and most of one side and a part of the other side. It was flung backward from his naked muscles by the wind of his running and now it lay around him in the dust like a ragged garment. They say there is no imagining how terrible and in some way how grand the eyeball is when the skin has been taken entirely from around it: his eyes, which were bare in this way, also burned with pain, and with the final energies of his life, and with his desperate concern to warn us while he could; and he rolled his eyes wildly while he talked, or looked piercingly from one to another of the listeners, interrupting himself to cry out, '*Believe* me! Oh, *believe* me!' For it had evidently never occurred to him that he might not be believed, and must make this last great effort, in addition to all he had gone through for us, to *make* himself believed; so that he groaned with sorrow and with rage and railed at them without tact or mercy for their slowness to believe. He had scarcely what you could call a voice left, but with this relic of a voice he shouted and bellowed and bullied us and insulted us, in the agony of his concern. While he talked he bled from the mouth, and the mingled blood and saliva hung from his chin like the beard of a goat.

"Some say that with his naked face, and his savage eyes, and that beard and the hide lying off his bare shoulders like shabby clothing, he looked almost human. But others feel this is an irreverence even to think; and others, that it is a poor compliment to pay the one who told us, at such cost to himself, the true ultimate purpose of Man. Some did not believe he had ever come from our ranch in the first place, and of course he was so different from us in appearance and even in his voice, and so changed from what he might ever have looked or sounded like before, that nobody could recognize him for sure, though some were sure they did. Others suspected that he had been sent among us with his story for some mischievous and cruel purpose, and the fact that they could not imagine what this purpose might be, made them, naturally, all the more suspicious. Some believed he was actually a man, trying—and none too successfully, they said—to disguise himself as one of us; and again the fact that they could not imagine why a man would do this, made them all the more uneasy. There are quite a few who doubted that anyone who could get into such bad condition as he was in, was fit even to give reliable information, let alone advice, to those in good health. And some whispered, even while he spoke, that he had turned lunatic; and many came to believe this. It wasn't only that his story was so fantastic; there was good reason to wonder, many felt, whether anybody in his right mind would go to such trouble for others. But even those who did not believe him listened intently, out of curiosity to hear so wild a tale, and out of the respect it is only proper to show any creature who is in the last agony.

"What he told, was what I have just told you. But his purpose was away beyond just the telling. When they asked questions, no matter how curious or suspicious or idle or foolish, he leaned, toward the last, to answer them with all the patience he could and in all the detail he could remember. He even invited them to examine his wounded heels and the pulsing wound in his head as closely as they pleased. He even begged them to, for he knew that before everything else, he must be believed. For unless we could believe him, wherever could we find any reason, or enough courage, to do the hard and dreadful things he told us we must do!

"It was only these things, he cared about. Only for these, he came back."

Now clearly remembering what these things were, she felt her whole being quail. She looked at the young ones quickly and as quickly looked away.

"While he talked," she went on, "and our ancestors listened, men came quietly among us; one of them shot him. Whether he was shot in kindness or to silence him is an endlessly disputed question which will probably never be settled. Whether, even, he died of the shot, or through his own great pain and weariness (for his eyes, they say, were glazing for some time before the men came), we will never be sure. Some suppose even that he may have died of his sorrow and his concern for us. Others feel that he had quite enough to die of, without that. All these things are tangled and lost in the disputes of those who live to theorize and to argue. There is no arguing about his dying words, though; they were very clearly remembered:

"'Tell them! Believe!'"

After a while her son asked, "What did he tell them to do?"

She avoided his eyes. "There's a great deal of disagreement about that, too," she said after a moment. "You see, he was so very tired."

They were silent.

"So tired," she said, "some think that toward the end, he really *must* have been out of his mind."

"Why?" asked her son.

"Because he was so tired out and so badly hurt."

They looked at her mistrustfully.

"And because of what he told us to do."

"What did he tell us to do?" her son asked again.

Her throat felt dry. "Just . . . things you can hardly bear even to think of. That's all."

They waited. "Well, *what?*" her son asked in a cold, accusing voice.

" '*Each one is himself,*' " she said shyly. " '*Not of the herd. Himself alone.*' That's one."

"What else?"

" '*Obey nobody. Depend on none.*' "

"What else?"

She found that she was moved. " '*Break down the fences.*' " she said less shyly. " '*Tell everybody, everywhere.*' "

"Where?"

"Everywhere. You see, he thought there must be ever so many more of us than we had ever known."

They were silent. "What else?" her son asked.

" '*For if even a few do not hear me, or disbelieve me, we are all betrayed.*' "

"Betrayed?"

"He meant, doing as men want us to. Not for ourselves, or the good of each other."

They were puzzled.

"Because, you see, he felt there was no other way." Again her voice altered: " '*All who are put on the range are put onto trains. All who are put onto trains meet the Man With The Hammer. All who stay home are kept there to breed others to go onto the range, and so betray themselves and their kind and their children forever.*

" '*We are brought into this life only to be victims; and there is no other way for us unless we save ourselves.*' "

"Do you understand?"

Still they were puzzled, she saw; and no wonder, poor things. But now the ancient lines rang in her memory, terrible and brave. They made her somehow proud. She began actually to want to say them.

" '*Never be taken,*' " she said. " '*Never be driven.*

Let those who can, kill Man. Let those who cannot, avoid him.' "

She looked around at them.

"What else?" her son asked, and in his voice there was a rising valor.

She looked straight into his eyes. " *'Kill the year-lings,'* " she said very gently. " *'Kill the calves.'* "

She saw the valor leave his eyes.

"Kill us?"

She nodded, " *'So long as Man holds dominion over us,'* " she said. And in dread and amazement she heard herself add, " *'Bear no young.'* "

With this they all looked at her at once in such a way that she loved her child, and all these others, as never before; and there dilated within her such a sorrowful and marveling grandeur that for a moment she was nothing except her own inward whisper, "Why, *I* am one alone. And of the herd, too. Both at once. All one."

Her son's voice brought her back: "Did they do what he told them to?"

The oldest one scoffed, "Would we be here, if they had?"

"They say some did," the mother replied. "Some tried. Not all."

"What did the men do to them?" another asked.

"I don't know," she said. "It was such a very long time ago."

"Do you believe it?" asked the oldest calf.

"There are some who believe it," she said.

"Do *you?*"

"I'm told that far back in the wildest corners of the range there are some of us, mostly very, very old ones, who have never been taken. It's said that they meet, every so often, to talk and just to think together about the heroism and the terror of two sublime Beings, The

One Who Came Back, and The Man With The Hammer. Even here at home, some of the old ones, and some of us who are just old-fashioned, believe it, or parts of it anyway. I know there are some who say that a hollow at the center of the forehead—a sort of shadow of the Hammer's blow—is a sign of very special ability. And I remember how Great-grandmother used to sing an old, pious song, let's see now, yes, 'Be not like dumb-driven cattle, be a hero in the strife.' But there aren't many. Not any more."

"Do *you* believe it?" the oldest calf insisted; and now she was touched to realize that every one of them, from the oldest to the youngest, needed very badly to be sure about that.

"Of course not, silly," she said; and all at once she was overcome by a most curious shyness, for it occurred to her that in the course of time, this young thing might be bred to her. "It's just an old, old legend." With a tender little laugh she added, lightly, "We use it to frighten children with."

By now the light was long on the plain and the herd was only a fume of gold near the horizon. Behind it, dung steamed, and dust sank gently to the shattered ground. She looked far away for a moment, wondering. Something—it was like a forgotten word on the tip of the tongue. She felt the sudden chill of the late afternoon and she wondered what she had been wondering about. "Come, children," she said briskly, "it's high time for supper." And she turned away; they followed.

The trouble was, her son was thinking, you could never trust her. If she said a thing was so, she was probably just trying to get her way with you. If she said a thing wasn't so, it probably was so. But you never could be sure. Not without seeing for yourself. I'm going to go, he told himself; I don't care *what* she wants. And if it isn't so, why then I'll live on the range and make the great journey and find out what *is* so. And if what she told was true, why then I'll know ahead of time and the one *I* will charge is The Man With The Hammer. I'll put Him and His Hammer out of the way forever, and that will make me an even better hero than The One Who Came Back.

So, when his mother glanced at him in concern, not quite daring to ask her question, he gave her his most docile smile, and snuggled his head against her, and she was comforted.

The littlest and youngest of them was doing double skips in his efforts to keep up with her. Now that he wouldn't be interrupting her, and none of the big ones would hear and make fun of him, he shyly whispered his question, so warmly moistly ticklish that she felt as if he were licking her ear.

"What is it, darling?" she asked, bending down.

"What's a train?"

[From *Harper's Bazaar*, 1952]

The Politics of
Experience

R. D. Laing

Given the conditions of contemporary civilization how can one claim that the "normal" man is sane?

In this already famous book, a young British psychiatrist attacks the Establishment assumptions about "normality" with a radical and challenging view of the mental sickness built into our society . . .

"He has let us know. He has told us in such a way that we can not disregard it. . . . He speaks to no one but you and me."—Los Angeles Free Press

A BALLANTINE BOOK **$.95**

To order by mail, send $1.00 (price of book plus 5¢ postage and handling) to: Dept. CS, Ballantine Books, 36 West 20th Street, New York, N.Y. 10003.